PRAISE FOR SOUNDING DARK

Faith, luck, and grit propel this ambitious space opera from Graham (*Black Ships*). // Graham amps up the action, constructs a rich mythology of gods, cultures, and societies, and develops evocative characters that will make readers cheer. This pure sci-fi escape proves a fresh experience for fans who are tired of clichés. — *Publishers Weekly*

Sounding Dark is tremendously exciting space opera. // It's the sort of book you stay up far too late finishing, and then go back to re-read so that you can savor the details. The thing that's hard to express how well *Sounding Dark* blends solid technical SF // with deep myths. // Jo Graham makes both aspects utterly believable and equally crucial to the story. — Melissa Scott, legendary pioneering SFF author of more than thirty novels, winner of multiple genre awards

Jo Graham's space opera is a richly imagined narrative which uses its spectrum of relatable heroes who face overwhelming odds with drive, determination, grit, and most powerfully of all, hope. // With its inventive use of Sumerian motifs in its intriguing worldbuilding, *Sounding Dark* soars to reach a liminal place on the boundaries of science fiction and myth. — Paul Weimer, SFF book reviewer and Hugo finalist

Sounding Dark is a hope-filled space opera with a classic feel. It has space battles, politics, and // vividly-imagined worlds in conflict. Enduring friendships and the deeply-held beliefs of the characters // make it a story with heart, as well. I'll definitely be looking forward to further books exploring this universe. — K.V. Johansen, author of the *Gods of the Caravan Road* epic fantasy series

Jo Graham specializes in writing gloriously epic yet deeply personal science fantasy, and *Sounding Dark* is the beginning of just my kind of saga: generational, political, magical. — E.K. Johnston, #1 New York Times Bestselling Author

Also by Jo Graham (selected works):

Black Ships

Stealing Fire

The Order of the Air
(series, Melissa Scott co-author)

SOUNDING DARK

Jo Graham

Candlemark & Gleam

For information, address
Athena Andreadis
Candlemark & Gleam LLC,
38 Rice Street #2, Cambridge, MA 02140
eloi@candlemarkandgleam.com

Library of Congress Cataloguing-in-Publication Data
In Progress

ISBNs: 978-1-952456-05-3 (print), 978-1-952456-06-0 (digital)

Cover art by Eleni Tsami

Editor: Athena Andreadis

Proofreader: Kelly Jennings

www.candlemarkandgleam.com

For Melissa,

who loved this story from the beginning.

CHAPTER ONE

The Steel Captain looked out across the debris field, and her face was still. Yes, the rest of the ship couldn't see her, but the bridge crew could, their couches arranged in a tight semi-circle on the modified merchanter, space that should have been left open for comfort packed tight with missile tube controls and two weapons officers. The main screen showed the forward view; drifting bits of debris, larger chunks that might hold lingering atmospherics or liquids, down to micrometeorites of flash-frozen blood and flesh. Not one person on the bridge of *Steel Nine* spoke a single word.

The Ivory Captain's voice was incredulous on the comm, clear as though he stood at her shoulder rather than on *Steel Nine*'s sister ship. "What happened here?" Tal Robber said.

"The Calpurnian Navy," she replied in clipped tones. Adelita Massacre did not trust her voice further.

Tal was scanning. The screens showed the pulse of his sensors, pinging once, twice, three times. *Ivory Three* slipped slowly further into the debris field, larger and older than *Steel Nine*, slower but better able to take the debris strikes.

The cameras showed a drifting arm, hand dangling by strings of flesh, and the officer of the watch cut the scene quickly to another view. Every person on either ship had loved ones missing.

"Drift pattern suggests twenty to twenty-four hours ago," Tal said.

Adelita nodded. "Butcher, scan for any atmospheric bubbles in the larger pieces." It was just possible, just barely possible, that there were survivors in sealed compartments. Someone might have gotten into a suit. Blast doors might have held. It could have happened.

"Captain." Butcher adjusted controls, scratching his bald head, for once short on backtalk.

Ivory Three was creeping deeper into the debris field. Adelita was silent, letting the scanners do their work. Tal was reading off numbers, vectors. Adelita turned the main screen to his cameras. A recognizable section swam into view, part of an exterior panel about six feet long. Part of the white stenciling against the black was visible, and a palpable wave of exhalation ran around the bridge.

"I have a section of *Horn Four*," Tal said. "Lady's Breath!" he swore quietly.

"*Horn Four* and *Bone Seven*," Adelita said. Her tones were clipped and formal. "Ivory Captain, we may consider both ships lost."

"Confirmed," Tal said. "We consider both ships lost."

Someone let out a sob at their post. She did not turn to see who. "Continue to scan the field," Adelita said. "We will retrieve survivors."

Butcher looked up from his board. "It's been twenty-four hours, Captain! There's no…"

"We will scan." She did not sit down on the edge of her acceleration couch. She stood, and she would stand until the scan was completed.

T*he solar wind had a voice. It begged and pleaded, speaking of heat and the flow of electrons, of warm worlds caressed with light. It lapped at her.*

It whispered like a lover, and yet she could not answer. There was Void, and it held her in eternal silence.

Sometimes there were others, her children in their skins of metal and fire, calling to her, reaching for her. She strained. Sometimes she touched them, her hands dark streamers reaching into their dreams, quantum effects of electrons reaching for electrons, firing neurons to show them in their sleep. They dreamed her, accretion disk in one hand, flaring nova in the other, her gown of stars. And yet she could not move. There was only cold. Only silence.

One twisted in emptiness, a tiny spark, slowed heartbeat, fading breath. A spark. A tiny touch. A bridge across the darkness, a chink in the walls of her prison….

"We have a life sign," Butcher said.

They had scanned for nearly two hours entirely fruitlessly. Adelita bent down to look at his screen. "A single life sign?"

"There." He pulled up the close view. "Way out to the side of the debris field, near the wreckage of the Calpurnian scout ship." Either *Horn* or *Bone* had given as good as they got. They'd taken a Calpurnian pinnace with them.

The Steel Captain frowned. "Pursue." She opened the channel to *Ivory Three*. "Ivory Captain, we have a life sign. One person in a suit."

"After at least twenty-two hours?" Tal sounded incredulous. "That's well beyond the air supply of a suit."

"Perhaps they were inside for part of the time. We will know when we have them aboard."

Adelita did not pace as they made their way to the edge of the debris field. She looked around her bridge instead. For all its clutter, it was well organized. Eight acceleration couches were tightly arranged, the arm controls for shipboard functions easily accessible when strapped tightly in, their reclining seats tilted forward for comfort while the ship was not jump-ready. The walls were pearlescent white between the large screens, though the carpeting beneath was a patchwork of dark red and light tan. *Steel Nine* had been a merchanter before she was taken, and no doubt the original tan flooring had been stained in the melee that took her. Eresh's shipwrights had left the sections that served. Waste not, want not. Now there would need to be *Horn Five* and *Bone Eight*.

"Permission to join," Tal asked. *Ivory Three* was closing. Of course he'd want to see the survivor too, as soon as they were brought aboard. Perhaps they could tell them what had happened.

"Permission granted." It would take nearly twenty minutes to come alongside and extend the guidance drones, then mate hatches. They'd have recovery completed by then.

Adelita watched until sensors showed the drones out, each towing a long line as they swam from *Steel*'s side like glowing fish in the dark, magnetic clamps seeing the black painted side of *Ivory Three*. "Adulterer, take the bridge," she said, and nodded to her second as she palmed the door open. She'd greet Tal at the airlock as was proper.

He was not quite aboard when she arrived, so Adelita stood in the corridor with its green stripe running in one direction and blue in the other, patting down her black shipsuit, her energy flail at her side. The airlock cycled and Tal Robber, the Ivory Captain, stepped through. He was a tall man perhaps five years her junior, his shipsuit brown with the grinning teeth of *Ivory* boldly displayed on each shoulder pad. Though he was no more than thirty-five, his pale face was drawn. He'd not been planetside for quite some time—every bit of color had leached from his face. "Permission to come aboard, Steel Captain?"

"Welcome aboard, Ivory Captain," Adelita said. Her smile was genuine. Tal was a true friend, not simply a colleague. "Walk with me." She led him away from other crew, following the green stripe aft.

As soon as they were out of earshot, Tal stopped. "How could this happen?"

"The Calpurnians guessed the jump coordinates," Adelita said. "They must have caught them at the transition. I don't see how else."

"But how would they know that? It's constantly shifting." Tal looked harried. "It doesn't look like *Bone* got a shot off. We found missile debris from *Horn* in a couple of places."

"*Horn* probably took out that pinnace," Adelita said. "But why they didn't pick up our survivor…?"

"No Calpurnians in ship suits, no Calpurnian pods." Tal sighed. "They picked up their own wounded and dead before they jumped. So if they left our survivor—"

"Hopefully it's someone from *Horn* who can tell us what happened," Adelita finished. "Two full ships and all their crew…."

"Don't say it," Tal said.

"I must. I fear they intend to retake Eresh."

"We've been little enough trouble to them lately," Tal pointed out.

"We are always trouble to them."

Adelita's communicator chimed. "Captain, the survivor is aboard and in Life Services."

"Calpurnian or ours?"

The medic's voice sounded perplexed. "Neither. She's Tainted."

Tal's eyebrows rose. "Why would a Tainted be on a Calpurnian pinnace?"

"We'll find out soon enough," Adelita said, striding toward Life Services.

She dreamed, and in her dreams there were ships. They voyaged far in interstellar space, far between the warm ionized pools of suns. Beyond heliopause there was the Void.

Yet they danced it bravely, these children in their generation ships, fragile shells holding life within. She was drawn by their joy. She sang to them. Surely such small creatures should not venture into the deep darkness alone!

They answered her. The dreamers in interface heard her, Navigators who followed their course, feeling the flow of electrons down the hulls of the great ships. Artists painted her in pixels and light, the Lady to guide our course, the Lady of the Void with her gown of spangled night and a newborn star in her uplifted hand.

She answered them. So brave, so small, so beautiful in their loving courage. Here were brighter streams. Dreamers felt them, the currents of distant suns. The First Captains were dead. Three generations had passed. She led them to Agni, cold and volcanic, but capable of supporting life at the margin of their needs. They debated then, ships locked in orbit while they explored. Some stayed, unwilling to try the great dark again, or perhaps in love with Agni's fire and ice.

The others put themselves in her hands, pouring wine like blood into the void, its icy crystals sacrifice to her, and with a vast, swelling music set forth again.

She knew better now what they needed: Menaechmi with its twin suns, a planet with vast oceans and desert continents. Some stayed, planting gardens along the shores, singing of the Lord of the Dance and his lover, the Lady of the Void.

Onward still into the night, but the pools were closer together now, rich Inanna, gentle Calpurnia, tide-locked Morrigan, sea-kissed Lono—nine worlds for her children. She sang to them, and they sang to her, dancing her praises as each set of golden solar wings unfolded, at each setting-forth....

"She's crying in her sleep."

Bister stirred. There was a voice, a dampness on her cheek. A man's voice, not the one she had been hearing. Not the voice that filled her dreams. Bister opened her eyes.

Three people bent over her, one in the ubiquitous green of Life Services. The man who had spoken bent closer. "Can you hear me?" His fair hair was cut short for a helmet and his shipsuit was brown, a badge of grinning teeth on the pauldrons.

Bister nodded. She could move her head. That was a good sign.

The third person was a woman perhaps a decade Bister's junior, tall and dark, her eyes enhanced with cosmetics, a contrast with her severe expression and black shipsuit. "Can you tell us who you are and what happened?"

Bister moistened her lips. "I don't know," she whispered. "Where am I?"

"She's lucid," the medic said. "That's a good sign that there's no lasting brain damage from the hypoxia. Our scans suggested little physical damage, but it's hard to tell what the impact has been until they regain consciousness."

"You are in the Life Center aboard *Steel Nine*," the woman replied. She came around to Bister's side. "You are safe aboard ship. There is nothing to fear."

"Aboard ship...." There had been the void, the endless bone-eating cold sinking into her, all other comm traffic ceasing gradually, one by one.

"*Ivory Three* and *Steel Nine* arrived at the site of the battle," the man said. "We picked you up."

"In a suit...." She had been in a suit, tumbling slowly in the dark.

"Yes," the woman said. "I am the Steel Captain. You are safe aboard my ship. Our medics have been treating you."

"I don't remember."

"You were unconscious when you were brought aboard," the medic said. The medic looked at the wall screens approvingly. "But you seem to be in surprisingly good shape, considering."

Bister lifted her head. She could see the medical pod around her, a white sheet pulled up just below her arms to cover her body, the tattoos on her shoulders bared. "My things...."

"Your clothing and effects are in the locker there," the medic said. "But don't get up just yet. I want to run another electrolyte scan."

"Can you tell us what happened?" the man asked. "What ship were you aboard?"

Eresh. They were from Eresh. Her thoughts were working so slowly. But then she had been hypoxic. "Not one of yours," she said.

"The Calpurnian pinnace?" he asked.

Bister nodded. "The *Carulin*. I was a prisoner." That part was clear. She remembered being taken aboard and why.

"You are from Inanna." That was the Steel Captain again. "Why were you a prisoner of the Calpurnian Navy?"

"I was arrested on the Adelpha Rim," Bister said reluctantly.

"Smuggling." The Steel Captain's voice was flat.

"It's illegal for a Tainted to be off Inanna," the man said. "Come on. Just being there was enough of a reason to be arrested." He looked at Bister with a diffident smile that women probably found charming. "I'm Tal Robber, the Ivory Captain. And you are?" He waited for a name.

"Bister."

"It's a pleasure to meet you, Bister. So you were a prisoner on the Calpurnian pinnace and then what?"

Obviously he was going to play good guy to the Steel Captain's bad guy. Bister sat up cautiously, keeping the sheet pulled up. "We were diverted. Different orders. I don't know what. They don't tell prisoners why the ship is going where it's going. We were just told to strap down for the jump." Bister thought back. "It wasn't a long jump. Maybe seven or eight minutes. When we came out we just sat there for a long time. Hours. And then suddenly we went to general quarters and battle stations. I didn't even know who we were fighting. You, I suppose."

The Steel Captain and the Ivory Captain exchanged a look. "You're right," the Ivory Captain said. "They knew the jump coordinates and were waiting."

"They took out two Name Ships," the Steel Captain said. "Nearly four hundred people. One of our ships didn't get a shot off. And to attack without warning...."

"I don't know if there was a warning. I couldn't see any of the ship's business," Bister said.

"There wasn't," the Ivory Captain said. "It doesn't look like *Bone* even went to battle stations. They must have fired the moment our ships came out of jump."

"Somebody fought back." Bister felt like she needed to say it, like it was some odd comfort. "I felt the pinnace take a hit and the power flickered. Then the power shut down." Alone in the dark, locked in a cell, the sound of the ventilation systems ceasing.... She took a deep breath. "But with the power off I forced the cell door. There was emergency lighting in the corridor. We were obviously breached. I could feel the wind." Wind on a spaceship was the worst possible nightmare. "I went aft because that's where the lock was, so I thought that's probably where the suits were." The Steel Captain nodded. Her face was grim as though she were filling in all the things Bister didn't say.

There had been a young man with a coolant burn on his face. He'd tried to stop her. Those moments in the flickering dark, his shouted words being torn away by the hardening wind, chest to chest, heart to heart like lovers as they struggled. And then the lambent flash as she got the energy flail from his belt, its tendrils against his ruined face.... She'd pushed him and run. The wind took his screams, the wind at her back blowing her aft toward the airlock. She slammed the first set of doors. There were three suits in their chargers. She got in one but stayed plugged in, doors sealed, suit lapping oxygen from still unruptured systems. How long? Minutes? Maybe an hour?

"You got into a suit and got out," the Steel Captain said. Bister nodded. "There were other survivors?"

"Yes." Kicking off from the pinnace's lock, its systems exhausted, on the suit's power alone, turning and drifting in the darkness amid a sea of floating debris.... "The Calpurnian ships were picking up survivors." Black forms almost invisible except where they eclipsed the distant stars, the comm shouts of the others loud in the void, the ships swam through the debris field. "I didn't have a Calpurnian transponder," Bister said. "They didn't pick up anyone without them."

The Ivory Captain ducked his head. "They left our people."

"Yes." Bister's voice sounded harsh even to her. "They deliberately left anyone without a Calpurnian transponder. They even picked up their dead. But they left us." Suits clutching at the drone lines as they pulled them in, lines slipping through their fingers as the great ships cruised silently through the night, as though they didn't hear the curses and pleas. "Did you get them? Did you pick them up?"

The Ivory Captain and the Steel Captain exchanged a look again, but it was she who spoke. "You were the sole survivor."

"What?"

"It was twenty-four hours before we arrived at the jump point. There were no life signs besides yours," the Steel Captain said.

"That's..." Bister could think of no words.

"We don't know how you survived." The Steel Captain shook her head. "Perhaps you remained attached to the pinnace's systems longer than you thought."

"No." She shook her head. "It can't have been two hours. I don't think it can be."

"Then what other explanation is there?" the Ivory Captain said. "A regular suit, even one that was full and topped up when you put it on, wouldn't last more than sixteen hours at most. Certainly not an entire day. You should have died long before we arrived."

"As the others did." One by one, the comm voices ceased. One by one, until she was alone in the void, drifting in and out of consciousness….

"As the others did," the Steel Captain said starkly.

Here. Now. "What are you going to do with me?"

"You've committed no crimes in our jurisdiction," the Ivory Captain said. There was that disarming expression again, even if it seemed a bit forced. "And frankly I don't care what the Calpurnians wanted you for."

"We are bound for Eresh," the Steel Captain said. "You are our guest, not our prisoner. I hope that when we get there you will tell the Council what happened since you are the only witness. And then you are free to return to Inanna or wherever you choose."

"Thank you," Bister said, breathing an inward sigh of relief. It could be much worse. "I will of course be delighted to testify as to what happened. And I appreciate your aid and hospitality."

"You need to stay in the Life Center for at least another four hours," the medic said. "Preferably more. I want to be sure you have no organ damage."

"I'd be a fool to refuse Eresh's life treatment." Bister lay back down in the medical pod.

The Ivory Captain looked at the Steel Captain. "I'd better get back to my ship. And prepare some things to say. They're bringing remains aboard."

For a moment the Steel Captain's face was still. "Yes, Tal," she said quietly. "That's best. We'll coordinate the jump times. Let me know when you're done."

"Of course."

Bister rubbed her arms with her hands, watching them. "If you're cold I can get you a blanket," the medic said. They had a reassuring smile. "You're going to be just fine. I want to run another course of mitochondrial stimulants. You'll be walking out of here by the time we get back to Eresh."

"A blanket would be lovely," Bister said. "I am tired. Would it be all right if I slept while you did the course?"

"Absolutely." The medic tucked a warmed green blanket around her. "You're perfectly safe."

Bister closed her eyes. There were the comforting sounds of the medic moving around, the electronic sounds of their equipment. Beyond it, she heard indistinguishable voices in the corridor outside, probably the two Captains conferring. Warm. Sleep. And beyond that, the sounds of the ship, the low subsonics of the engines at one quarter as they moved slowly through the debris field, the whisper of ventilation systems, the faint sad pings of micrometeorites against *Steel Nine*'s skin…. How could she hear that? Bister wondered for a moment, hovering just this side of sleep, but the warmed blanket was so comfortable, so unlike the void. She slept.

Adelita Massacre only hesitated a moment before she keyed open the bridge door. Her face was calm. She stepped in. Every head swiveled to face her. The screen showed the debris field. Butcher's big nose was red from crying. Oxa Usury had streaks of tears down his face.

"Adulterer, put me on shipwide," the Steel Captain said, stepping up to her post. "Visual and audio both, please. Usury, calculate the soonest jump window for Eresh."

"Captain," Adulterer said. "You are live in three seconds, two, one."

"Crew of *Steel Nine*, Ship's Company all, I am sure you are aware of the attack that destroyed *Horn Four* and *Bone Seven*." The Steel Captain's words were measured. "It is my duty to inform you that we know with certainty that the attack was carried out by the Calpurnian Navy, and that the state of conflict which has waxed and waned between us has now escalated to open war. We are certain of this due to the eyewitness testimony of the attack's sole survivor, now aboard *Steel Nine*. Sadly, the survivor is not one of our Company, and so I must dash the hopes of all who held out faith that it was someone in particular." She paused for a moment. "The survivor is, however, one of our allies rather than a Calpurnian, and is willingly cooperating to help us get a fuller picture of what transpired. What is certain is that we must count both ships lost with all hands."

Adelita glanced around her bridge. Solemn faces, but no more tears. No curses. They were holding together, something one could not always count on. *It is not anyone you wanted it to be*, she thought. *It is not any of your friends, your lovers, your kin. You are hearing the cruelest thing I can say.*

"As soon as we have recovered what remains we can, we are jumping for Eresh at the first opportunity. We will mourn the lives of our *Horn* and *Bone* siblings when we have left the field of battle. In the interim, I know that we shall act with the strength and fortitude that *Steel* is known for." She nodded sharply, and Adulterer cut the comm. Adelita took a deep breath. "Usury, give me an estimate as soon as possible."

"Captain."

Adelita sat down on the end of her couch and pulled the swinging control arm to her. Usury would send her the options, and until then she would check the rest of the systems. She did not look up. They did not need her to watch them. They needed to see her going about her work, and they would go about theirs.

It was a good five minutes before Usury sent her three options, and she opened the external comm to send them to Tal without comment. One was too soon. She doubted they'd be ready in eleven minutes. The second, forty-three minutes out, was most likely, and Tal would probably come to the same conclusion quickly. Technically each ship was an independent entity. She could not appear to order Tal around without causing him to lose face.

He had only been elected Captain the year before, and that after Marisol's breakdown. He'd done a good job of rebuilding *Ivory's* crew and morale, but his authority was a great deal more tenuous than hers. She'd served aboard *Steel Seven*, then *Eight*, and now *Nine* for nearly twenty-six years, since she had reached the minimum age for service at fifteen. She'd been elected Captain four times, two before her brief break stationside and two after. Only Butcher had been in the bridge crew longer, and he'd probably stay until they had to carry him out.

Butcher cleared his throat. "Captain? How do we know the Calpurnian fleet isn't at Eresh already?"

She looked up. "We don't," Adelita said simply. "That's why we're going to jump prepared for the worst. However, it isn't likely. That's not their protocol, and the Calpurnians are very, very wedded to their protocols."

That caused a whisper of amusement to run around the bridge. Everyone knew the Calpurnians would stick to protocols, sometimes even when it made no sense. They might call the Ships' Companies pirates, but there was no denying that one-on-one Eresh's ships were much more nimble and less orthodox. It made up for the technological lag.

"We'll jump at battle stations and we'll choose a run-in point that puts Inanna between us and Eresh so that we have time to see what's going on, and to deploy and integrate into whatever situation awaits us. Remember, *Silk Five* and *Salt Seven* are insystem. They're not going to just surrender. If we get there and they're engaged, we'll support them."

Butcher nodded. Behind him, she saw Distribute nodding at her post. Distribute was the youngest of the bridge crew.

"*Ash Five* may be there too," Adulterer said. "They may already be in."

"So we may have as many as five Name Ships. That's quite a fleet." Adelita smiled with more confidence than she felt. They wouldn't be outnumbered by more than two to one. "So we can handle it if the Calpurnians are there. But I don't expect them to be."

The comm binged. "Steel Captain," Tal's voice said formally, "Would you care to coordinate our jumps for the second jump window?"

"It would be my pleasure, Ivory Captain," Adelita said. "If you would care to jump first, we will follow you—" she glanced down at her screen "—the recommended seventy seconds later."

"Acknowledged and agreed," he replied.

"Butcher, sound the first chime at fifteen minutes until jump," Adelita said. "And the second at three minutes."

"Yes, Captain."

"Captain, we have a ping from *Bone*'s logbox," Usury said.

"Close enough to recover," Adelita said. "Bring it aboard. And be wary of debris." And mines, she thought, though *Ivory* had been wading through the debris field without any hint of ambush. She was more worried about accidentally hitting unexploded munitions from *Bone* than a Calpurnian mine.

"I'll put the docking drones out to clear a path," Usury said.

"Good plan."

It took most of the time before the jump to recover the logbox. They maneuvered it aboard just as the chime sounded. For a moment Adelita considered waiting for the third jump window, but thought better of it. It was nearly a full hour later. If there was any chance the Calpurnian fleet was at Eresh, that was time they didn't have.

"Adulterer," Adelita said. He opened the comm. "*Steel Nine*, we will jump in fifteen minutes. At your stations, everyone." She glanced around the bridge. "Secure for jump."

Oxa Usury was putting bowl and drinking flask into the compartment by his station. Adelita checked her own for stray objects. Nothing. She hadn't eaten anything on the watch today.

No one had except Usury. Well, who felt like it? By the time the second chime sounded she had folded her couch back from the sitting position to reclining at seventy degrees to the floor. With practiced hands, she fastened the straps, first the shoulder belts and the sternum pad where they crossed, each buckling at her waist on the opposite side, then the lower belts that started at her waist and fastened at opposite sides of her lower thighs. Lastly, she secured the neck piece that cradled her head and prevented the kind of spine injuries that were the most common mishap in jump. Reaching up, she pulled down the heads-up display and swung the control arm so that her right arm rested comfortably along it, controls beneath her fingers.

"Captain, we are secured for jump," Usury said.

"Adulterer, you may engage when ready," Adelita said as the third chime sounded. There was the sudden sensation of pressure against her chest, the rumble of the engines beneath her, a powerful purr rising to a roar with the enormous energy required to accelerate into the gravitational slingshot for subspace travel. "The clock is running," Adelita said.

Light flared behind her eyes and she closed them, the momentary pressure on her eyes making it seem as though there were sudden flashes. There was the sudden sense of unreality, of being held, pinned, caught between. Jumps were always like this. This was a short one, as they were less than a light year from Eresh, only a minute of subjective time in the jump. Short jumps were preferable. While jumps lasting hours or days were theoretically possible, it was too hard on humans both mentally and physically. Anything over thirty minutes was considered a long jump, grueling and painful. She'd had to make a few in her lifetime, but the Captains much preferred to make several shorter jumps rather than one long one, skipping from one jump point to another, from one convergence to another, like an insect making its way across a pond.

Adelita opened her eyes. The ship's systems would bring them out of the jump automatically at the elapsed time. Ten seconds to go. "Prepare for reversion in ten," Adelita said. "Confirm battle stations readiness."

There was a chorus of responses, sections confirming. For a moment the sensation of distortion increased, and then as abruptly as it begun, it ended. There was a profound silence. The main screens flickered, then came back to life. Ahead was the familiar starfield, Inanna rising three-quarters full ahead and to the left, Eresh out of sight behind it, eclipsed by the larger world it orbited. Inanna's seas and green continents were dotted with clouds, beautiful and welcoming.

Adelita resisted asking for a scan. Butcher would be scanning as she spoke, Usury monitoring the auditory channels. "Captain, I am seeing no unusual traffic," Butcher said. Adelita's control arm screen shifted, showing a schematic of insystem traffic. With Eresh obscured, there was only the flare of a small ship rising from Inanna and what looked like a mining shuttle about its business. *Ivory Three* was off to their beam on the right.

"Captain, we are being hailed by Eresh control," Usury said.

"Put it on speaker."

"*Ivory* and *Steel*, we have you insystem," the controller said. "Welcome home."

"Control, we are inbound to Eresh," Tal Robber said from *Ivory*.

"Understood." There was a brief pause. "*Ivory*, you are cleared for Greengate. *Steel*, you are cleared for Glitter Port Two."

"Acknowledged," Adelita said. "Please give my regards to the Captains and Elders. And request that the full Council meet in session as soon as we have docked. We have urgent news."

Chapter Two

Tal Robber was glad they were in the Greengate Dock instead of one of the Glitter Rim ports. It limited the number of people who could mob the outer airlock to meet members of Ships' Companies. He waited behind the door while the lock cycled. There would be dozens, as many as the area could hold, family and friends of everyone on *Horn* and *Bone* wanting news, answers, comfort. And how was he supposed to give it?

But it wasn't like he could delegate this task to anyone else. He was the first one off, before the rest of the crew, for a reason. The halves of the airlock peeled back, retracting into the walls. The crowd surged forward.

"Captain! Captain! Tal! Captain!" They pushed forward, shoving one another, reaching out for him. "Are there any survivors? What happened? What happened? Captain, what happened? Where is my daughter? Captain! Are we in danger here? Captain! Do you know where Ku Manslaughter is? He's in *Horn*'s crew. What happened?"

Tal held his hands up. "Please. Everybody! Don't shove. We're all brethren here and we all want answers. I don't have all the answers you need, but I will gladly tell you what I know." He waited a moment, still at the top of the ramp with the height that gave him, waiting for relative quiet. Three heartbeats. "First, and most important, *Horn* and *Bone* were lost with all hands." A shockwave spread across the crowd, almost like a physical blast wave, people reeling back, grabbing onto one another.

"I'm sorry. There is no way to soften that. There is no way to encompass the tragedy." Tal shook his head. "There are no survivors from their crews. None. I am sorry. I am sorry for every loss." His voice was not loud, but it carried. A woman suddenly slouched as her knees gave way, people beside her catching her. A child screamed.

"Who did this?" a bearded man shouted. "Who killed them?"

"As best we can tell, it was the Calpurnian Navy," Tal said. Looking across the crowd, he saw three of the Council Guard making way for an older woman with white, flyaway hair. "And no, I don't know where they are now. As to what happens next, I am ordered to report to the Council immediately." The woman caught his eyes. "Here is the Ivory Elder now."

The crowd parted somewhat reluctantly.

"Ivory Captain," she said, "You are required in the Council chambers. We are all gutted by this. I'm sure you know that all of us had family and friends aboard *Horn* and *Bone*. My granddaughter was aboard *Bone*." Her chin went up. "So we all stand together in our losses. Please let the Ivory Captain through. We need to get information in an orderly way, and in an orderly way we will release it."

At that they parted, a murmuring throng of misery. Tal clasped every hand that reached for him. "I'm sorry. I'm sorry." Sorry that he could do nothing, sorry he had not saved them, sorry.... He reached the door that led to the back corridors. They went through, leaving the guards outside. He turned to her. "Doro. I am so sorry about Nysia."

"Don't," Doro said. "I can't now."

"Of course." He had known Doro all his life, born to Ivory's Company as he was. In fact, she'd been his first teacher thirty years ago, sitting on the little stools beside him at the short table, opening jars of paint for him to draw fantastic creatures. Instead he put his arms around her. She barely came to the middle of his chest. It had used to seem to him that she was so big.

She clasped him tight for a moment. "Thank you, Tal."

"Doro, I...."

"I know there wasn't anything you could do."

"It was too late." Tal shook his head. "We have one survivor. The Steel Captain is bringing her to the Council."

"One of ours?" He tried not to notice the breath of hope in her voice.

"One of the Tainted. She was a prisoner on the Calpurnian ship we destroyed. She can tell us a limited amount, but she's cooperating completely."

"That's something," Doro said. "You can imagine what this meeting will be like."

"I can." Tal nodded solemnly. "I'm at your disposal, Elder."

They made their way along the corridors and down a short lift to the Council chamber, a room in the first tier below ground. No doubt long ago this had been one of the mine superintendent's offices, but the Calpurnian superintendents were long gone, the walls decorated with antique weapons from the Taking—boarding pikes and prisoner-made knives fashioned from eating implements. Now it was filled with four curved tables that left space between them, a circle with aisles to the center. Fifteen chairs surrounded it, and along the walls were another thirty chairs for aides and speakers. There was no need for a gallery. The Council's proceedings were on open channel. Tal could bet that nearly everyone was watching.

The chairs were almost all occupied, two chairs for each Ship's Company, an Elder and a Captain. The Elder was elected by the Ship's Company, all who had birthright or houseright within the Company. The Captain was elected by the Name Ship's crew. And the fifteenth seat was the Navigator. That seat was empty, to Tal's surprise. The other two empty seats were conspicuous—the seats for the Horn Captain and the Bone Captain. They were dead.

Across the room he saw Adelita seating Bister in one of the wall seats behind Steel's Chairs. The Steel Elder was already seated.

Ash's Elder was the moderator and called the meeting into session, speaking not just to the twelve at the tables but to everyone who was no doubt watching all over Eresh. "Brethren, we are in council. We are here in crisis unprecedented since our parents and grandparents took Eresh from our jailers and declared us free. For sixty-one years we have governed ourselves according to our Compact. Last year, Calpurnian autarchs declared that we had no right to self-government or self-determination, that we were merely a treasonous and rebellious installation. Today, they have attacked us with all the power at their command. Two Name Ships have been lost, and we mourn with their Companies. We are gathered in council so that all may hear, as is their right, what we know of what occurred. Steel Captain, you have a report for us?"

"I do." Adelita stepped out into the center, into the lights. Her black shipsuit was somber and her back straight and unyielding, as expressionless as her voice. Tal was glad she was giving the first report. She was always better at this sort of thing than he was. And of course she'd been doing it for more than a decade. Her words had weight even with difficult personalities. "In accordance with our previous agreements, *Steel Nine* and *Ivory Three* proceeded to a jump point just beyond our system for an intended rendezvous with *Horn Four* and *Bone Seven*...."

She laid it out starkly. Tal watched the faces of the other eleven, the play of emotions betraying horror, sorrow and fear. They asked few questions. They simply let her talk, her words emphasized by screens showing pictures and data collected by Steel's cameras and sensors. When she finished, she gestured to Tal. "Ivory Captain, do you have things to add?"

Tal got up, stepping out into the lights to take her place, acutely aware of all the eyes on him he could not see. He bent his head for a moment. "*Ivory Three* has recovered remains of some of our people. We respectfully ask that these remains be transferred to Central Life for identification." Someone around the circle of tables caught their breath.

"I think that would be advisable, Ivory Captain," Ash's Elder said quietly. "A motion?" Every hand was raised. "Carried," Ash's Elder said.

"Other than that," Tal said, "I believe the Steel Captain has described the situation perfectly. I do think it would be worthwhile to hear from the sole survivor of the attack who has been released from *Steel*'s Life Center and is more than willing to tell us what she knows. Her description of the attack and its aftermath is of more use than a repetition of my impressions." He looked across to her. "Bister of Inanna, if you will come forward?"

She got up uncertainly, wiping her hands on her pants legs, and came to stand beside Tal, a small woman in middle age with weathered skin. Tal stayed beside her encouragingly. "Bister, I understand that you were aboard the Calpurnian pinnace *Carulin* as a prisoner when it was ordered to join the fleet?"

"That is correct." Her voice was surprisingly firm and clear. She lifted her head, making eye contact with the unseen cameras. "I was aboard the *Carulin*. We were told to strap ourselves in for the jump...."

Though he supposed technically he should have gone to his seat when she began, Tal stayed standing beside her. After all, she'd been through a lot in the last day. When at last she finished her account, the Council had a number of questions which she answered calmly, though many of her answers were that she didn't know.

"They don't tell prisoners how many ships are in the fleet," Bister said. "I would guess ten or so large ships from what I saw afterwards. But could be eight. It could be twelve. Remember, I was floating in a suit. I couldn't positively identify any of them."

"We understand that," the Silk Captain said perhaps more harshly than she intended. "Your best guess."

"Ten," Bister said. "And perhaps four smaller ships. The pinnace I was on, at least one other, and a couple of dispatch boats."

"Which by now will have taken word of their victory back to Calpurnia," the Salt Elder said, looking sharply at the Ash Elder.

"That is speculation," Doro said. "Let's save our speculations for the closed session."

The Horn Elder stood. "Bister, we appreciate your presence at this Council. Brethren, I think we should recess. Our Companies need time to consider what was said here, and at least two of our Companies will spend the night in Vigil. I respectfully request that we recess until the fifth hour of tomorrow."

"That's awfully early," someone began.

"Respectfully, Elder," the Steel Captain said, standing up, "We do not have time to mourn. The Calpurnian Navy will follow up this victory. We must respond now."

"Emotion leads to ill-considered action," the Steel Elder said. He looked up at Adelita. "Captain, your energy is appreciated, but we must make good decisions, not hasty ones."

"Elder, we do not have time," Adelita began.

"You have given us no indication that the Calpurnians intended to jump directly for Eresh," the Ash Elder said, "and if they had, they would already be here. I see no reason not to recess so that we may mourn our dead."

"Seconded," the Bone Elder said. He looked ragged and his voice broke as he spoke. "My place is with Bone Company now."

"Show of hands?" the Ash Elder asked.

Adelita shook her head as the vote split nine to three for recess. She had not carried her own Elder, or in fact anyone but Tal and the Salt Captain.

"What's going to happen next?" Bister asked Tal quietly as people began to stand up and talk, the cameras now off.

"The Council is going into recess until tomorrow. And then we'll talk more," Tal said. And where was the Navigator? Presumably with some of those who had lost family.

Adelita came over to them. "This is ridiculous," she said. "We need to make decisions now. Not just postpone the entire business ten hours."

"They're not going to do that," Tal said.

"The Calpurnians aren't waiting ten hours!"

"They probably are, actually," Tal said. "If they assault Eresh, they want to do it in good order and be prepared. Time is on their side."

"I know it." Adelita shook her head. "But we…"

"Can't do more tonight," Tal said.

B ister watched the discussion between the Captains, trying to gauge exactly who led whom. The Steel Captain certainly seemed to have seniority, but clearly she valued Tal Robber's opinions. She'd heard a great deal about the Council in her years in and out of Eresh, though she had to admit that the labyrinthine politics of the Ships' Companies escaped her. People were born to a Company, though they might move between Companies if they joined a different household or had some specialty that recommended them to a Company. They might even be recruited if they were especially distinguished. It was highly unusual for someone not born to Eresh to join a Company. The Glitter Rim was full of residents from other worlds who weren't in a Company but who lived on Eresh.

Still, the Captains had treated her well. They'd certainly saved her life, and *Steel*'s medics had put her back on her feet. She had her effects such as they were, everything she'd been allowed to keep as a prisoner: her old shipsuit, the underclothes beneath it, the pouch she wore against her skin with a currency card, a little data card with nothing more than some images on it, and a square of worn flannel the size of her palm. Of course the Calpurnians hadn't let her keep weapons.

"So I can clear out now?" Bister asked.

The Steel Captain frowned. "I hope you will stay for the remainder of the meeting when it reconvenes. I think it would be useful for the Council to be able to ask you questions."

"I'm not sure what more information I can give you," Bister said. Not that she had anywhere else to be, but it was instructive to find out if she was free to go. Her head was starting to hurt. How long had it been since she'd eaten? There had been water and a protein drink in the Life Center, but the last meal must have been several hours before the battle.

"Still, if you would remain until the Council comes to a decision, it would be appreciated," the Steel Captain said.

"Of course. I'm happy to stay in a transport pod like I have before," Bister said, her mind on her exceedingly low currency balance.

The Steel Captain and the Ivory Captain exchanged glances. Was it that they mistrusted her wandering freely around the station or something more complicated? "She could stay with me," the Ivory Captain said. "I've got more room than you do since you have Galion and Cielo."

"I don't want to be a bother," Bister began. Among her own people failing to offer hospitality would be a terrible social sin, but on Eresh it was usual for visitors to pay for lodging, especially since few people had much personal space.

"It's no trouble at all," the Ivory Captain said. "And you can call me Tal. Everyone does. Well, everyone except my crew."

"Because they shouldn't." The Steel Captain's mouth twitched as though she almost smiled. Surely the woman smiled sometimes? Nothing Bister had seen suggested any sense of humor or for that matter any life outside the work of the ship, though apparently she shared her quarters with two people.

"If you truly don't mind." Bister made the conventional demurral, agreeing but indicating her debt. It seemed they were playing by something close to her rules. Everywhere she'd been had different ones, but she had thirty years' practice in sorting them out.

"Not a bit." Tal Robber—the Ivory Captain—straightened his shoulders. "Let me show you where I live. It's just me most of the time, so there's plenty of room. No need to waste your currency on a pod, and more comfortable too."

"And we will see you tomorrow," the Steel Captain said. "For the Council."

"Of course." Bister followed Tal's tall, lanky form through the doors and into the maze of corridors that was the heart of Eresh.

Unlike ships, which were laid out in an orderly, logical fashion, Eresh was a living place. It was almost organic, the way that sections from different cultures, different eras, different purposes had been welded together. Tunnels went down into the crust, either parts of the old mines that were played out near the surface, or as intentional living space. Habitation domes and parts of derelict ships had been attached however seemed best, stuck on randomly wherever it was convenient. There was the Glitter Rim, which was the only part of Eresh she'd visited before, the traveler's pale where the commercial docks were and the merchants who serviced them, the hangars that held small ships and the docking tenders that went back and forth to the blackened landing pads three kilometers away for the big ones.

But Eresh was much more than the Glitter Rim. She'd never been down in the mines or in the areas where the locals lived, much less the Council chambers and the official quarters of anyone with rank. Travelers' speculations alternated between the locals living in decadent and forbidden luxury to crowding in squalor in dank caves. Bister imagined it was something in between; most things in life were.

"It's this way," Tal said unnecessarily, leading her up a ramp with a bright floor plasticized to prevent slipping, then turning sharply left through doors into a corridor that looked nothing like the one they'd left, resembling instead the gray metal of old engineering sections. They went down a long corridor, bare except for doors to the left, then a sharp turn to the right and through a set of airlock doors that slid open at their approach.

Bister caught her breath. It looked like nothing so much as one of the cliff cities transported to a strange place. A wide four-sided plaza with fountains filled the center of the dome, trees reaching up to the fifth-story balconies that overlooked it. Running water, real running water, cascaded down from the second floor through a series of pools that were stocked with bright blue fish, making its way around islands of greenery artfully irregular to mimic nature. Of course, on a closer look, nothing was mere ornament. Every plant was edible. Even the tall trees had clusters of unripe nuts of a kind she didn't recognize. Most of the balconies had plants trained over the edges or climbing up strings to the bottom of the balcony above, making a green and edible screen. Amid the greenery, strings of lights crossed the courtyard, the overhead ambient lighting dim, so that it resembled a village at twilight.

"What is this place?" Bister asked. It was so unlike any of her imaginings.

"This is Ivory Junction," Tal said. "I guess once this was where the original Ivory ship connected to the old mining colony. But we've made a few improvements." He looked at her sideways and smiled. "In the last sixty-one years. A ship's Company isn't the literal ship anymore. Though of course there's always a ship named *Ivory*."

"So this is…"

"The Ship's Company." There was quiet pride in his voice. Children ran here and there, intent on some game. Adults were clustered around a communal sideboard, some serving and most helping themselves from a variety of offerings.

"Oh, I suppose it is dinner time," Tal said. He scratched his head. "I'll ask someone to bring something up in a little bit."

"Of course," Bister said, though the smell of the food was mouthwatering and reminded her sharply just how long it had been since she had a decent meal.

Tal glanced at her. "Or we could go ahead and eat."

"If…" Again, the lack of currency presented a dilemma.

"Just come get a plate with me," he said. "The meal is for the Ship's Company, but I can have a guest."

Just like it would be for a clan, Bister thought. She'd seen far more different ways of living in her travels. This was surprisingly like home. Or perhaps not so surprising. Although the people of Eresh claimed no kinship with the Tainted, the boundaries between had never been impermeable.

They went down the sideboard, Tal pointing out what various dishes were, while Bister loaded her plate as high as she thought polite. Everyone had something to say to Tal. She had wondered how he'd been elected Captain with his diffident style, but it seemed that it was part of his charm. He was every older woman's son, every child's self-effacing hero.

They found a small table by the cascade far enough removed from the crowd, the sound of the water covering conversation. Everyone left Tal alone once he sat, the invisible walls of the clan politeness apparently holding firm here as well. Bister bit into the bread. "Don't tell me you grow grain here. I can't see how you could do that."

Tal looked vaguely sheepish. "We trade for it with you. With Inanna, I mean. There's a lot of trade, actually."

"I know. I've done a bit of it."

"Of course you have." Tal frowned. "Bister, I don't want you to think I've got anything against the Tainted."

"Says the man named Robber."

"I've never robbed anyone. It was my great-grandfather." Tal took a bite of his fish. "He was a repeat offender on Calpurnia, beating people up and stealing their valuables. So he got sent here. I'm a Usury and a Mutineer and two Pornographers and a Crime Against Nature too." He sounded quite cheerful. "But Adelita's got it on me. She's the Lindorn Massacre three times. A lot of Steel Company is. But robbing? I'm not sure I'd make a very good thief."

"It's a surprisingly skilled profession," Bister said with a smile so that he wouldn't know if she was joking or not.

Tal laughed. "I'm sure it is."

Tal's rooms were nothing like Bister had expected. She had supposed a man who must spend much of his time aboard ship would have rooms half-empty and devoid of personality, with perhaps simply the basics for sleeping and grooming. Instead, when he opened the door for her, Bister positively boggled.

Every square inch of wall space was taken up with cupboards and shelves, each door lacquered with elaborate designs in a variety of colors so that the effect was nothing so much as being inside a giant tiled box surrounded by intricate pictures. His screens were nestled amid them, each screen showing yet more pictures that shifted constantly—sunrises and trees and the night sky over a waving sea of grass. She recognized that one. It must have been made on Inanna near Taralis Beacon.

The furniture in the front room was deep and comfortable: a couch longer than Bister was tall taking up the main space, the entire thing done in a patchwork of different colored leather, each patch no larger than her hand, and with no rhyme or reason to them, a crazy quilt of a couch. On top of this were piled three fringed blankets in different colors and an array of pillows. Plants hung from the ceiling in pots on strings, descending in tiers to the floor, while a stand held another series of plants ascending as though green stalagmites and stalactites competed.

"So this is home," Tal said. "Make yourself comfortable. The bath's in there. My room's the one through there. You're welcome to the couch and I promise it's big enough."

"It certainly is," Bister said.

Tal went into another room, still talking. "I'll get you some more pillows. And here's another blanket just in case you're cold."

"It's very comfortable in here," Bister said. "It's not as though we're on the plains and the temperature will drop at night."

"No, it stays where it's set. Usually. Unless there's a power issue. Which there isn't very often anymore." Tal came back out of the other room with a big green blanket and two more embroidered pillows. "We used to have brownouts sometimes when there was a dust storm. But we've got enough backup batteries now that it isn't much of a problem."

"It must be an entirely different set of challenges living on an airless moon," Bister said.

"Yes, well. Of course. And the Glitter Rim has its own power sources too. But the main problem of course is maintaining structural integrity. There's the constant problem of micrometeorites. They'd burn up harmlessly in atmosphere, but since Eresh doesn't have one…." He shrugged. "It's patch, patch, patch." Tal put the pillows and blanket down on the couch arm. "I've got some things I need to catch up on. If you need me, yell."

"Thank you," Bister said. She didn't ask if he lived alone. There was no other person here and there did not seem to be other rooms. This living area was spacious, and there was a private bath, something that in the Glitter Rim denoted great luxury, but certainly there was no evidence of multiple people. Perhaps a lover then, who had their own rooms? Or perhaps Tal was single either by design or accident.

Tal went in the back room and closed the door. After a bit she heard a mechanical mumble, as though he were on some device. Entertainment? Work? Bister went around the room methodically before she settled down on the enormous couch. It was wise to learn as much as possible. And she needed to wait a bit until he was fully involved in whatever he was doing before she slipped out.

Chapter Three

The corridors that led to the Glitter Rim were well marked. Late on station night, it was still easy to find her way to the wide grated gate, the arch lit with bright lights that shifted slowly from lavender to deep indigo. Purple Gate then. She knew where that was in relation to the port rim, though she'd never been on this side of the gate before. It slid open at her approach. She'd figure out how to get back through later if she needed to.

Bister drew herself up, feeling the swing return to her stride. Back on familiar ground everything was making much more sense. She started off along the rim toward the more populated areas where transients lived and worked and played. There was very little foot traffic. Admittedly it was late in the evening, but even the bars and eating places seemed unusually empty. Eresh kept Calpurnian Standard Time, as it had when it was a penal colony. On an airless moon there was no local diurnal cycle to adjust to, so this counted as night on Eresh. Shops that were still open, catering to ships' crews who were on ship time rather than station time, were all but deserted. She glanced in Yuli's Hygiene and Joy, surprised to see Yuli there himself.

It was a tiny space that fronted on the Rim itself, purple and green lights embedded in the glass front lighting in a variety of patterns. Inside, there were shelves along the walls with one sample of each of his wares and a door that led to the back area. You could try the sample all you liked, then have someone get it from the back—nothing but samples for anyone to walk off with. Bister assumed most of Yuli's space was the workshop behind where he made his concoctions and stored materials. She strolled in. The front space was given to a display of one of her favorites, Orange and Green Herbs, and she took the sample bottle of Oil for Body, Bath and Pleasure and sniffed it appreciatively. The oranges were grown on Eresh. The herbs probably came from Inanna, as Yuli did himself.

He looked up from the datapad on his lap, a hefty man on a tiny chrome stool by the door. "Holla, Bister. Didn't hear you were in."

"Just got in today," Bister said, which was Lady's truth. She put the cap back on the bottle somewhat regretfully. There would be no luxuries for herself until she'd built up a stake again. "Why are you watching the shop? Where's Chrys?"

"Gave her the night off. She may live in the Rim, but she's born to Horn's Company. She's at the Vigil."

"Oh right." Of course there were Vigils. Of course everyone from Horn and Bone's Companies would be there, along with everyone who had friends or relatives in them. There was no reason those born to a Company had to live in it. There were plenty of people who chose to live in the Rim, just like those who crewed or owned merchant ships that didn't belong to the Company and weren't Name ships. Lots of people wanted to be their own boss in the Rim rather than join the official ventures. Most of the bar and shop owners were in that category. Yuli was Tainted, but he'd come to Eresh and married here. He wasn't part of a Company, but he had resident rights to rent property and engage in commerce. Certainly there was always plenty of demand for Hygiene and Joy, and he was something of a genius for fragrance in her opinion.

"I've got a new one with resin and smoked daritt leaves," Yuli said. "The base is lightly filtered fruit oil. Very dark, very smoky, very mature. Interested?" He handed her a dark red flask labeled in elaborate script, "Essence of Smoke and Blood for Body, Bath and Pleasure."

Bister sniffed appreciatively. It did conjure up bonfires and autumn nights, roasting meat and the musk of the dancers around the fires. And it reminded her of something else, something she couldn't actually place, some warm memory that escaped her. "That's lovely." She handed the bottle back to him. "I'm afraid I can't right now, but it's on my list for later. Actually, I was wondering if you'd seen anyone from *Naga* or *Perisad's Pleasure* on the Rim in the last few days."

"Not that I can think of," Yuli said. He heaved himself off the stool and put the bottle into a wall niche which lit up when he put it down, bathing the flask in sparkling red light. "It's a sad business, don't you think? Two ships lost. Makes you think about life and death and the reason for it all."

"Yes, I suppose." And that was about the last thing Bister wanted to think about.

"They're all in her hands now, the Lady of the Void. Or at least we can hope so, since there's nothing of them to burn."

Right. Not a conversation she was having. "I expect so." Bister headed for the door. "Sorry I've got to dash, Yuli. I'm looking for someone."

"Holla round then."

"I will." She lifted a hand to him and hurried back out onto the Rim, following the bright curve counter-clockwise.

Not quite fifteen minutes later she was sitting on a pink metal chair under the circulating lights of the tram that ran around the Glitter Rim, a bored young man slapping a drinks menu in front of her. She ordered a warm fruit wine and asked, "Any chance you've seen the crew of the *Naga* or *Perisad's Pleasure* in port?"

He frowned, his eyes actually focusing on her. "I think Captain Ravit was in last night. You could page her on the net if you want."

"No thanks. I'll just wait." Bister wasn't entirely certain what her status was. Tal Robber hadn't exactly forbidden her to leave and she hadn't been locked in, but she was quite certain that she wasn't going to be given permission to just leave Eresh without complications. Best not to advertise that she had a way off. Jamila Ravit would let her work off the passage or pay her back later. That Jamila was around was a stroke of luck. She'd probably be by sooner or later. Best to get comfortable.

Bister took a sip of her wine and ran her hands through her hair. The medics had said she was fine. And she supposed she felt fine. There was still something strange, though that was only to be expected after nearly dying. Her hands felt odd. She looked down at her left hand circling the flowered pottery cup. It didn't seem hers, somehow. Or rather, it seemed like she wasn't quite used to it. Like it was a perfectly nice hand but somehow unfamiliar. Bister closed her fingers, lifted the cup. And yet everything worked perfectly. There was no tremor, no loss of sensation. She was absolutely fine. And wasn't that odd in itself? Surely prolonged hypoxia ought to leave some symptoms? And yet she was completely recovered.

"Well, look what wandered in!" a big man rumbled.

Bister got to her feet, reaching around the table to give him the embrace of greeting. "Shee! It's good to see you."

Jamila Ravit was right behind him, her slight body dwarfed by Shee's leather-clad bulk. "I thought you were on Menaechmi, Bister." She leaned in for the embrace as Shee pulled back. "Did problems come up?"

"You could say that. Join me?"

"Of course." Jamila slid into the chair across from her, while Shee attempted to perch on the one next to Jamila.

"I thought you were going to the Cities of the Coast for a load of pharma," Shee said.

"I was. I had a nice packet of anticoagulants, cholesterol inhibitors and antihistamines. Only I got caught getting through

Adelpha. I'd be awaiting sentencing now if the customs pinnace hadn't suddenly been ordered to join the fleet." Bister took a long sip of her fruit wine. For some reason it seemed especially pleasing, as though she hadn't had it in a long time. Surely not more than a week. And yet the warm wine, the depth of the fruit—it was luxurious, amazing.

Shee blinked rapidly. "Wait, you're her."

"Shee, you know who I am."

"No, I mean you're her. The sole survivor."

"Has that story already gone around the Glitter Rim?"

Jamila shifted on her chair, pouring herself a cup of wine. "Of course it has. Don't you see half of Eresh in mourning? Two ships lost and several hundred people? And whispers that there was one sole survivor, one woman who was picked up in a suit hours after her air should have run out." Her dark eyes were very serious. "Was that you, Bister? How did you do it?"

She took a deep breath. "It was. And I have no idea."

"What do you mean, you have no idea?" Shee leaned forward.

"I mean I don't know what happened," Bister snapped. "I've told everybody from the Steel Captain to the sanitation tech everything I know. We came out of the jump. I was in a cell. We went into battle mode. I couldn't see anything. Then there was a hit. The power flickered. I got out of the cell when the power went out. I got in a suit. That's it." There was more. But nothing worth telling. Nothing worth knowing or remembering.

"You're incredibly lucky," Jamila said.

"Don't I know it?" Bister drank again.

"So let me guess," Shee said. "You're flat broke."

"Nearly. I had most of my currency in that shipment." Bister shrugged. "I could probably get another stake on Inanna. But that's not a good idea right now." She leaned forward, though there was no one at nearby tables. "I think you need to get out of here as soon as you can. The Calpurnian Navy is coming."

Jamila frowned. "To check enforcement of the Isolation?"

"I don't mean a customs pinnace. I mean the fleet." Bister felt her hands shaking and stilled them under the table. "I think…the Ivory Captain thinks…they mean to take back Eresh."

"What for?" Shee asked incredulously. "They haven't bothered in sixty years."

"The volume of trade through the Glitter Rim," Bister said. "Think how many deals are made here. Not just pharma and mech for Inanna. Everything. Stuff outbound for Morrigan. Stuff for the Freyar. Not to mention everybody smuggling stuff into the Calpurnian Mandate. It all goes through Eresh because the Ships' Council doesn't care. More than doesn't care. They do everything but actively encourage it. When was the last time you saw Council guards down here for anything except a fight? Cargo inspection is minimal. They just read the manifest and take your word for it."

"That's why I do business here," Jamila said dryly. "Most of the time I don't have any outlay in bribes."

"That's what I'm saying!" Bister bent forward over the table. "Calpurnia can't afford it. The word I was hearing was that it's not just the cost in duties, but the political cost. Some of the Altissimi are making a big play out of ending lawlessness. Two of them have both sworn up and down to end piracy and smuggling. They're rivals to clean things up."

"And we're the thing they want to clean up," Shee finished.

"That's the size of it." Bister took another drink. She couldn't quite shake a slight feeling of distance, as though some part of her sat just behind her, listening and applauding her logic.

"So they attacked Eresh's ships first," Jamila said.

"Hoping to cut the fleet up piecemeal before engaging at Eresh," Bister said. "And since they won a big victory and took out two of the Name Ships without losing more than a customs pinnace, there's no reason they won't attack Eresh as soon as possible."

Shee swore. "We won't be fully loaded until tomorrow."

"If I were you, I'd ask for clearance tonight," Bister said. "I'd rather jump half-loaded than be here when the Calpurnian fleet arrives."

Jamila nodded. "That makes good sense." Her eyes met Bister's. "Need a ride?"

"Absolutely. I was hoping you'd ask."

Jamila pushed back her chair. "I'm going to go see if I can get the heavy metals from Agni loaded tonight. Pay double time or whatever. I'll ask for a jump window in six to ten hours."

"Where are we jumping to?" Shee asked.

"Wherever's open." Jamila stood. "Beggars can't be choosers. We'll jump and then work out our final course later." She glanced down at Bister. "Be aboard in three. I owe you for the tip."

"Thank you." Bister took a deep breath. She'd made the deal. She should be relieved. Instead, she felt a nagging sense that something was wrong. Should she hunt a ride to Inanna instead? But then she'd be stuck. If the Calpurnian Navy decided to enforce the Isolation, she might not be able to leave Inanna for seasons if not years.

She lifted a hand to Jamila and Shee as they hurried out. And if she was stuck off-world for seasons or years? Griff would worry, but what good would it do for her to be stuck there too? She would miss him, but sooner or later, and probably sooner, the Calpurnian fleet would be recalled. They'd leave a governor on Eresh and maybe one ship for enforcement. It would be possible to run that blockade. It wouldn't be years. Seasons, maybe. And deadly dangerous to get in. But that would make what she had all the more necessary.

And yet. If she were on Inanna, it might be easier to run the blockade out, if Griff could be persuaded to help. He could be incredibly stubborn sometimes, and one of the things he was stubborn about was leaving Inanna. For a moment she wished he were there with her, sitting across from her, nondescript and sober in his stolid workman's clothes, only the shape of fine bones beneath his beard betraying how handsome he truly was. Or at least she thought so.

Bister took another drink of her fruit wine, surprised the cup was nearly empty. The bar was very quiet. Jamila wasn't joking that Eresh was in mourning. It was usually much busier at this time of night. Two ships and their companies. How many more before this was over? Certainly the Steel Captain looked like a woman who wouldn't go down without a fight. Five Name Ships against the Calpurnian Navy? It would be a battle but ultimately the outcome wouldn't be in doubt. Calpurnia could put fifteen ships in action if they wanted to. How many had been at the battle in which she'd been an unwilling participant?

Ten, something whispered in the back of her mind, *ten capital ships and five smaller ones*. A flash of fire bright against the void, main thrusters firing, sleek black shapes accelerating away while she floated....

Bister pulled herself back. She was on Eresh. It was over. It was fine. She'd somehow survived and it didn't matter how. The only important thing was what to do next. Jump with the *Naga* to wherever or try to get to Inanna—that was the real question. Her hands were shaking on the empty cup. But were they hers? For a moment they looked bony, attenuated, flesh and muscle shrunken....

"This is ridiculous," Bister said aloud. She was not going to fall apart. It was just one more close call.

"What's ridiculous?" Someone stood across the table from her behind the seats Jamila and Shee had vacated, and Bister looked up.

They were perhaps Bister's height, black hair flowing down their back from a golden headband nearly to their waist. A sleeveless scarlet vest fastened in the front with intricate gold knots above floor-length skirts made of tiers of red and magenta and orange embroidered silk, five tiers from the tight waist to the wide ruffles beneath which peeped the gilded toes of little sandals. Their eyes were rimmed in kohl black, arched beneath golden powder. "Do you mind if I join you?" They did not wait for an answer before they sat down, the flashing pink lights reflecting on the iridescent glitter on their arms. "I am the Navigator."

Bister blinked. "I'm sorry?"

"You and Tal Robber left the Council meeting before I arrived. I did not have the pleasure of meeting you earlier." The Navigator raised a hand for the stunned bar boy to bring another cup. "And a flask, please," they said. "You are drinking fruit wine?"

"Yes," Bister said. She felt that she was gathering her wits rather slowly. "How did you know where I was?"

"I thought I might find you in the Glitter Rim." The Navigator poured for them both from the new flask. "After all, it is where you would have friends and contacts, yes? So it was simply a matter of walking the Rim until I found you. And people do tend to tell me things."

"I expect so," Bister managed. She took a sip to buy time. This flask was a rather better vintage than what she'd been served. "Who are you, exactly?"

"I am the Voice of the Gods on the Ships' Council." The Navigator lifted their cup. "I was chosen when I was seven to speak for them, and since then I have trained in their service ceaselessly. I learn still from the elders, though it has been many years since I took my seat. I am dedicated to the Lord of the Dance."

Bister put her head to the side. That explained the garb at least. "It must be challenging to serve the lord of green and growing things on an airless moon."

"Perhaps that is why I was needed," the Navigator said. "Why I was born to this service now. In this time, perhaps what we need is to bring forth and cherish life in all its messy complexity."

"Perhaps so," Bister said. The vast and beautiful interior environment she'd seen at Ivory Junction was a work of art. "Why are you called the Navigator?"

"The Navigator is a guide," they said. "Each ship used to have one, a person whose job was to understand the vast currents of the stars, to guide the ship through space 'with their heart and dreams' as the stories tell us. Of course nowadays we navigate by mathematics. It takes millions of calculations to determine the positions of every celestial body with a gravity field along a line of transit and to work out the constantly shifting jump points that will allow faster than light travel using those fields without colliding with any of the bodies along the way. There are no dreams involved."

"No, clearly not," Bister said. She'd never had the technical background for navigations herself. Big ships might have crew members who had other specialties, but the small ones she travelled aboard generally required the entire crew to be able to take a bridge watch. She'd always done her smuggling as a hitchhiker, a paying passenger, or support crew that did the dirty work, handling cargo or something. After all, somebody always needed to clean and cook. "So the Navigator is now a priestly title?"

The Navigator nodded. They took a sip of their wine. "We are chosen based on certain omens, and of course vocation. I've been in His service for twenty-two years, though I still have a great deal to learn. There are many priests, but only one Navigator at a time. Who that Navigator serves generally gives a tenor to a certain era. We speak of the era of the Golden Lady before this, when the Glitter Rim was opened. You can see her likeness by all the main airlocks. She led us to commerce. When we threw out the jailers, took over Eresh for ourselves and welcomed the mutineers who brought us the first Name Ships, that was the era of the Warlord."

"That makes sense." She sipped from her cup. "We worship the Lord of the Dance on Inanna too."

"But that is not who you serve." The Navigator's eyes were

sharp over the rim of their cup. "The Steel Captain said you had the accretion disk on one shoulder and the nova on the other, tattooed in the way of your people."

"It's true," Bister said. "We wear their marks on our bodies." She glanced at the Navigator's finery. "It's practical."

"You serve the Lady of the Void."

"So I have sworn," Bister said cautiously. "But I am no priest. Just a worshipper who was marked in accordance with tradition."

"The only god who has no voice in our councils. The only one who has no era." The Navigator put down their cup. "Why do you suppose that is?"

"I haven't the faintest idea. Nor do I have any idea why you're posing theological questions to me."

"Don't you?" the Navigator asked. Their dark eyes were very steady.

A frisson ran through her. "No," Bister said. "I don't think so."

"How did you survive in space so long?"

"I don't know," Bister snapped. "I've told the Steel Captain, the Ivory Captain, your Council, everybody. I don't know why I'm not dead. Yes, I know the suit's air should have given out several hours before I was picked up. I don't know why it didn't. I lost consciousness."

The Navigator nodded. "And then what?"

"I was picked up by *Steel*."

"Before that."

"I told you, I was unconscious!" Bister took a deep swig of the wine. If there was ever a reason for drinking, this was it.

"Did you dream?" the Navigator asked. "I'm merely curious."

"I…" Bister hesitated. "…I suppose I did. But it's not important."

"May I ask what?"

"I dreamed I was floating through space. Which isn't strange, because I was. But I was a ship. I was just gliding through the void on momentum alone, no propulsion activated, just continuing on my course. Like a fish underwater, you know? When they're just traveling with the current. I was listening. I was listening to the music between the stars, and I heard them singing." Bister stopped, taking another long drink. It wouldn't do for her voice to break. "I heard the music no one can hear." She shook her head. "And then I woke up in *Steel*'s Life Center. That's it. I dreamed when I was unconscious from hypoxia."

The Navigator was sitting up very straight, their face suddenly taut with tension. "That is extremely interesting," they said.

"Why?"

The Navigator got to their feet. "It will be easier to show you than to tell you. Will you come with me? I think you will find it… moving."

"Where are we going?"

"To a part of the station you haven't seen," the Navigator said. "And I do think it will answer some of your questions, Bister. At least I hope so."

"I'll come then," she said.

They went back into the station proper through the Greengate, the Navigator merely waving a hand at the screen with their control ring. There was a click and the gate slid open, two elaborate panels twelve feet high with bars wrought to look like growing vines, painted and gilded in green and gold. The actual doors were open in their tracks, airtight doors seven inches thick that could withstand hard vacuum or a cannon blast.

"We'll be going up through Salt," the Navigator said. They led the way to a lift, its doors likewise ornamented with flowering vines.

"Up?"

"Into one of the oldest parts of the station." The Navigator swiped their ring at the control box, ring and box both lighting. "Twelve, please." The lift began to rise with a soft whirr.

Bister suppressed a question. Most of the station was built down rather than up, or at least no higher than the two to three stories of the Glitter Rim that surrounded it, docking ports built into the Rim, with the cargo movers and towmasters beneath it. Even if the lift went down five or six levels beneath the surface, twelve would be the very top, or close to it.

The doors opened into a small room. It was semi-circular and quite dark, the walls painted a rich deep blue that absorbed the light of the single lamp on a table beside a door. The door was plain dark steel, without markings of any kind, strange in this elaborately ornamented place. The room was also nearly empty, a distinction that did not escape her. On Eresh, nothing was more valuable than space. Every inch had to be useful.

"A moment," the Navigator said, and approached the door to enter a code into an old-fashioned keypad beside the door. "There."

The door slid back, jerking a little on its track. Bister followed the Navigator in, turning about, her hands out from her sides. It was entirely round, a dome of many panes of clear, thick silica crazily pieced together, making a hemisphere that rose from knee height on all sides. In the middle of it was a couch covered in fine red brocade fabric, shaped like a fantasy of a ship's acceleration couch, with graceful curving back and a throw of purple silk fringed in gold. It was the only thing in the room besides two small cabinets on either side of the door, each with sconce above it giving off a dim light that did not compete with the stars above.

"What is this place?" Bister asked.

"It is called the Array," the Navigator replied quietly. "And it belongs to the Lady of the Void." They slipped off their sandals and left them beside the door. "Will you? It is a matter of courtesy. We wear no shoes or gloves here."

"Of course," Bister said. She had to hop on first one foot and then the other take off boots and socks. The floor was steel and cold, but one should always be polite to the gods.

The Navigator walked out into the middle of the room. "Long ago," they said, "when Eresh was first founded as a mining colony from Inanna by the Corporation, this was one of the earliest things they built. Come and see for yourself."

Bister walked over to join them. Looking down, the shape of the station was clear—the great crater almost obscured by the patchwork of hulls and habitat domes, the Glitter Rim that ran around it in a perimeter lit up with the lights of ships at the ports. From here you could see almost three hundred and sixty degrees around. There was *Steel Nine*, its bulk dwarfing the docking port and Rim beside it. Clockwise, another of the Name Ships snugged up to the station, dorsal missile tubes plain to see. A merchanter was next, then two smaller ships, then the familiar shape of Jamila Ravit's *Naga*. A drone loader was out and three mechanics in suits worked beneath her launch cradle. Jamila had obviously gotten the early clearance she wanted.

It was beautiful and intricate, the pattern of the station, of all the lives it touched. How many lived here? There must be thousands in the Ships' Companies, ten thousand maybe? Fifteen thousand? And perhaps as many again who lived here as transients or permanent residents, Tainted and drifters who had washed up here. Beneath the fragile skin, life happened. "Eresh," Bister said. She supposed the Navigator had brought her here to see what the stakes were. Indeed, it was beautiful.

"Look up," the Navigator said.

And that was uncanny. A few inches of silica separated her from the void. She had seen the stars from space many times before, but only on screens. Nobody put actual windows on starships. There was no need for that kind of hull weakness. It was nothing like the night sky. There was not one molecule of atmosphere to Eresh. The darkness was so profound that it had depth. You could see how far it was between the stars.

For a moment it was disorienting. The only time she'd seen the stars like this was when she was drifting in the suit, and Bister put out her hands for balance, suddenly feeling the room around her tilt as though she were in freefall, tumbling purposelessly, helpless and alone....

The Navigator's hand was beneath her shoulder. "Easy," they said, and helped her to sit down on the couch.

"I was drifting," Bister said. She closed her eyes, leaning back on the couch, its carved back supporting her. The world seemed to pitch nauseatingly beneath her, and she held onto the edge of the couch. Of course it wasn't moving. "And I heard a woman singing. She was singing back to the solar wind. I couldn't understand the words, but she was singing. And I wasn't scared anymore. I knew the suit indicators were nearly on empty. I knew the other voices had stopped. I knew I was going to die. And it was like going to sleep. It was like going to sleep in my mother's arms." Bister felt a tear form and squeezed her eyes shut. "I don't remember my mother. My parents died when I was a baby. They were trying to get our wagon out of a flooded creek. They should have just left the wagon. But it had everything in it, you see. Everything they had. And then the wheel shifted." Bister felt the tear spill over. "They were young and stupid and they should have left the wagon. But my cradle floated. It was wood. When the water came up it floated free."

Alone on the tide, the gray rain pelting down, the bodies face down in the water beside the tilted wagon.... She saw it as from above, as though the sky could see and hear the frantic screams of the baby carried away on the flood....

"I heard her singing," Bister whispered. "And I knew I was safe."

"The Lady of the Void chose you," the Navigator said. "She took you in her hand and saved your life."

Bister opened her eyes. The Navigator was sitting at her feet on the couch, their spangled skirts spreading around them. "There is no way the suit could have lasted as long as it did. The Steel Captain examined it herself. Our techs have examined it. It's just an ordinary Calpurnian suit. It has a sixteen-hour capacity. *Steel* got your signal twenty-one hours and twenty-eight minutes after *Bone* registered missile impact. Even if you'd stayed on the Calpurnian pinnace for an hour, life support would have run out long before *Steel* arrived. Your survival is literally a miracle."

"I don't understand," Bister said.

"Nor do I." The Navigator shook their head, heavy oiled curls against their shoulders. "Except that the Lady of the Void does as she wishes for reasons that are her own. Or at least it is said that she used to before she was lost to us, as so many things have been."

"How do you lose a god?" Bister said. "Besides, she's not lost. We revere her. I mean, not commonly. It's kind of unusual that I chose her marks to wear. Most of us choose the Hunter or the Lord of the Dance who brings the rains, or the Lady of Fires."

"Why did you?" the Navigator asked. "It is, as you say, unusual."

Bister shrugged. When she looked up she could still see the starfield above, but the world didn't move. The couch was as solid as an acceleration couch. "I suppose because I've always wanted to travel. I could never reconcile myself to just staying on Inanna. The idea that there were all these worlds out there, places I'd never be allowed to visit because of the Isolation…. When I came of age and got my marks, I took it as a kind of defiance. Out there was where I belonged. And I made it happen." Bister smiled. "One of the free traders from Eresh landed. That was right after we set up Taralis Beacon so we could call them when there was a clan there ready to trade. I talked him into bringing me with him back to the Glitter Rim." It hadn't been hard. She was sixteen and pretty.

"And then?"

"And then the whole galaxy was mine." Bister smiled as though it had been easy. "I've been to Calpurnia and Menaechmi, Morrigan and Lono, the Adelpha Rim, even Freya. I've been a lot of places and seen a lot of things in the last thirty-four years."

"And now you're a free trader yourself." The Navigator steepled their hands.

"You could say that. But why a goddess would save me...I mean, surely there were better people who died." It sounded stark when she said it that way.

"There probably were," the Navigator said quietly. "People I have known all my life. People who were kind and loving, and who have families who miss them very much. But the Lady of the Void makes her own choices, even though she is lost to us."

"I don't understand what you mean by lost."

"When the war came between the Corporation and the Alliance two hundred years ago, both sides had mighty fleets." The Navigator put their hands at their side. "We know how the war ended, of course. Inanna was ruined and the Isolation was imposed. Eresh became a penal colony for Calpurnia rather than a mining installation for the Corporation. But both sides had ships. Both sides had those who worshipped the Lady of the Void. And there was one ship more." The Navigator paused, then went on. "One of the First Ships had remained in the system. Maybe it had been the one that first brought colonists to Inanna. I don't know. But what the oldest records say here on Eresh is that it was a temple, a place of pilgrimage. It remained on a long orbit around our primary, an orbit decades long, but once in a while dipping back into our system. When it did, it was a time of enormous celebration, the turning of an era. It was named *Sounding Dark*."

Though nothing had changed, it felt to Bister like a vast bell had tolled just beneath hearing, its vibrations spreading under her skin.

"Pilgrims would seek it out in ships. Those who had the favor of the Lady of the Void might find it. They might be allowed to go aboard and walk its corridors and make their petitions to her in the holiest of holy places. Sometimes—often—she answered their prayers." The Navigator sighed. "But of course when the war came, both sides wanted it. They both wanted to say they had it and had her favor. So her priestess at the time, her avatar, took it away into the Long Night. She and *Sounding Dark* both disappeared."

"I don't see...."

"A few times in the last two centuries someone from Eresh has claimed to see it. Maybe it was a sensor ghost. Usually it was when the ship was in distress. Twice the crew was saved when logically they should have been lost. But no one, no one who deliberately sought it, has ever found *Sounding Dark*." The Navigator's eyes rested on Bister's face. "I think you are a sign to us that she has not abandoned us. I think you were chosen by the Lady of the Void to return her to us."

"That's ridiculous," Bister said. And yet she squeezed her eyes shut because the starfield above tilted gently, as though a massive creature moved through the night, golden wings furled, singing to the lost.

"Do you have any other explanation of how you survived?"

"I'm not a priest! I'm not an avatar! I'm a smuggler, a dealer, a sometime thief!" Bister opened her eyes and sat up. "If the Lady of the Void wants an avatar, why doesn't she pick you? Why didn't she pick any of the other people who were dying?" Her voice caught, and she could say no more, the pain in her chest overwhelming her.

The Navigator's arm was around her back, young and strong. She held on, a silent scream inside her. "We can't know why some live and some die. We can't know why she chose you. We only know she did." The Navigator's voice was gentle. "And because she chose you, you have a duty. You owe her for your life. You must serve her as best you may. You must pay the debt."

Bister found her breath. "She holds my debt-service."

"If you like to put it that way. You owe her. And you must repay her."

Bister looked up. The Navigator's arm was still around her. They smelled of flowers and smoke. "I have no idea how to do that."

"Find *Sounding Dark*."

Chapter Four

Tal was surprised to hear his front door open. Nobody had the code but him and one other, so he stuck his head out of the bedroom. Surely the Navigator was busy? Yet there was the Navigator and Bister coming in. Bister looked solemn and stressed, and they were clearly finishing some conversation. "Yes," she said, "I'm just going to go to sleep now."

"That's probably best," the Navigator said, giving Tal a look he supposed was intended to be significant but actually conveyed nothing. "Good night, then."

Bister went into the bathroom and the Navigator followed Tal back into his bedroom, the door shutting behind them. "Before you ask, I found her in the Glitter Rim arranging passage off. And yes, telling her friends the Calpurnians were coming," the Navigator said tiredly.

"What else could you expect her to do?" Tal said. "Of course she's going to warn her friends. And as far as passage off, I'd like her to stay for the meeting tomorrow, but it's not urgent if she does. Bister's not a prisoner. She's free to go."

"It's much more complicated than that," the Navigator said. "And I don't have time to explain it now. I've got to be at *Horn*'s Vigil in a few minutes."

"Come back after?" Tal asked. He put his hand on the Navigator's arm. It was firm and muscular despite the scatter of golden glitter on it. "You can at least sleep here."

"For a few hours." The Navigator's eyes smiled, though their face looked drawn. "You've set the Council meeting early."

"A few hours' sleep is better than nothing." Tal gestured to the rumpled bed, the lights still on, his datapad activated. "I'm having trouble sleeping too."

"It's been a day, and tomorrow will be worse."

"Prophecy?" It was sometimes disconcerting, the things the Navigator just came out with.

They smiled then, reaching up to ruffle Tal's hair affectionately. "It doesn't take a prophet to see that we're screwed."

Tal laughed. "Well, then. Come back after the Vigil. And don't wake me."

"I won't." The Navigator opened the bedroom door.

Bister was just settling on the couch, pulling up the pile of blankets as though she could disappear under their weight. She looked up, startled, coming up on her elbows.

"Goodnight," the Navigator said, and went out.

"Er, call me if you need anything," Tal said.

"I will. Thank you." Bister lay back down again.

Tal went back in the bedroom. He'd give it fifty/fifty odds that she'd be there when he woke up, but it was her right to go. In fact, why the Navigator wanted her to stay was opaque. Yes, it would be nice to have her at the meeting tomorrow, but hardly critical. Unless they were worried about the panic that rumor might spark on the Glitter Rim? But it would be better if the merchant shipping could get clear of a battle. There was little doubt there would be one. Five Name Ships would put up a fight. They had to.

This may be my last night here, Tal thought, looking around his comfortable room. *Tomorrow night I may be in a Calpurnian brig awaiting execution like my great-grandfather before me. Or I may be dead.* The latter didn't truly frighten him. He'd faced death in space since he joined the ship's crew. It was the former that…

Tal sat down on the bed, pulling out a hidden drawer and hunting through a series of datasticks until he found the one he wanted. He didn't look at it much, but his father had made him a copy when he moved out. Yes, there were the images. There was the first one, nearly a century old. It was cropped sharply, a head shot of a man staring unsmilingly at the lighting source, wavy fair hair and two days of beard stubble, something defiant in the tilt of his chin. The watermark across the bottom read Ithen, Robber. Whatever his family name had been, it was lost. No one had names. Just crimes.

But he had held to Ithen. He was bad news, a young man in search of a fight, Tal would have said if he'd seen him on the Glitter Rim. He'd been fifty and the father of three children born in prison by three different women when he'd been in the Taking and fought the jailers. He'd been killed. His daughter, Ema Robber, had slashed the man who'd killed him to shreds with an energy flail, or so the story went. Tal found it hard to imagine Gramma Ema slashing anyone to death, but he supposed it was possible. She'd been born when her mother was in solitary.

"Tal," she'd said when he was a child, "no matter how bad it gets, remember it could be worse."

Of course it wasn't bad at all. He had parents who loved him and all of Eresh was his playground. He had Doro as a teacher and a snug classroom with red and blue walls deep in the mines where the radiation didn't penetrate, friends and a playcenter with fake trees made out of plastics that you could climb all over and pretend you were anywhere. Eresh was a wonder and they'd made it so.

And now it was his to defend. Now it was his to die for. Tal turned off the image of his great-grandfather. He wouldn't be the one who let them down. He was a Robber.

The Navigator came in just when Tal needed to get up. "It's after four," Tal said, scrubbing his hands across his face.

Looking tired, the Navigator sat on the edge of the bed. The dark makeup around their eyes was blurred with use and tears, their finery drooping. "I've been with the families all night." Tal put one arm around the Navigator's waist, silent comfort he knew could not possibly suffice. "But I wanted to see you before starting again."

"Of course," Tal said. "And you wanted to make sure I didn't oversleep?" It was an old joke between them, that Tal could sleep anywhere and at the most inappropriate times.

"That too," the Navigator said with a wan smile.

"You've got spare clothes here if you want to clean up," Tal said. "And by the way, is Bister still there?"

"Asleep on the couch," the Navigator said. "I gave her quite a bit to think about last night."

"Oh?" Tal opened one of the lacquered compartments in the wall and started rummaging for a shirt. He'd wear an Ivory shipsuit over it, but the shirt beneath should be clean and decent.

"Tal, we can't beat the Calpurnian Navy."

He turned around. "That's helpful. Thank you for the vote of confidence."

"I mean we can't beat it alone." The Navigator shook their head. "It's a fool's mission."

"So what do you suggest? Surrender? I take *Ivory* and run?" Tal heard the anger in his voice. "We have to fight. And I don't see any allies around."

"We need to find *Sounding Dark*."

"That again?" Tal said. "*Sounding Dark* has been missing for nearly two hundred years. *Sounding Dark* is a legend, if she ever existed at all. Yes, sure, in theory one of the First Ships would be great! But people have looked for her for centuries without any luck. I don't think she's going to just turn up fortuitously right now."

"I think she is." Tal spun around, shirt in hand. "I think Bister was saved by the Lady of the Void and she means us to recover *Sounding Dark*." The Navigator's voice was firm and tired. "How else do you explain her survival? I think the Lady of the Void chose her. I think Bister is a message for us."

"I can't explain her survival," Tal said. "But to call it direct intervention from the Queen of Night? That's taking it really far. I know you want this to have something to do with *Sounding Dark*, but we have to make some decisions today about how we're going to fight and we have to make them on facts, not faith."

"Faith is my job." The Navigator stood up. They raised their hands, letting them rest on Tal's shoulders. "Look, if it's a straight-up fight we can't win. Five ships on ten or more? You are going to die, your crew is going to die, and they're going to take Eresh anyway. There has to be a better alternative."

"If I could think of one, I would," Tal said. "I know you're scared. I'm scared too. But we can't expect the gods to save us."

"If they don't, who will?"

Tal swore. "I don't know, but it won't be me. I can't turn a seventy-year-old converted merchanter into the match for a Calpurnian ship of the line! I will do my best and I will fight to my last breath, but I can't do better than take some of them with me." He shook his head. "And maybe some people will say it's a good idea to surrender. But I don't think that's better."

"Some will," the Navigator said. "So what do we have to lose? If we search for *Sounding Dark* and don't find her, we're no worse off than we are now."

"*Ivory* has to fight. We can't go off chasing a ghost ship. We couldn't any of the other times you asked me to, and we certainly can't now when every ship is needed to defend Eresh."

They tightened their hands on Tal's shoulders. "Let's take it to the Council and see. I doubt the Council is going to want to fight a pitched battle. Let's see if they're open to alternatives. The Lady of the Void has given us one. It would be foolish not to use it."

"And Bister's on board with this?" Tal asked skeptically. "The Lady's chosen is a Tainted smuggler?"

"She is." The Navigator brushed one hand across his cheek. "And she's willing to try. So let's dress and do this."

"In a minute," Tal said, drawing the Navigator in for a kiss and trying not to think it was the last one.

Adelita Massacre strode into the Council chamber not quite fifteen minutes before it was supposed to convene. The aura of fear and grief could almost be tasted, like a contamination in the air that could be perceived with both nose and mouth. Her black shipsuit was pristine, her eyes rimmed in black. Her face was set. Nobody would note any weakness in the Steel Captain. She was Justice's Hand for the Council, and there were expectations. She could almost feel people standing up straighter when she passed.

Bister was back in the company of the Navigator, Adelita noted. She supposed that was as well. It was going to be a difficult meeting. She sought the Ash Captain, a tall man in his early fifties, his long hair halfway down his back—an affectation for a man who served shipboard. It was the same steel gray as his shipsuit. "We fight?" Adelita said quietly.

The Ash Captain grimaced. "I don't see we have much choice."

The Salt Captain joined them, his forehead creased. "I think we have to use the Name Ships to evacuate as many people as we can. There are a lot of people who are wanted in the Calpurnian Mandate. And the children and the old, of course."

"Evacuate to where?" Adelita asked. "Inanna?"

"Maybe temporarily," the Ash Captain said. "But if Eresh falls, the Calpurnians will be all over Inanna soon enough."

"Somewhere not allied with Calpurnia," the Salt Captain said. "Agni?"

"The Agnen won't welcome us," the Ash Captain said. "It has to be Morrigan. We've deep trading ties there."

At that moment the Ash Elder called attention for the Council to go into session, and Adelita excused herself to find her seat. The cameras were off. Perhaps, she thought, it would be bad for morale for everyone to see the Council flailing and debating fruitlessly. Better to put on a show of resolve and unity later.

"Brethren, we are gathered in solemn council," the Ash Elder began, "to make a decision as critical as any we have made since the Taking. It is likely that in the next hours we will be tested by the might of the Calpurnian Navy. What will our response be?"

Everyone began to talk at once. It seemed to Adelita that every member had an opinion to expound, most of them loudly and a few with table thumping as the volume and stress grew. She remained seated and silent. They'd blow themselves out and then they'd listen to what they had to. The Ash Elder futilely called for order. The thing about free people, the thing about pirates, Adelita considered, was that leading them was near to impossible.

"We have to evacuate!" the Salt Captain shouted. "In good order. While we can!"

"Coward!" the Silk Captain snapped. "And you're to lead this retreat I suppose?"

"We need to prioritize," the Bone Elder said. "The most vulnerable need protection."

"Surrender is an option," the Silk Elder said, and the Silk Captain wheeled around as if stabbed. Adelita shook her head, her lips pursed. "If we fight," the Silk Elder continued, "there is no reason they won't just destroy the station. They don't need us. They could blow up the whole thing. If we surrender, at least the children will live. They may arrest the adults and execute some of us, but they won't execute children."

"So you suppose," the Steel Elder snapped.

"We can win," Tal said.

"That is full of shit," someone replied. "You think you're the hottest Captain there is and you've only had it a year. If you knew what a real battle looked like…."

Adelita got to her feet. "I do know what a real battle looks like. And I do not think anyone here can fault my experience." Her voice was level. She did not shout. And yet heads turned to her. "We must fight. But we must also consider evacuating. I know my ship and my crew as well as any. We are willing to die to buy time for those we love to evacuate. *Steel Nine* will not lead the retreat. We will cover the retreat."

That shamed them into silence for all that it was true. The Ash Captain took a deep breath. He, at least, would stand with her. Tal looked solid.

"Three ships can slow them down," Adelita said. "We will hold them off. We will give them the fight of their lives. And in the meantime, an evacuation can be completed."

The Ash Captain nodded. "We will spill their blood into the Void, and ours will be the sacrifice. We will die free." Those were the words of the Taking, and a resonance ran around the room.

"There is another way," the Navigator said. Their voice was quiet, but in the sudden still it carried. "As the voice of the gods among us, will you hear me out?"

"Of course, Navigator," Adelita said, inclining her head and retaking her seat. If she did, others must.

"Siblings and friends," the Navigator said, stepping into the space between the tables, "you all know of *Sounding Dark* and you all heard yesterday of Bister's miraculous escape…."

Adelita listened as the Navigator spun their tale, her eyes moving from one of her colleagues to another. Some were incredulous, others planning what they would say next. Some were afraid. Some felt a stirring of hope. Some hoped for surrender. And Bister, the Tainted, sat quietly in her chair along the wall, leaning forward slightly. Adelita's eyes kept returning to her.

As the Navigator finished, Tal Robber stood up, coming to stand at the Navigator's shoulder. "When I suggested we fight, I didn't mean that we should throw our lives away needlessly. I meant that we could hold until *Sounding Dark* could join the fray."

"Hold? Hold?" The Silk Elder was incredulous. "How is that supposed to work? And we're supposed to expect a mythical ship to join the fight at a certain time? This doesn't make any sense."

"Do you believe in the gods?" the Silk Captain snapped.

"I believe the gods gave us the good sense not to do something ridiculous," the Silk Elder snapped back.

"We have lost too many already," the Bone Elder said. "We must surrender."

"If we surrender the Name Ships, we have nothing!" the Ivory Elder said.

Bister was still sitting quietly. Her head turned, her eyes meeting Adelita's, dark as infinite space, her expression waiting. Just as in a battle, there is no time for thinking. There is only time to do what you must.

Adelita got to her feet. "We surrender the station," she said. "But not the Name Ships. We take the Name Ships outsystem. And when the time is right we strike." Every head turned to her, including the Tainted, her lips slightly parted, expectant. "We cannot defeat ten capital ships with five," Adelita said. "But they cannot keep ten ships at Eresh for long. They will have to reduce their force fairly promptly. When they draw down, we strike. And in the meantime, we find *Sounding Dark*." She lifted her hand to forestall comment. "Whether she is one of the First Ships or not, she possesses ancient armament and at the very least gives us another capital ship in the mix. The Lady of the Void has shown us the way. We cannot win in a straight fight, and evacuation will destroy us as a people. So we dissemble. Have you forgotten that they name us pirates? Have you forgotten that our ancestors were scoundrels all? We lie. We sucker them. We let them think they have won and then we hit them hard!"

Bister was smiling, a faint and knowing smile that did not belong on the face of the Tainted, as voices erupted again. But the tide had turned. The Ivory Elder was speaking for Adelita's plan. The Ash Captain was on her side. Tal had been on board all along.

Adelita pressed it home. "The Name Ships need to launch before the Calpurnians get here so that all they see is a contrite and weak station that surrenders meekly. There's no reason for reprisals or a single shot. And yes, they might destroy the station if it resisted, but if it surrenders? That's wasteful. The Calpurnians may waste lives but they don't waste currency."

"We're to leave our families while we run?" someone asked.

"While you prepare for battle," Adelita said. "Make no mistake, even when they draw down their forces, even when we have *Sounding Dark*, it will be a battle and many will die. Those on the station will be much safer than on the ships. They can go into the deep mines."

"It's a good plan," the Ash Captain said. "They'll pull down to five or so. In an even fight we can take them."

"Or with *Sounding Dark*," Tal said.

The Ash Captain eyed him. "What if there is no *Sounding Dark*?"

"*Sounding Dark* exists," the Navigator said. "That is historical fact."

"What if you can't find her?" The Ash Captain gestured at Bister. "I'm not hearing the Tainted saying she knows where *Sounding Dark* is. Nor anybody else. We have to count on our own strong backs and good sense. The Steel Captain has a plan that makes sense."

"Do you know where *Sounding Dark* is?" the Ivory Elder asked Bister.

Her expression changed, almost as if someone different were looking out of her eyes than the person who had been. She was just an ordinary middle-aged woman in an old shipsuit. "No," she said. "But I am willing to try to find her." She stood up. "If Eresh falls, Inanna will suffer too. If they enforce the Isolation, we'll die just like you. We have a stake in this. I'm in."

The Navigator's face betrayed their satisfaction. "I will go with Bister to find *Sounding Dark*."

"And how do you plan to do that?" the Ash Elder asked. "We can't send a Name Ship off on a fool's errand." He looked at Tal. "And don't you even say that *Ivory Three* will do it."

"I wasn't," Tal protested.

"Tal has to stay here and surrender the station," Adelita said. Every head turned to her, including Tal's. "They're not going to believe that we just rolled over that easily. If only one Name Ship is here when they arrive, of course it would be stupidity for that single ship to fight ten! That ship is *Ivory*. Tal surrenders knowing he's hopelessly outgunned. He professes he doesn't know where the other Name Ships are—they're off on errands or they ran at the rumor of war—whatever makes sense. But somebody has to stay here and surrender and keep the Calpurnians confident so that they'll draw down their forces promptly. Maybe even say that the Name Ships intend to attack a Calpurnian station somewhere. They'd need to detach two or three ships to answer that."

"I don't want to surrender," Tal protested.

"Why the Ivory Captain?" the Ivory Elder said. "Why not you?"

The Ash Captain laughed. "Can anybody believe that the Steel Captain surrendered? I've known Adelita Massacre all my life. Adelita, you're smart as a whip and strong as iron, but you can't act for shit. You'd never pull it off. They'd see through it in half a day." He looked at Tal. "Now Tal's canny as well as brave. He could pull off the craven. He's a nice, agreeable young man who looks like he could lick boots."

"I resent that," Tal began.

"It's true that I cannot act," Adelita said, forestalling him. "And you can, Tal. This part requires a robber who can lull the mark into complacency. Steal their wits, Robber."

"That's almost a plan," the Silk Elder said.

"It is a plan," Adelita said.

"Except for how we find *Sounding Dark*," the Navigator said. "Bister and I need a ship, and neither of us is a pilot."

"We can't spare one of the Name Ships," the Steel Elder said. "Maybe an interplanetary shuttle?"

"That doesn't have the range…" the Navigator began.

Adelita looked past them at Bister. There was that strange look again, a little smile as though she silently asked, *Adelita, what do you believe? Do you truly believe, or is it all a pretty metaphor?*

"I don't do metaphors," Adelita said under her breath. Then, more loudly, "I will take them."

"*Steel Nine* is our largest ship," the Ash Captain said.

"Not *Steel Nine*. I will take them. Oxa Usury will command *Steel Nine* in my absence." Adelita lifted her chin. "And if it is a fool's errand, we will return fools and rejoin the Name Ships."

There was a great deal of shouting and joggling, and Adelita could not see Bister. She was rather small, behind Tal and the Navigator and so many others.

And then suddenly there was an alarm, Eresh Control's voice coming over the Council speakers. "Ten ships have just come out of jump in the inner system just beyond Baal's orbit. Repeat! Ten ships have come out of jump in the inner system!"

The Calpurnian fleet had arrived.

Bister had been watching the Council meeting with a growing sense of unreality. Tal's couch was comfortable enough, but even fruit wine hadn't made sleep come easily. She'd dreamed too much, searching through rooms that led into one another in an endless maze, the floor suddenly falling out from under her so that she startled awake, grabbing at the couch and blankets. Tal might have had a soporific stronger than fruit wine, but she hated to wake him to ask for it, and she hated even more for him to think she needed it. Now, as the meeting dissolved into controlled chaos, she wished she'd had enough sleep.

The Steel Captain's plan seemed to be the one they were going with. Everyone was charging around, Elders directing evacuations of various people, some on ships and some to the mines. The Ash Elder was talking to the Portmaster on the comm while the Portmaster also dealt with every merchanter still in a Glitter Rim gate begging for launch. Bister was glad Jamila Ravit had lifted an hour earlier. At least *Naga* and her crew were clear.

And if they didn't go, they wouldn't be able to. There were only so many launch crews and so many ships that could fit on the pads at once. If the Portmaster didn't get a hold on it, ships would start taking things into their own hands.

The Steel Captain was talking on her private comm, apparently to her ship, and Bister grabbed her other arm. "We need a ship," she said. "And we have to get out of here fast. Otherwise the traffic will mean we can't. And it has to be a ship with jump capability."

The Steel Captain cut the comm. "There's a venture ship at Cyan Gate that belongs to Steel's Company. We can take that."

"Then let's go." Bister looked around for the Navigator. They were on the other side of the room having a heated conversation with Tal Robber.

The Steel Captain's mouth set in a thin line, her voice carrying as they approached. "We need to go now, Tal!"

Tal drew himself up, presumably terminating whatever tender farewell he'd hoped to have. "You've given me the worst job."

"It's the job that has to be done," the Steel Captain said. "Besides, don't you think I'd rather be with my ship than chasing a ghost?"

"Trade you."

"You wish. Navigator, are you ready?"

"Yes. Absolutely." They looked at Tal. "Good fortune."

"And to you."

Everybody wanted time, but now there was none. Bister knew that in her bones. "We need to go now. Captain, where is this ship?"

"This way." The Steel Captain led the way along the wall to one of the doors out of the Council chamber, Bister slipping between people as she went. Everyone was talking at the top of their voices, many of them to people who weren't there. The comm systems must be nearly overwhelmed.

As soon as the door slid shut behind them, it was quiet. The Steel Captain led them quickly down the corridor, around a corner, through a door and up a set of metal stairs. Their feet clanged on the perforated plates. *An older part of the station?* Bister wondered. She'd seen steps like this in Corporation ruins on Inanna. This seemed like an aged service corridor.

The Steel Captain keyed open a blast door that looked like it had once been a ship's outer airlock. "We're passing from Salt to Steel," she said by way of explanation. "I've got the codes."

"Of course," Bister said. You wouldn't want unauthorized people running around in the service areas, not with the patchwork of ships and habitation areas and mines. Someone who didn't know what they were doing could make a real mess in a sensitive area. The Steel Captain probably had the override codes for all the sensitive areas of Steel.

The Navigator brought up the rear, their sandals making a lighter sound on the floor. Another turn, and the next door looked like an ordinary one.

It opened onto chaos. The Glitter Rim was full of people running in different directions, all shouting and dragging things and people. The crews of every merchanter in port were trying to get back to their ships, dogged by residents and travelers trying to get passage off Eresh. Shop owners were closing down their businesses, hauling down metal shutters over their storefronts. Parents were herding frightened children toward ships or lifts or gates that led to the inner parts of the station.

"Bister! Bister!" She heard a shout close behind. Yuli was elbowing his way through the crowd. "Do you have a way off? I've got to get a way off!" Of course. He was Tainted. Being off Inanna was reason for arrest.

"I'm sorry," Bister said. "I don't. I mean…" They were being dragged apart by the crowd, the Steel Captain pushing the Navigator ahead of her.

"She is on official business for the Council," the Steel Captain said, "We cannot take passengers."

"But I…"

"Go down into the mines with the residents," the Steel Captain said. "We are not asking questions about where people were born, and you have resident rights. Go to Steelgate and tell them I sent you." She grabbed Bister's arm. "Come on. We have no time!"

Above, a slow pulsing alarm sounded, the lights flickering. "What is that?" Bister shouted, dragged away from Yuli.

"It's the evacuation signal for the mines. We have meteorite strikes from time to time and need to get people out of breachable areas." They rounded a corner into an empty docking lounge, the crowd left behind. The docking port was dark, the airlock sealed.

"I hope your codes work on the main port docks," the Navigator said tersely.

"So do I." The Steel Captain entered a code into the airlock, then sighed with relief as the lights turned blue, the hatch cycling and checking equalized pressure. It opened into the short tube that ran toward a pinnace-sized venture craft. "Come on," she said, hurrying them through and setting the hatch to seal behind.

The ship sat quiescent, the hatch open to the tube and umbilicals attached so that it drew power from the station. Bister followed as the Steel Captain hurried forward, apparently knowing exactly where she was going. "I hope you don't think I can take second seat," she said, following her into the command center. "Also, where is the crew?" With everyone scrambling to get off Eresh who could, why wasn't this ship's crew ready and waiting?

The Steel Captain was already on one of the couches, swinging a control arm over her waist. She looked at the screens and swore, the first time Bister had heard her utter an unprofessional word. "No fuel."

"What?" the Navigator said.

"No fuel." The Steel Captain's fingers raced across the control screen. "We're empty. We need a launch crew and a tug." She opened a channel. "Eresh Control, this is the Steel Captain. We need a fuel crew and a cradle tug at Cyan Port for *Fortunate Son* immediately."

A man's voice replied, "Sorry, Steel Captain. We have no tugs available. They are all in use. Also the ETA on the fuel crew is uncertain. We've got three crews out, but they're all busy. At least forty-five minutes."

"That's not acceptable," the Steel Captain said. She looked at the Navigator, something like actual worry cracking through the makeup she wore like a mask. "Countermand one of the assignments. We need a fuel crew now."

"Negative, Steel Captain. All fuel crews are busy." There was a pause. "And even if I did order one to stop what they're doing, they're not going to."

"Everyone is trying to get off," Bister said. She shook her head. Through one of the cameras she could see the flares of light out on the pads, tugs positioning larger ships for launch well away from the habitation areas. The big ones couldn't reposition themselves—they were simply too large to dock at the station and withdraw from the docks without tugs. And every tug was busy. Even if they tried to commandeer one themselves.... "We need another ship,"

Bister said.

There was a sudden flash out on the field, one of the Name Ships lifting. It was impossible to tell which one it was. It rose bright-stemmed into the atmosphereless sky.

"There aren't going to be any except mining shuttles left," the Steel Captain snapped. "Not that are already fueled and don't need a tug crew."

"Then we get a mining shuttle." Bister turned off the camera screen. "You can fly one, surely?"

"Yes." The Steel Captain stood up.

"But we need a jump-capable ship to find *Sounding Dark*." The Navigator sounded perplexed. "A mining shuttle isn't going to get us anywhere except around Eresh to one of the outer mines."

"Or Inanna," Bister said.

"And if we're stuck on Inanna?"

"I can find us a jump-capable ship on Inanna," Bister said. "But not if we don't get off Eresh." She looked at the Steel Captain. "It's the only chance."

She nodded. "You're right. A mining shuttle it is."

They scurried back along the Rim, then down to the lower ports. The crowds were absent there where the industrial loaders were parked, some full of the precious ore that made Eresh's mines a going concern. The Steel Captain went down the row, stopping at the third one. "This one's been emptied and restocked, so it's been fueled too."

The Navigator scrambled aboard in a flurry of multicolored skirts, Bister following and manually closing the hatch. By the time she'd confirmed it was shut, there was already the vibration of the Steel Captain bringing the engines online.

"Strap yourself in," the Steel Captain directed as Bister hurried forward into the cramped crew compartment. It was tiny and uncomfortable, built to take only four crew, most of the ship's space left for cargo. "We're making a cold launch."

The Navigator had settled into one of the rear seats and Bister took the other, pulling the worn, greasy straps across her. "Cold launch?"

"I don't have time for a full run up." The Steel Captain didn't glance back, her eyes on the screens ahead of her. "The lead Calpurnian ships will be in bombardment range in a little less than fifteen minutes." She opened the comm again. "Eresh Control, this is the Steel Captain. Requesting a launch clearance for the shuttle BH-9 immediately."

The same voice as earlier replied, "Steel Captain, the pads are full." Bister could see the lineup, seven or eight ships with tugs being towed toward the launch pads a safe distance from the station. One of the Name Ships had jumped the line, its massive missile tubes dwarfing the tug and the merchanters around it. The red swish on its side identified it as *Silk Five*. If the Name Ships didn't get off…

"Then we will launch from the taxiway." The Steel Captain turned the shuttle under its own power, rolling along on its built-in undercarriage, away from the line and toward the perimeter. The purple and indigo lights of the Glitter Rim flashed across the camera.

The Navigator clutched their couch arms. Bister leaned back, settling the sternum pad correctly and pulling the neck protector into place. If it was going to be a rough launch, best to be prepared. Her heart was beating very fast.

"…can't confirm, Shuttle BH-9. Regulations require…"

The Steel Captain snapped off the comm. "Flail your regulations." There was a bump as the shuttle rolled over the lane barrier into the taxiway for the maintenance area. "Bureaucrats!"

The Navigator and Bister exchanged a look from the two rear seats. The Navigator shrugged as if to say, *She has always been hotheaded.* As far as Bister was concerned, the only surprising thing was that the Steel Captain was supposed to be part of the hierarchy. But then things were different on Eresh than most places.

The ship tilted, undercarriage elevating the nose as the forward momentum ceased. "Initiating launch procedure," the Steel Captain said.

Bister closed her eyes. The shuttle's vibrations increased, the built-in undercarriage shaking like it would pull apart. Logically it wouldn't, Bister thought. It must launch all the time from mining claims with a full load, not with an empty cargo section and only three crew. Logically, it would be fine. The rumble grew. Before she expected there was the surge of momentum, gravity pushing down on her chest as the shuttle rose. Bister opened her eyes. Already the cameras showed the field retreating beneath them.

The Steel Captain swore. The shuttle was unloaded and light. In her haste, they'd climbed more quickly than she'd expected, almost on the tail of a much larger ship. Its engine blast filled the forward camera.

The comm crackled again. "…crazy shuttle pilot! Get off my ass!"

The shuttle pitched as it slid beneath the larger ship, passing beneath its belly, the red swish of *Silk Five* showing clearly. "Sorry, Mira!" the Steel Captain said.

"Adelita? You are certifiable!" the woman's voice replied. "Go do this Void-Damned thing and get back here!"

There was a smile in the Steel Captain's voice. "I will do that. Good hunting, *Silk Five*."

They passed the nose of *Silk Five*, veering away as they gained altitude from Eresh. Ahead, beyond visibility from the camera, was the Calpurnian fleet. Bister shivered.

"All right, Bister," the Steel Captain said, not glancing back over her shoulder. "We're clear. Where's this jump-capable ship you were talking about?"

Bister took a deep breath. "Make for Taralis Beacon. You can land the shuttle there."

Chapter Five

The sun edged above the horizon; Taralis Beacon faded out in its sudden, slanting light across the rolling seas of grass. Birds took flight, small ones that dipped and soared in the new light, and larger ones that called to one another in the grass with oddly mournful voices. The grasses were knee high. It made it hard to see their footing, though there was little to see; just these endless rounded hills covered in grass and the distant shapes of mountains on the western horizon. They looked purple and lowering in the slanted light. The sun rose, the high clouds flushing scarlet.

Adelita could hardly believe it was the same sun that gave its distant light to Eresh, pale and dim. She was not going to think about what might be happening on Eresh. She was not going to consider it at all. She had her work to do. She must trust Tal. She must trust Galion. She must trust all the rest. They would do what they needed to do. Even now her Second, Oxa, would be beating outsystem as fast as possible. Tal would be rolling out the red carpet for the Calpurnian Navy.

And Galion—hopefully he was simply doing his job. They would send the children into the deep mines as a precaution. Cielo would be in the deep mines with the others, safe if frightened. But Cielo would be less frightened than many. He was too brave for his age, always wanting to do things he wasn't old enough or strong enough for yet. Yes. The children would be in the deep mines. Tal would do that until the Navy personnel were on station, until they were fully occupied. Until he was certain there would be no orbital strike.

Adelita raised her head. Bister had ranged ahead. Her stride was shorter than Adelita's, but she scrambled up each hill effortlessly, followed much more slowly by the Navigator and Adelita. "Where exactly are we going?" Adelita asked. "Away from the beacon, yes. But we cannot get so far on these plains that we are not easily seen on a flyover."

"If anyone is looking for us." Bister stopped at the top of a wildflower-crowned hill, glancing up at the sky. "I expect the Calpurnian Navy is more than busy right now. One mining shuttle isn't worth much."

"Not with four Name Ships heading outsystem as fast as they can," the Navigator said. *If they can* remained unspoken.

"They are probably trying to intercept." Adelita could visualize all too easily the battle of maneuvers above, trying to keep out of range of the Calpurnian ships. Oxa Usury was good. He would be fine. And Mira had gotten off with *Silk Five*. She knew that.

The Navigator was at her shoulder. "You are needed here," they said. The Navigator's beautiful face showed worry that was not in their voice. "No one else can do this."

"No one else was willing," Adelita said. "To put our faith in this legend…."

"To put our faith in faith," the Navigator said. Their smile was warm. "Adelita, you believe."

"I…." She glanced at Bister, still scouting ahead. "I want to. I want to believe that the gods are real and they care for their children. But for the Lady of the Void to choose her…. Why not you?"

"Why not indeed?" the Navigator asked. "Perhaps because I lack the necessary skills? I've spent my life in holy service, not pharmaceuticals smuggling." They shook their head. "I'm not jealous. We each have our part to play. Yes, you as well. You are chosen too. You chose yourself because you are the only one who would do this."

"And what if I am wrong?" Adelita asked. "What if I have deserted my post at the time I was needed most?"

"The fleet has many officers. But for this…" the Navigator shook their head. "We need your clear eyes and your moral compass as well as your piloting skills. And without you, how would we even begin to find *Sounding Dark*?"

"How we are going to find *Sounding Dark* without a jump-capable ship is the pressing question at the moment," Adelita said.

Bister had stopped just ahead, clearly hearing the last exchange as they approached her. "I know where we can get a ship."

"A ship of the Tainted?" Adelita's brows rose. "The Tainted aren't supposed to have any ships."

"You know perfectly well some of those little insystem gigs that dock at the Glitter Rim are Tainted-owned," the Navigator said. "*Steel* ignores them just like everyone else as long as they don't break any laws."

"It is not up to me to enforce the Isolation," Adelita said. "I don't ask for owner's papers."

"Well then." The Navigator smiled. "Nor does Tal. Nor the Dockmaster. Nor anybody else. If some half-derelict shuttle belongs to a Tainted, who's to say anything?"

"A half-derelict shuttle isn't going to get us to *Sounding Dark*," Adelita pointed out. "If it exists, and I hope to the stars it does, it's on such a long orbit that we're going to need an interstellar craft, a ship that can go beyond heliopause. Those shuttles couldn't do it if they spent five years at top speed! We'll all starve or asphyxiate, and Eresh will be completely subjugated long before we get there."

"I know that," Bister said somewhat impatiently. "I know where we can get an interstellar ship. So if I'm your precious chosen one, how about trusting me for three minutes? Believe me, it has occurred to me that we need to breathe and not take five years to find *Sounding Dark*." She turned away, clambering down the rounded hillside.

Adelita looked at the Navigator and they both shrugged. "We follow her to the ship," Adelita said. Practically speaking, there was no other choice.

The sun rose high. The sky was cloudless, a wide expanse of blue over the endless grass. It was unnerving to one who had spent her life bounded by walls. Ships have walls. Stations have walls. Even mines have walls. This endless, open, lidless place made Adelita feel naked. Anyone could see them.

However, the only things circling above were clearly organic, some kind of large birds that floated high above, looking down at this featureless world, the endless undulations of prairie. Some of the hills were strangely regular. Were they a geological feature, or did they mask ruins beneath? History said that Inanna had once had cities, the cities where millions toiled in debt-servitude, leading to the Righteous War and the Isolation. The cities had been razed, never to be rebuilt. The Tainted were forbidden settlements of more than five thousand individuals. Were these the traces of those cities? Or was it simply that planets with grass and rain were shaped this way?

Adelita followed Bister. She would not ask for a rest. Her boots were made for shipboard, not for hiking. But she would not be the first to complain. If the Navigator could do this in their little sandals, she would never complain. Even now, on Eresh…no, she would not think of that. She would put one foot ahead of another and get up the next hill, sweat running beneath her black shipsuit in the heat of the day.

There seemed to be some sort of small watercourse ahead. A copse of trees grew along it. Beyond it there was what appeared to be a dilapidated building. A barn or a dwelling? The weathered wood looked deserted.

"It's not much further," Bister said. "We're almost there. Navigator, how are you doing?"

The Navigator was breathing hard, but they looked up and smiled. "I'll manage. It's just some blisters."

Bister looked almost apologetic. "We can take care of that when we stop. There really wasn't anywhere closer that would do, Steel Captain."

"Please call me Adelita." Adelita helped the Navigator down the bank, no more than waist high. The stream was only a few inches deep, running swift and clear over the stones. It reminded her how thirsty she was. "Should we drink?"

Bister grimaced. "I wouldn't. There can be heavy minerals even if the water looks clean. There's filtered water just ahead."

"At that house?" Adelita asked. Closer, it looked like a falling-down farmhouse, though there was a windmill that turned smoothly with no squeaking. Someone was maintaining it. Water and shade would be welcome, even if there was nothing else. And hopefully there would be people. She took the Navigator's arm and helped them up the opposite bank. "It's not far. You can do it. Just a little farther."

The building stood on a little rise over a flat pasture with a wooden fence, though no animals grazed there. A barn stood just beyond, doors closed though there was no one around. It was exceedingly quiet. Bister didn't bother to knock. She just opened the door to the farmhouse and went in. There was no lock anyhow. Adelita followed her.

There was nothing there. Or rather, there was a stone fireplace long cold, an old trestle table and a couple of benches. That was it. No food, no bedding, no people. "Where is everyone?" Adelita asked. "Does anyone live here?" She wondered if she sounded as dismayed as the Navigator looked.

"In a manner of speaking." Bister gave her a sideways smile and she scuffed the floor near the fireplace with her foot, brushing away the dust and straw that had blown in. "Here we go." She reached down and slid her fingers into a recessed handle. Quickly, she lifted a section of floor back on hidden hinges. Beneath it, a couple of feet down to make up for the height of the house's foundation, was a metal hatch with an electronic keypad on it.

"Oh, really?" Adelita smiled.

Bister jumped down and entered a code quickly, then opened the hatch outward. Cool air rushed out. "I'll close up behind us. Adelita?"

"Of course." Adelita slipped around her. The ladder going down was very standard, as were the cool intermittent lights on the walls of the tunnel. This was much more like it. She climbed down quickly, the Navigator following more slowly. Above, the natural light was cut off as Bister closed the trap door and then the hatch in turn.

It was quite a way down, perhaps two decks if this were a ship's auxiliary corridors. Adelita had nearly reached the bottom when she heard a sound and looked between her feet. A man stood at the bottom, his hands on the ladder as though he meant to come up. He was a big man, bearded, with sharp blue eyes. "Who in the name of the stars are you?" he asked.

"They're with me," Bister called down from above. "Holla, Griff!"

"Holla yourself." He stood aside and let Adelita descend. The bottom of the tube opened out into a wider space, and the Navigator reached the bottom next. Griff looked up. "What are you doing here? I thought you were outsystem."

Bister clambered the last few feet down. "It's an incredibly long story. Griff, this is Adelita Massacre and the Navigator of Eresh. Adelita, Navigator, this is Griffin. He's a friend."

"Adelita Massacre? The Steel Captain?" he asked incredulously.

"I said it was a long story. Best told sitting down with water," Bister said. "We've had quite a hike from Taralis Beacon."

"Oh, of course. This way." He gestured for the Navigator to precede him through another airlock door, their skirts grubby with dust. "Water and quiet and then the story. If you've walked from Taralis Beacon this morning, you must be tired."

"Just a bit." It didn't escape Adelita that Bister gave his waist a quick squeeze as she passed him, and that he caught her hand for a moment. "Griff," Bister said. "I need a favor. A big one."

They ate in a dining room obviously meant for more people, with an old scuffed concrete floor and walls that had recently been painted with fantastic murals. Imaginary creatures flew over spired landscapes while flowers grew tall as houses. There were eight big wooden trestle tables. They settled at the one nearest the kitchen door, only one set of electric lights turned on, the fluorescents flickering fitfully. Adelita repressed the question of why someone didn't just change them as they would on Eresh— the bulb was nearly spent. The answer was obvious. These were probably Eresh's castoffs. After all, somebody was selling the things that were almost used up. Getting a bit more wear out of them by selling them to Tainted traders was a very Eresh-like thing to do.

The food, however, had nothing to do with Eresh. There was bread and sour cream, cold smoked duck sliced thin, green watercress so fresh it tasted of chlorophyll and sun. Bister spread the sour cream on the bread with gusto and piled the rest on top. Adelita followed suit. It tasted wonderful, especially after a long hike.

"Did you harvest this today?" she asked Griffin. "The cress, I mean."

"A couple of days ago," he said, trying not to talk with his mouth full. "We have refrigeration now."

"It tastes different than it does on Eresh."

"You probably have hydroponics," Griff said, gesturing with his bread. "Not the same as grown in earth. Perfect mineral balance and all that. Natural things aren't perfect."

"Oh yes. It's all hydroponics. Though we can do quite a lot with that." Adelita smiled involuntarily. "My husband is Steel Company's Chief Pescador. The fish co-nurture in the hydroponics tanks. We have nearly nine thousand fish at any one time in various stages of growth. After they reach hatchling size they go into the Citrus Forest."

"The Citrus Forest?" Griffin looked bemused.

"It's a bay of hydroponics tanks that grow lemons, oranges, limes, and grapefruit in ascending frames. Citrus trees are amazingly adaptable, though of course some varieties are better than others. The fish swim through the tanks co-nurturing and their waste fertilizes the citrus. Lemons are actually the easiest. Right now we've got so many trees that we're producing a considerable surplus of lemons, more than Steel Company can possibly use. So we sell them through one of the Company's ventures and they supply the Glitter Rim and who knows what else? Well, certainly the culinary needs of Silk Company, because they don't grow citrus." She stopped. "I'm sorry. I'm used to my husband, Galion, talking shop. I know far more about hydroponics and pisciculture than one really wants to hear!"

"It's interesting," Bister said. "I'm always curious about where things come from and how they're made."

"You're always curious about everything," Griffin said. Bister shrugged, her mouth full of sliced smoked duck. "Your husband is a hydroponics engineer?" Griffin asked Adelita.

"In a sense. He apprenticed in hydroponics before he moved over to pisciculture. But they're interrelated." Adelita took another bite. The cress did taste very different. "Galion is the one who convinced Steel Company to make it a venture. They already did pisciculture on a smaller scale in Horn Company where he was born, but he officially joined Steel when we married. That was seventeen years ago." Adelita couldn't help but smile at the memory. "We've been together twenty-one years, since we were teenagers."

"You are fortunate," Griffin said, "to find a lasting relationship that gives you joy."

"I know." Adelita wondered if it were polite to ask, and then decided that Bister was unlikely to take offense. "Are you and Bister…?"

"We're something," Bister said cheerfully. She wiped sour cream off her chin. "I reckon he'll do."

"As you say," Griffin said with a grin.

The door to the dining room opened. "I thought I heard voices," an old man said. A middle-aged woman pushed the door wide and held it for him as he made his way slowly in leaning on a cane. Like Griff, he wore a loose homespun shirt and trousers, the shirt bunched up over a hump on his upper back, bent forward at sixty degrees over his cane. Arthritis, Adelita thought, or childhood calcium deficiencies, and probably treatable on Eresh.

"Holla, Dads," Griff said. "Holla, Melly. Bister's back and she's brought a couple of friends."

"I see she is," Melly said. "Holla, Bister. And nice to meet you folks." She stayed at his elbow as Dads maneuvered himself toward the kitchen door.

"Little Bister," he said. "In trouble again I expect." He raised watery eyes to them all. "She's always been unruly. Going to get yourself into big trouble someday if you don't change your ways, young woman!"

She dropped her voice, watching him move toward the kitchen door like a very slow steamroller. "Don't mind Dads," Melly said.

"Bister, we decided not to go to the summer pastures this year. The trip was too much."

"I understand," Bister said. "And no offense taken, of course."

"It's just that he's seventy-three," Melly said.

Adelita started. She would have guessed two decades older.

"Melly!" he shouted as the kitchen door swung shut behind him.

"Coming, Dads!" She raised a hand to them all. "Sorry. And Bister, we'll catch up later, all right?"

"Anytime," Bister said as Melly followed Dads into the kitchen. She turned back to Adelita with a shrug. "He's been saying that for thirty years. I've certainly lived up to expectations."

The Navigator cleared their throat. "I hate to bring it back to business, but Bister said that there was a ship that would be capable of interstellar travel?"

Griff's expression closed. "And why would you need such a ship?"

Bister put her head to the side. "Griff, have you ever heard the legend of *Sounding Dark*?" He shook his head. "It's quite a story," Bister said. "And it has to do with the big favor I need. Navigator, if you would?"

"Long ago," the Navigator began, "in the days when our ancestors first set out among the stars…" Adelita listened while the Navigator spun the tale out. She had always found it interesting. Bister listened attentively, though surely she had just heard it from the Navigator a matter of hours before.

Griffin listened first with skepticism, then with increasing fascination. "And you think this ship exists and you can find it? Now?"

"I do," Bister replied instead of the Navigator. "I think *Sounding Dark* wants to be found. I think the Lady of the Void wants to help us."

He shook his grizzled head. "Lots of people think the gods will intercede for them, and if it ever happened in times of legend, it doesn't anymore."

"It does," the Navigator said. "It's just that the gods aren't a vending machine. You don't put an offering in and get a favor out. They have their own reasons and their own limitations."

"Griff, I should be dead." Bister leaned forward, her hand on his knee. "I don't have any rational explanation for why I didn't die. Nobody does. I can't doubt that I'm here and I shouldn't be. I believe she saved me for her own purposes."

"I'm glad you are."

"I have a debt to pay," Bister said. "She saved my life. I need to do what she wants me to do."

"Find a ghost ship and use it to defeat the Calpurnian Navy."

"That's the size of it." For a long moment their eyes met.

Then Griffin started laughing. "Okay. Sure. Why not? You've done some crazy things and gotten away with them."

"And you think that this is the only way you're going to get me out of here and clear of capture by the Calpurnian Fleet, who will probably execute me as an escaped prisoner if they decide to crack down on Inanna," Bister said.

"Maybe I think it's the only way I'm getting out of here," he said.

Neither of them looked away. "I don't believe that for a moment," she said. "I think you'd stay on Inanna if I weren't here."

"I think you wouldn't be going anywhere without my ship," he said.

Bister smiled. "So we're going then."

"Reckon we are."

The Navigator looked at Adelita bemusedly. Adelita shrugged. "Where is this ship? I can't imagine where you'd hide an interstellar ship here. I would think we would have seen it on approach. Is it one of the little traders? If so, I don't think that will work."

"It's an interstellar ship," Griffin said quietly. "I'll show you when we've finished eating."

After the meal, Adelita followed the others into the kitchen and washed up the plate she'd used. There was hot water on tap, though it made alarming noises when Bister turned the tap on. When everything was washed and put away, they made their way through a set of doors off the dining room, down a winding stair and along another corridor.

"What was this place to begin with?" the Navigator asked, clambering down the steps in their hampering skirts. "And why doesn't it have a mechanical lift?"

"It does," Griffin said. "But we don't use it unless I've got something heavy to move or Dads needs to get up and down. It's a power hog."

"We turn it on in the winter," Bister said. "It's easier for old folks and people carrying children. But Griff is right, it's a power hog."

"You're on battery?" Adelita asked.

Griffin nodded. "We have the windmill and it turns a generator. We've also got a turbine on the stream a little ways down. We store the power in six Class 5 batteries from Eresh and a pair of old Class 2s."

Adelita whistled. "How'd you get Class 5s? That's the newest model we use on the Station. They're expensive."

"We have our ways," Bister said with a smirk.

"I do not even want to know how you smuggled six Class 5 batteries onto an Isolated planet."

"I won't tell you about the other seven of them then," Bister said. "Two at Cor Landing, four at Windmark, and one at Illen's Glen."

"I did not hear that," Adelita said. The Navigator laughed. "I am very good at not hearing things." Griffin opened a door ahead and stepped through. Adelita followed him. "Oh my," she said.

It wasn't a room. It was a launch tube. Sitting upright in its cradle was the silver and black shape of a Calpurnian dispatch boat. Nearly four stories tall from thrusters to pointed beak, it shone sleek and lethal. Above, as far from its nose as it was long, a retractable door showed an iris shape like a missile tube on shipboard.

"We think it was a launch facility for the Corporation," Bister said. "Probably a military installation. For whatever reason, it wasn't destroyed completely by the Alliance, just buried. My clan found it twenty years ago, so when Griff needed a place to keep a ship and the installation needed somebody to keep it up…."

"It made sense," Griff said. "I've been working on getting things functional again. It's a big job."

"A lifetime's work," Adelita said. How Griffin had stolen or commandeered the ship was another question she wasn't asking. Lots of people came through Eresh with things that didn't quite belong to them, and the fewer questions, the better.

"The clan arrives with the harvest," Bister said. "This prairie land is terrible for farming. The soil is shallow and blows away. We farm in the bottomland and follow the herds. But it's good to have a place to overwinter that's safe and warm. We can get the livestock in too. It doesn't smell nice, but the animals we're keeping after Bloodtide are safe all winter. And winters are harsh here."

Adelita nodded solemnly. "I suppose the part of Inanna I had visited before was warmer."

"Further north," Bister said. "Closer to the equator. There are so many clans and septs now, people you'd never meet except for the illegal traders. Eight hundred kilometers might as well be on another planet to most of us."

"And yet you share a common culture," the Navigator said.

"We did once, two hundred years ago. We haven't drifted so far we don't know each other yet." Bister smiled grimly. "But believe me, we remember how to fight. Septs get into it all the time over grazing rights or foraging lands and fighting is in our blood. Tainted, remember? We love to fight."

The Navigator looked vaguely shocked. "With what?"

"Fists, knives, bows and arrows," Bister said. "You don't need energy weapons to kill someone. There's always somebody with a grudge or somebody with something to prove."

"That is true of the Glitter Rim as well," Adelita said. "And the Companies, though if someone misbehaves too badly they'll be exiled." She glanced at the Navigator. "And the Tainted aren't the only ones who carry knives." She patted the long leather sheath at her belt. "Remember, we don't use projectiles on shipboard. Anti-personnel weapons only. We fight with knives too."

Griffin nodded solemnly. "That's why the Calpurnian Navy uses energy flails. They hurt flesh and blood but won't damage machinery too much. Can't risk hulling your own ship." He glanced up at the ship in her cradle. "Going to have to do some things to get her ready for launch."

"How long do you think it will take?" the Navigator asked.

"Several hours. But that's for the best. Right now Eresh has just risen; so if we lifted, our boost would be in full sight of any ships around Eresh. Twelve hours from now it will be going round the opposite side of Inanna. It's our best chance to get off without the Navy catching us in boost."

Adelita nodded. "Reluctantly, I agree that it is best to wait. If we launch into the teeth of the Calpurnian fleet, we will simply be destroyed."

"I can show you to a visitor room," Bister said. "I'm sure you and the Navigator could use some rest if it's going to be that long."

"It isn't necessary…." Adelita began, though nothing sounded better than a soft bed.

"I have imposed on your hospitality on Eresh," Bister said. "You must impose on mine."

"If you insist."

"I do insist," Bister said. "I'll show you. And there is a washroom, which I expect you'll want too."

"That would be greatly appreciated," the Navigator said.

"And you'll want to get on the shortwave," Griffin said to Bister. "And at least warn Cor Landing and Windmark about what's happened."

Bister shook her head regretfully. "I can't risk it right now. It's shortwave, but it's better to wait until Eresh is setting at least. We're not supposed to have radio."

"In the morning, then."

"In the morning." Bister turned toward the door. "Navigator, Adelita, let me show you to a room."

"Thank you," the Navigator said.

Holy Lady, show me my soul…. Bister sat on the steps of the old farmhouse, looking off across the prairie to the east, a thread of old litany coming back to her like the ghost of her childhood borne on the evening wind. The sun was behind the mountains. The stars were appearing to the east, bright against the cool indigo sky. Eresh hung three-quarters full, silver against the darkness.

Bister took a deep breath, letting the place sink into her, or her into it. There was the smell of growing grass, the sound of the wind across the plains where nothing would stop it short of the mountains, the soft whispers of the leaves of the bushes along the creek. Home. For better or worse, Inanna was in her blood. Quite literally, she thought. The Taint was evident in the isotopes present in her bones, in the residue in her teeth. There was no escaping it. Anyone who ran the simplest medical scan could tell she was from Inanna.

She heard a sound behind her and turned to see the Steel Captain coming cautiously out of the hatch in the floor. She closed it behind her, then stopped as she saw Bister.

"I thought you and the Navigator were going to sleep," Bister said. "Planetary time is so far off Eresh that you and the Navigator are well into tomorrow morning."

"So are you," Adelita said. "Yet you are not sleeping."

"I couldn't sleep." Bister shrugged. "And Griff is working on the ship, getting it ready to lift tomorrow. So I thought I'd come out here for a while and listen."

Adelita frowned. "Listen to what?"

"To Inanna." She looked up at the tall woman in her black shipsuit, her shorn dark hair still damp from the shower below. She patted the step beside her. "Come sit. It's nice."

The Steel Captain did, stretching her long legs out. Her boots were scuffed from the walk on the prairie. "I don't spend a lot of time on Inanna."

"I expect not." Bister worked her shoulders. "You have a lot to do."

"Yes." Adelita looked up at the darkening sky. "On ship and station. It is a lot of work." She searched the sky. "There is Eresh."

"Yes." Bister tilted her head back. The stars glittered, the last traces of gold and peach behind the mountains. She glanced sideways at Adelita. "You're worried."

The Steel Captain took a deep breath. Her eyes did not leave the sky. "Yes. My son…"

"You have a child?"

"Cielo is nine years old." Adelita didn't blink, just stared at the stars. "My husband will try to keep him safe. But if there is a bombardment—"

"There won't be," Bister said reassuringly. "They want to capture the station, not destroy it."

"I know. And Tal will play his part. He will surrender most convincingly. He will give us the time we need. It's just…"

"That you are worried," Bister said. "I understand. I would be too. If my son…" This time it was she who broke off. The stillness was utter, as if someone was very quiet just behind her.

"You have a son too?" Adelita turned her head and smiled. "How old is he?"

"He would be twenty-four," Bister said. There was no tremor in her voice, none at all. "He died when he was ten."

"Oh My Lady," Adelita breathed. "I am so sorry. I didn't mean to be so tactless."

"It's all right." Bister lifted her head to the sky again. This time she heard the lash of anger in her own voice. "He died of tetanus. He stepped on a rusty piece of metal that worked its way loose out in the field. Tetanus!" She glanced sideways at Adelita. "You are thinking nobody dies of tetanus. There are vaccines and even if someone were unfortunate, there are life centers, medicines…. Not on Inanna. We are the Tainted. We must maintain a pre-industrial society, per the terms of the Isolation."

She shook her head, looking out across the even, rolling hills. "My ancestors were Corporation. They brought people here under debt-servitude. How many? I don't know. Dozens? Hundreds? They worked in their shops and their restaurants and their mines and their factories. And my ancestors oversaw them. Maybe they managed the shop or directed the kitchen. Maybe they were oligarchs who lived in luxury seventy stories above the streets. Or maybe they were some of the few who managed to pay their way out of debt or be chosen as so excellent and gifted that they should be lifted up and sent to universities. I don't know. I just know that when the Righteous War came, when the Alliance separated the perpetrators from the victims, my ancestors were perpetrators." Bister took a deep breath, flattened her hands against the weathered beams of the steps. "And so we have no life centers and no vaccinations. We are to live simple, pure, agrarian lives so that we may never again subjugate others. My son died because my ancestors held others in debt-service." She shook her head. "I'm sorry. It's not your fault."

Adelita frowned. "Do not be sorry." She paused, as if considering her words, then went on. "I have always felt that the

Isolation was wrong. I know that is radical. It is far to the side even on Eresh to think that it should be abolished, but I believe what I believe and say what I think. And what I think is this: I think I am not responsible for the Lindorn Massacre." Her jaw tightened. "Two of my great-grandmothers and one of my grandfathers stood in that snow and shot those civilians. But that was ninety-four years ago! When I was born, it had been fifty-three years. No one alive did it. No one alive was sent to life at hard labor in the mines of Eresh. I do not question the justice of the sentence. They killed without mercy those who supported a different government, and they were sentenced to life at hard labor."

"But you did not do those things," Bister said.

"I did not." Adelita lifted her chin. "And I believe we are responsible before the gods only for our own actions, not for the actions of our ancestors. I am not my grandfather. I did not even know him. And Cielo is not responsible for his actions. My ancestors were criminals, all of them. And they were sent to a penal colony for the rest of their lives. But it is not justice to condemn innocent people because of the actions of others, whether that was decades ago or centuries."

Bister nodded slowly. "And that's why you don't enforce the Isolation."

"I do not enforce it because I think it wrong," the Steel Captain said. "These were not our laws, Eresh's laws. These were the terms of the Alliance, the terms that Calpurnia enforces to their own benefit. I cannot change the law, but I will not be responsible for injustice myself. Not knowingly, not willingly."

"Do many feel as you do?" Bister asked.

"Enough to elect me Steel Captain." Adelita's mouth quirked. "I am a radical. I do not hide my beliefs."

"That's..." Bister looked for the words, "...encouraging," she finally said.

"And it may be our death," Adelita said. "Calpurnia might not have come down upon us if we had enforced the letter and spirit of the Isolation. I may have led us down a terrible path."

"You can't know that," Bister said. "Their need for a quick and painless war may have as much to do with their internal politics as anything that Eresh did."

"That is true." Adelita stretched out her legs. "We do not know as much of what passes in the Calpurnian Senate as we should."

"I've been in the Calpurnian Mandate recently," Bister said. "Mind you, I don't move in rarified circles. But there are at least two autarchs who are vying for power. Both Altissimi need a swift victory to make one of them a great warleader. A swift victory requires a weak enemy."

"We are not so weak as they think!"

"No, I think not." Bister smiled. For a moment she thought her voice had a strange timbre, as though the thought was hers and not hers at once. Was that what the Navigator had meant? Was it true she carried some fragment of the Lady of the Void in her?

Adelita tilted her head to the side. "Is that what you think? Or what she thinks?"

"I don't know," Bister said honestly. "It's very strange."

"I hope it is enough to find *Sounding Dark*."

"So do I. No, I think it is. If I didn't think so…"

"You would what?" Adelita asked.

"I would have told you not to trust me. I would have said this plan was cracked."

"As I recall, you did." The Steel Captain frowned. "But the Navigator said…"

"I think it will work." Bister sounded more confident than she felt. Or maybe it was that she did. "And really we have no choice."

Adelita huffed. "Not at this point, no. We all lose everything if Calpurnia takes and holds Eresh."

"There will be no more Captains ignoring pharma and mech and the rest of the terms of the Isolation." Bister leaned back on her elbows. "If we have to run a blockade every time we come in or out, or Lady forbid if they decide to do planetary sweeps…. That's a thing we need to prepare for. I'm going to put that word out before we go, just in case." She looked up at the cloudless sky. It was full night now. Her body was tired even if her mind kept going. *The body must rest.* She must rest. They must rest.

"I owe you an apology." Adelita shifted to face her. "I am sorry, Bister. When I met you, I thought you were just a criminal."

"I am a criminal."

"Yes, but you smuggle pharma because…"

"I smuggle pharma because I want no one else's son to die like mine did," Bister said evenly. "I don't give a shit about what's legal or just. I want nobody else to die on my watch. That's it. I don't care whether it's right or not."

"Then we believe the same thing for different reasons," Adelita said. "I, because I think the Isolation is unjust, and you because…"

"Because it hurts people, and it's not going to hurt mine while I have the means to stop it." Bister shook her head, smiling. "So there we are. And if that means being a criminal and a rebel, so be it. And by the way, welcome to the club! You've joined the Most Wanted List all on your own now."

Adelita laughed. "I suppose I have! Galion always says I will get into trouble with my radical ways."

"I'm not sure you could get into much more trouble." Bister stood up. Her body was stiff. She ought to rest as well. "I know it's early by planetary time, but I'm still on station time. I'm going to bed. You?"

"I will be down in a few minutes," Adelita promised. "I think I will sit here and worry a while longer."

"Suit yourself," Bister said. She trailed her fingers across the Steel Captain's shoulder as she turned. "And thank you."

Chapter Six

Bister stepped into the cool quiet of the shower cube and turned the lights down. Nothing hard and glaring. She turned the water on and stepped into the stream, droplets falling from the muted blue light above and running down the gray tiled walls. They were natural river clay, made at Two Bluffs fifty kilometers north, each stamped with a wavy pattern that meant the water ran down them as if over a silted stream bed. Bister tilted her head back, closing her eyes.

Much as she loved the luxury of all this tech, warm water whenever anyone wanted it at the touch of a finger, she also loved the communal bathhouses used in the winter, the water heated to steaming by a wood fire, the scent of the fragrant logs the house was built of released by the heat. Whole families would be there, laughing and telling the same old stories, though if you went late enough at night the stories wouldn't be at all suitable for children. Still, that was for winter. Now it was high summer and the clan was on the move. They'd not be back to camp here until the first frosts touched the grass and the butterflies were gone. They left and then the birds followed, great flocks of fat waterbirds well-fed on southern shores, ranging north as the winter crept up from the pole. When the butterflies left, the clan would be back.

In her childhood they'd wintered in dugouts heated by the dung of animals and people. Sometimes the snows were so deep that days could pass when it wasn't safe to go out, but someone had to, because if the chimney were stopped with snow everyone would suffocate in their sleep. Climbing up on curved dugouts, the snow to her hips, ice crusting on her hair, to clean the chimney pipes wasn't something she missed. This old installation could fit the entire clan comfortably and safely, running water and enough power for heat. Now they'd gotten one of the big refrigeration rooms going again with mech from Eresh and there was even a limited supply of perishables that could overwinter, a change from endless root vegetables and dried meat. It was possible to think about more than surviving.

Which of course was the point, wasn't it? Bister turned, letting the water run down her back. People who have no time to think about anything but survival can't plot or plan. They can't invent or create, much less consider political changes. The Tainted hadn't been farmers or herders when the Isolation had been enforced. They'd all lived with modern tech and done all the jobs that entailed. Suddenly being a pre-industrial agrarian society had meant that almost everything had been lost. Who has time for universities even if you were allowed to have them? Who cares about anything inessential when people are starving while they try to learn to plow without mechanical assistance and harvest enough food to stay alive? It was very effective. And if people died, they were the guilty ones anyway.

Bister opened her eyes. That was Calpurnian logic. You didn't have to kill them yourself, not in nasty ways that would cause unfortunate testimonies to crop up at home. You could simply leave them to die.

...dark ships pulling away into the void, their main engines flaring, oblivious to the comm signals around them....

She was not going to think about that. Bister poured wash into her hands, lemon-scented and made on Eresh, and scrubbed her hair and face. Well, that accounted for all those surplus lemons

Adelita had been on about. It was little things like this that changed their lives as surely as the old installation and Griff's help getting it running and maintaining it as year-round caretaker. If they stopped being able to get things through Eresh—well, that wasn't going to happen. And it was certainly useful political news to know that the Steel Captain wanted even fewer restrictions. Provided she wasn't captured and executed for piracy by the Calpurnian Navy. They'd call all the Name Ships pirates, and they wouldn't be entirely wrong.

No more politics tonight. No more. It was time to try to turn it off. Bister stepped out of the water and stopped it, found her faded robe on the hook by the door. She slipped it on and trotted quickly around the curving corridor to their room.

Griff was already there, sitting up on the bed that took up most of the space. His hair was still knotted in the hunter's knot at the back of his neck, but he'd traded work clothes for a pair of loose pants in the same homespun as her robe. The thick mat of hair on his chest was as much gray as brown; he was her age to the year. He looked up from the expensive datapad, the same novela playing on it that they'd watched twenty times. "I thought you were talking to the Steel Captain."

"I was." One step brought her to the bedside and she sat down on the well-worn padding. "I thought you were getting the ship ready."

"It's ready." Griff turned the datapad off carefully to save battery power. She glanced at the screen with a smile.

"You're watching that again?" He shrugged. "Sorry I didn't bring anything new this time."

"You got a little busy." He shifted the cover aside for her, and she slid in beside him. He reached up to turn the light strip down.

"Not all the way off," Bister said quickly.

"Sure." He only dimmed it to a moonlight level, not to the dark of the Void.

"Were you worried about me?"

"I didn't know to be until you were back." He settled on his back and she curled against his left side, one arm beneath his neck and one around him.

Bister took a deep breath. "Yes. This."

"I would have been if I'd known." He rested his face against the top of her head. He paused. "I'm worried now."

"What, just because I'm either carrying a goddess around inside me or suffering severe symptoms from a terrible, traumatic event, that was what, three days ago?" She tightened her hand on his chest. Real. Warm. "I figure if it's the latter I'll get over it eventually. If it's the former…." She looked up, trying to see more of his face than his chin. "What do you think, Griff? Do you think the Lady of the Void chose me?"

He was quiet a long moment, and she waited. Griff often wanted to think through things before he said them. His arm was around her back, his hand absently rubbing her shoulder. "I wasn't raised to think anything about the gods."

"I know. But…"

"That said, there might be a third explanation somewhere between gods and crazy. We don't know a lot about how those old ships worked. We know they had technology that was lost in the first generations of the Nine Worlds, when we lost contact with each other. We know they had charts and ways of navigating and from the stories it sounds like they had energy-beaming technology that worked over longer distances than the width of this room. It was centuries before Calpurnians invented the modern jump drive. Now we don't have anything that can communicate at faster than light speeds, but how do we know they didn't?"

"I don't see how that explains it," Bister said.

"You were floating in a suit. We don't have anything that could have communicated with you without being nearby. Or anything that could have helped you. But what if this ship the Navigator is talking about, *Sounding Dark*, did? If it still exists like they think, if it's still got systems on automatic, wouldn't one of them logically have been to help a person who was spaced? You'd want the ship to recover crew who were lost. Maybe *Sounding Dark* did help you. Maybe there is an old ship on automatic. Maybe it's even one of the First Ships, like the Navigator's legend says."

"That could be…." Bister frowned. She lowered her face against his shoulder again. "But why me? Why not the Calpurnians or the other survivors they left?"

"The Calpurnians took their people, you said. As to why you and not the other survivors…. You were in range? You fit its parameters somehow?" Griff shrugged. "I don't know. But I'm perfectly willing to believe there's a ship. I just don't know if a goddess lives in it."

"A goddess is trapped in it," Bister said. "Except for the part that's in me. It does sound crazy when you put it that way."

"I don't think you're crazy," Griff said. "I think you've had a rough time. And you'll be fine. You always are. But if there's a First Ship out there, we need it now, because we can't let Eresh fall."

"And I have an idea that you might not want to see the Calpurnian Navy either," she said carefully. That was treading close to things they didn't talk about.

He huffed mirthlessly. "Not so much."

"Well, since at this point we're all incredibly wanted, except maybe the Navigator, we'll have to avoid them. Think you can do that when we lift?"

"There's not a one of them born that can catch me," he said.

Bister laughed, curling closer. "Now that's my proud mess."

"You do court trouble." She felt him smile.

"And you're trouble."

"So are you." His arms tightened around her. Yes, he was worried, more than he'd like to admit. He'd never said a word about her off-world trips other than *Good luck*. That was part of their deal.

He never tried to stop her going, and she never tried to get him to come. Not until now. He'd said he would spend his life on Inanna and she respected that. Where he'd come from, what his reasons were for being in the middle of nowhere—those were questions she didn't ask. He knew a lot about tech and was good with his hands, working unstintingly to get the jury-rigged systems put together from two-hundred-year old tech and new stuff randomly brought through Eresh. He never asked for compensation, just a place to live and a share at the fire.

And he had been her lover these last six years, her friend and her companion. If she clung a little closer tonight than usual, he was right that it had been a bad time. She reached up, turning his face down to hers. "Make me remember I'm alive, Griff."

She felt his smile, his mouth almost against hers. "What, no honor bonding?"

"I'll work you over another time," Bister said. "But now…."

"You're alive," he said, and drew her tight against him.

The Calpurnian ship hovered over the Maingate dock at the apex of the station. It had plenty of berths to choose from. Only Greengate was occupied, *Ivory* the only one of the Name Ships present. All of the merchant ships had scattered, some still showing on Eresh's sensors, heading outsystem and presumably madly calculating jump windows. The Calpurnians pursued, though it was unclear to Tal how many they actually might manage to catch. *Invincible* had her choice of docking ports.

Tal Robber waited in the Rim, conspicuously unarmed. Behind him, three of the Elders waited as well, including the Ash Elder. There was no one else in sight. Nobody wanted to witness this, and certainly nobody wanted to be in the front if the Calpurnians came out shooting. All along the Glitter Rim plain metal plates protected the shop fronts, every place closed.

The gate lit, showing that *Invincible*'s hatch was cycling. Tal squared his shoulders. It opened. Four battle-armored troopers poured through, two to each side, their weapons at the ready, boarding pikes in hand. Four more followed. One shoved Tal in the chest, pushing him back and to the side, while the others pinned the Elders against the wall.

"We are here to surrender," the Ash Elder said.

"You'll be searched first." The trooper's blast helmet distorted their voice so much that it was impossible to guess their gender. Roughly, they began a pat-down.

"Why are you doing this?" the Ash Elder asked. "We're here to surrender." Tal knew the answer but thought it better not to say. It was at odds with the persona he had to claim.

"You might be an assassin," the trooper said. "Altissima Gnea takes no chances."

"I wouldn't either if I were the Altissima," Tal said.

The trooper paused, helmet leaning close, rendering whatever ordinary features were beneath it inhuman. "What does that mean?"

Tal spread his hands. "The powerful must be cautious," he said.

The trooper sneered. "Of a bunch of rabble who ran at the sight of us. We saw you. We saw you running away as fast as you could." Tal said nothing. He was supposed to say nothing. "And why didn't you run?" the trooper asked. "Stayed here to grovel instead?"

"Maybe I knew that fighting Calpurnia was useless," Tal said flatly.

In the airlock there was a sudden movement. It was a man backing out slowly, a recording device held in front of him. Beyond him, a pair of spotlessly attired officers stepped forwards, their energy flails activated in their hands, humming with the lavender light that played along each strand. "…Altissima Gnea prepares to disembark in the rebellious penal colony of Eresh!" he said. "With only two guards, she is the first to step onto the station here since they communicated their desire to surrender when offered mercy and quarter. The Altissima graciously granted it."

"Kneel," the trooper said to Tal, poking him with the handle of his energy flail. Reluctantly, Tal went to one knee.

The Autarch appeared in the hatchway, pausing a moment to make a dramatic entrance for the communications net. The recording would no doubt be sent to Calpurnia on the first dispatch craft. She was not tall, but her regal bearing and confident air rendered imposing what should have been an ordinary face. She was older than she looked too. Careful makeup and no doubt selective medical procedures created the illusion of a woman perhaps thirty, though he knew she was twenty years older. She had been a force in politics on Calpurnia that long.

"I will spare your lives," she said coolly. "Since you submit utterly."

"We surrender, Altissima," Tal said.

"And submit utterly to Calpurnian justice."

"Yes, Altissima." The words were ashes in his mouth, but Tal spoke them clearly. If they weren't clear on the recording, she'd make him repeat them.

"Excellent." She stepped out of the airlock onto the station. "All adult residents of the station will confine themselves to their living quarters beginning immediately, with the exception of those who are required to maintain environmental systems. We will begin an immediate review of all residents to weed out the criminal elements. Those residents under the age of fifteen will report to a central facility for review. This exempts only those under the age of three years, who will be moved to the medical facility for examination."

One of the Elders behind Tal caught their breath. "Altissima, if I may...."

"You may not. You are all presumed criminals unless investigation clears your names of all wrongdoing. This entire station is under arrest." The Altissima's eyes roamed over the gathered assembly. "We are here to purge this station of the disease which has flourished here—criminality and license. Unsurprising, given an inbred population descended from those with abnormal tendencies. You should never have been allowed to pass on flawed genes." Her eyes returned to Tal for a moment. "Today sterilization is mandatory for convicted criminals. Mental conditions that lead to anti-social behavior must be eradicated for the safety of the general population." She gave a tight smile to the recording device. "Calpurnia is a place of peace and plenty. We cherish it and protect it, a burden I gladly assume on behalf of my fellow citizens." Her eyes turned to Tal again. "You will escort my party to your governmental center. I will need full computer access."

"As you wish, Altissima," Tal said.

"You may prove useful yet," she said. The Altissima swept through the kneeling figures, the recorder following her.

One of the guards looked down at Tal, their expression unreadable behind the blast shield of their helmet. "Craven," they said. Tal closed his eyes.

Bister startled awake, grabbing at the mattress beneath her. She had been falling, falling through endless dark…. But it was a dream. She was in her own bed, Griff snoring beside her. The electric light strip had turned off, as it was supposed to after a certain amount of time. The candle in its holder of salvaged blue glass had burned down and gave off a fitful light. Bister took a deep breath. She unclenched her hands from the coverlet. She wasn't lost. She wasn't falling. She was home. She stretched naked against familiar sheets, Griff's leg against hers.

"You okay?" he asked sleepily.

"Yes."

He rolled over, not really awake, draping an arm around her. She curled back against him, tucked against his chest.

"What are you thinking about?"

Evidently he wasn't as much asleep as she thought he was. "I was thinking," Bister said slowly, "about what would happen if I just didn't. What if I just stayed right here, on Inanna where I'm supposed to be? What if we didn't do this?"

His arm tightened. "Well, I suppose the Calpurnians would finish taking over Eresh. Then they'd start doing planetary sweeps and scans of Inanna."

This wasn't his home. He was Calpurnian by birth, but he talked as if Inanna was his homeland. And maybe it was now. "You say that like it's yours."

Griff shrugged. "I told you I was never leaving." He was quiet for a minute. "I thought… It's not like I thought it would be, living among the Tainted. I never thought I'd make so many friends. So many people I care about."

"And who care about you." That was true enough. He fit in like he belonged, more than she ever had with her eternal wanderlust.

"I didn't grow up this way." Bister waited. He never said much about the past, and so when he did the best thing was just to wait him out. "On Calpurnia nobody starves. Nobody freezes. There's basic food and a basic place to live and basic clothes even if everybody knows that's what they are. And you can just live like that, year after year, decade after decade, with nothing to do. There are so many people and no work for most of them. No way out. No way to go anywhere you can do anything that matters to anyone." His voice was quiet. "I like fixing this place up. Year-round caretaker suits me."

"How did you get out?" she asked, her voice casual.

He glanced at her as if seeing through her false lightness. "The

Navy. But I expect you know that. In the Navy it matters what you can do, not just who you are. They appreciate hard work. They reward excellence. And the war with Morrigan provided a lot of opportunities." He shrugged. "It's not a bad life if you're willing to pay the price." His arm tightened around her. "If they crack down on Inanna, there will be no more mech from Eresh. A whole bunch of settlements have stuff they're not supposed to have. You don't think they'd be allowed to keep it, do you?"

"And if they found this place the clan would have nowhere to overwinter," Bister said, thinking through the chain of consequences. "We don't have dugouts now. All our surplus stores are here. And our pharma and supplies and things like the readers that hold everything we've saved and reclaimed and brought in from the rest of the Nine Worlds."

"I wouldn't stand here and watch them destroy every bit of work I've done for the last seven years," Griff said. "They'd have to kill me first."

"I expect so." She closed her hand around his arm. "I don't mean that I won't. I'm just scared." And that was a thing she never said. You never tell your fears their names. It gives them power.

"You were just spaced. Of course you're scared of going back into it." Griff twined his fingers with hers. "But I'll watch out for you. You can bank on that. I'm not going to let anything happen to you."

Bister closed her eyes. "What if I fail?" So many failures, so many losses, her son taking his last labored breath in her arms while she whispered to him that she loved him so, that he was her sweet boy, the light of her life....

"We just have to play the cards, babe." His arms were tight and warm. "Fold and we lose. It's that simple."

"And if we do it, there's a chance." Breathe the scent of him, feel the real, here and now.

"That's all we've got. That's all we've ever got. Just try and hope," Griff said. "But I won't let you fall. I won't let you down."

"I know that." And she did. Griff was solid. Whatever choices had brought him to Inanna, he was solid as the planet beneath them. "I do love you."

He huffed against the back of her neck. "I love you."

She opened her hand against the softened sheets. There were so many things to lose. That was the problem with loving things. "Do you think we'll ever be back here?"

"Yeah. Yeah, I do."

Bister wasn't sure if she believed him or not, but it was enough for now, enough to sink into. Morning would come soon enough.

Chapter Seven

Adelita made her way into the launch silo feeling much the better for sleep and food, though also of course guilty. Who knew what was happening on Eresh? It was so close, and yet it might as well have been on the other side of the galaxy. Bister said they didn't dare open a low-frequency channel because it would give away the location of the installation, and anyway Eresh's orbit had now carried it around Inanna where it was out of direct contact without a satellite boost. And at this point the satellites were under Calpurnian control if they had Eresh. So the entire idea was a bust. No, she just had to carry on with the plan and hope that everyone else was too. She could count on Galion and Tal. Everyone else…well, most people would try their best. She was sure of that.

Bister was there ahead of her, the Navigator and Griffin nowhere in evidence. Bister had changed her dirty shipsuit for brown pants and a white linen sleeveless shirt. A brown leather jacket and utility belt were slung over her shoulder as she checked out the launch cradle. A Calpurnian military energy flail hung from the utility belt.

"Where is everyone?" Adelita asked.

"Griff is already aboard. He's running the preflight. He said to come on up when you were ready. The Navigator's not here yet." Which made sense. The Navigator had nothing to do with the launch.

"And you're checking the cradle?"

"Yep." Bister looked reasonably cheerful. "Griff checked already, but procedure says two checks, two pairs of eyes."

"Absolutely," Adelita said. She climbed up the short ladder to the little ship's hatch. Because it sat in launch position, everything was ninety degrees off. She was climbing in the side of the aft chamber above the drive pod, the two acceleration couches already adjusted so that people strapped into them would be facing upwards, the g-forces pushing them into the seats in the safest way. Adelita noted that the two couches could tilt to become forward-facing chairs or to recline completely as beds. Well, on a ship this size there were no crew quarters. This compartment was it. The closed cabinets no doubt held all sanitary facilities and food preparation and storage. It was barely big enough for two people to move around in, the ceiling panels marked with instructions for troubleshooting a missile system. A tiny corridor ran forward, or rather up, a grid along the outer wall serving as a handrail when the ship was in level flight or a ladder in the launch position. The other side of the corridor held the sensor array and a cargo compartment.

Adelita climbed up. The cockpit was tiny, a screen wrapping around the ship's sharp nose, two couches with barely eight inches between them nestled among controls, each with flexible control arms built into their white foam. Everything was white except the controls themselves, very spiffy but in her opinion not very practical.

Griffin was leaning back in the far seat, a panel off above his head as he manually checked connections. "Come on in," he said, which she supposed served as welcome aboard.

"You will be taking first seat." Adelita made it a statement.

"Absolutely." He looked at her, multitool in one hand. "Any problem with taking second seat, Steel Captain?"

"I have taken second seat many times," Adelita said, and maneuvered herself to lie back on the white foam, pulling the control arm across her so she could reach the touch sensors. The forward screen lit at her touch, showing a camera view straight up the silo, the heads-up display a schematic of weapons system. It was fairly standard, not much different from the ships Eresh operated. In fact, some of theirs had started out as Calpurnian, taken as prizes at one time or another.

"Second is navigations and weapons on this ship," Griffin said. "It's designed to be able to be flown by one person in a pinch, though it usually carries a crew of two. And it can take two passengers if it needs to in addition to a small amount of cargo. It's a dispatch boat. It's the smallest interstellar craft the Calpurnian Navy has."

She frowned, her eyes on the display. "You only mount a single 60 launcher? And you've only got two missiles in ordnance?"

"I used the other four." For a moment Griffin's teeth showed between beard and mustache as he grinned. "For some reason or other. Yeah, one launcher. It's not that big a ship."

"Two shots. We have two shots." Adelita shook her head at the display.

"We're not going to outgun the Calpurnian Navy, Steel Captain."

"Adelita, please," she said. "It seems foolish to stand on ceremony when we are to be shipmates."

"Griffin, then," he said. "And since you've only got two shots, I trust you can make them count."

"That I can," Adelita promised.

He turned his attention to closing and sealing the overhead panel. "So how many missile launchers does *Steel Nine* mount?"

"We have six 900s," Adelita said. "And a pair of 250s. We usually carry twenty-four missiles for the 900s and eight for the 250s."

Griffin whistled. "Planning to take out a capital ship?"

"Absolutely." Adelita cracked a smile. "*Steel Nine* is a match for a ship of the line and maybe a bit more. We've got the range on most of them."

"Most of them are still mounting 750s," Griffin agreed.

"You know a lot about the Calpurnian Navy," she said. She raised one eyebrow. "Deserter?"

"Let's just leave it that I know a lot about the Calpurnian Navy." He didn't lift his eyes from his work.

"As you like," she said. She checked the displays again. Yes, that range was what she thought it would be. "With 60s I'd have to be practically aboard their ship to hit anything. They don't carry enough propellant to do more than accelerate at a stationary target."

"Yeah, but those ships are so big that any kind of evasive maneuver takes forever," Griffin said. "If you're close enough to hit them, it won't matter if they try evasive maneuvers."

"Nice," Adelita said. She'd never served aboard a small ship. Even *Steel Seven*, the first ship she'd served on, had carried a crew of a hundred although it was half the size of *Steel Nine*.

"I'm going to hope we don't need to shoot at anything," Griffin said. "We'll have Inanna between us and Eresh when we lift, so they shouldn't see where we came from, but sooner or later they're going to detect the boost. We've got to get far enough out of Inanna's gravity well to make a microjump to the outer system and then figure out where we're going. So if we're lucky…"

"If we're lucky, there won't be any Calpurnian ships in our flight path and we can jump before they get around Inanna," Adelita finished. "Good plan."

"Thanks." Griffin shot her a quick look. "The only problem is that if there's one sitting practically overhead we won't know until we lift. If I turn on the active scanners…" He spread his hands.

"They'll know exactly where we are now and get us in the boost phase."

"And we'll compromise where Bister's clan lives. Not okay."

Adelita nodded. "Got it. So I shouldn't turn on targeting or anything other than passive sensors until we're suborbital?"

"Wouldn't be much use in boost anyway."

"True enough." She ran her fingers down the checklist. Both the missiles were ready to arm, one in the launch tube and one in the compartment behind. The navigations system was online. "Want me to calculate a couple of microjumps? I'm going to need a window."

He nodded. "Yeah. Let me see how soon we'll be ready to lift." He leaned over her awkwardly, looking down the ladder. "Bister? You ready, babe?"

"Just about," Bister called back. "The Navigator is aboard. I'm helping them into the acceleration couch and then I'll seal the hatch. Give me three minutes."

"Got it," Griffin replied.

"So I'll do six runs starting ten minutes from now," Adelita said. "That'll give us some options depending on the situation topside."

"Sounds good." Griffin leaned back into his seat and began methodically strapping himself in, adjusting the headpiece and bringing the piloting plots onscreen. Another series of touches, and the forward camera suddenly blazed with light. The massive doors at the top of the silo were sliding open, chunks of dirt and grass falling past the dispatch boat. "We are preparing to lift. All crew, we will lift in five minutes. The clock is running."

"Confirmed. The clock is running. Final check," Adelita replied. Her fingers flew over the touch screen, eyes flicking to the forward screen to confirm. On the main camera, sunshine streamed down, light touching the little ship's nose.

"If they're watching up top, they'll see that," Griffin said absently, his eyes covered by the headpiece.

Six runs to calculate jump windows. Adelita shook her head. The first was too soon after boost. They wouldn't be out of the gravity well that fast. Then three that were reasonable, though the last was getting out there if there was a Calpurnian ship anywhere close. The last two were more than fifteen minutes after boost. If they had to play tag with the Calpurnian Navy for better than fifteen minutes, they were screwed. It had to be the second, third or fourth window. They'd just have to make it work. She glanced at Griffin. "We need to clear out by nine minutes from boost. There's a hole in the jump windows. We're going to get interference from Eresh's gravity field and the last two windows are too long."

"Okay. By nine then." He nodded sharply. There was nothing lazy or calm about him now. Every movement was crisp. "Second warning. Lift in one minute."

"We're ready," Bister said, her voice now on an internal comm, sounding like it was right beside Adelita.

There was a rumble beneath as Griffin brought the main engines online. It was boneshaking. A dispatch boat didn't have the deck upon deck between control and engines the way *Steel Nine* did. The rumble increased. She felt the jerk of cradle release, and for a moment the dispatch boat stood unsupported on its own ignition. Then it slowly began to rise. The sunlight sliced across the camera, momentarily blinding before the filters darkened it. Adelita fought back a grin.

"All engines full," Griffin said, and the dispatch boat rose on a column of fire, streaking into the cloudless blue sky. G-forces pressed Adelita back into her seat, foam cushioning and cradling her, straps holding her tight. The sternum pad was a weight on her chest.

Blue darkened to purple, stars appearing. For a moment it seemed that she hung upside down as Griffin put the ship into its roll. Then with a stomach-turning flip the ship's gravity systems engaged. Now instead of lying on her back she was strapped with her feet toward the floor, the screens ahead of her rather than overhead.

Passive sensors pinged, plots and vectors resolving on the heads-up display. "Lord's balls," Griffin said. "There's a frigate in our flight path."

"I see it," Adelita replied grimly. She could see all of them. Eight capital ships surrounded Eresh. One frigate was in high orbit around Inanna, just coming into view over the curve of the planet on a converging course. It must have corrected toward them when it detected the burn of their lift. Eight capital ships. Nine, with the frigate. And where were *Silk* and *Salt* and *Steel*? The sensors didn't have them in range. Of course this little boat didn't have *Steel Nine*'s sensor array any more than it had its weaponry.

"How long until the first jump window?" Griffin asked, spinning the dispatch boat around to try to gain distance as well as altitude.

"Fifty-five seconds," Adelita replied.

"Can't do it. We're too low."

"I know." Adelita's voice was calm, her eyes on the display. "They're clearing the forward missile tube. Open to vacuum."

The engine rumble increased, Griffin opening it to full speed, trying to put the curve of the planet between them again while angling for altitude. They had to get out of the last vestiges of atmosphere before they could jump.

"We have launch," Adelita said. "Live missile running. Looks like a 250."

"Let's try this, then." Griffin put the ship into a dive, dipping deeper into Inanna's atmosphere.

"It might skip on the ionosphere," she said. "That's a plan."

"Probably skip," Griffin said. "Those 250s have trouble with ionization. It acts just like countermeasures."

The camera showed the contrail flowing from their nose. They must be visible across half a continent below, a streak of fire and vapor. Adelita's eyes were on the display. "There we go," she said calmly as the missile wavered, losing its lock as it slipped into the ionosphere.

"Yeah," Griffin's long fingers moved over the touch controls. "Only problem is we've gone too far around the planet. Stay on that course and we'll join the party." Two of the other capital ships were ponderously getting underway, moving toward them from Eresh. Griffin pulled up hard, fighting for altitude again. "How's our jump window?"

"Missed the first. Seventy-three seconds to the second. Ninety seconds to the third."

"Going to be the third," Griffin said.

"And we have another launch," Adelita said. "250 running live."

"Don't want to waste the big missiles on us," Griffin said with a grin. He flipped the little ship into a barrel roll, reversing course and gaining altitude at the same time. "Let's see if we can intercept it before it arms." And that was a pirate trick if Adelita had ever seen one, straight out of Eresh. "Calpurnian procedure is to not arm until you're ten thousand meters away."

"And they love their procedures." Adelita's eyes went from screen to screen, watching as they converged, missile, dispatch boat and frigate. They were going to do it, slide the dispatch boat between the missile and the frigate. "We're going to cross their bow point blank."

"Steel Captain, the honor is yours," Griffin said. She'd swear he was smiling but couldn't spare a second to look.

"Arming missile one in the tube. Clearing the tube." If they got hit now the missile would go up before launch. On the other hand, as small as they were, if they got hit they'd be blown to a million pieces anyway.

Converging. Converging. Six thousand meters. The ping as the second jump window was reached and passed. Three thousand meters. "Firing." The missile streaked away as they crossed the frigate's nose, the dispatch boat dwarfed by the larger ship. And then it was behind them, nothing but stars before.

The explosion behind was close enough to rattle the internal gravity for a moment. Adelita watched the hit with satisfaction, the missile straight into the frigate's sensor array, a plume of atmosphere showing that it had pierced compartments behind, the frigate bleeding gasses into space.

"Nice shot, Steel Captain," Griffin said.

"Nine seconds to the window. Eight. Seven."

"Punch it," Griffin said, "here we go."

"Five, four, three…"

There was the momentary disorientation of the jump, the sudden pressure and then release as the dispatch boat skipped into subspace for exactly twenty-six seconds. And then it released. The cameras adjusted, compensating, and showed nothing but the starfield. Eresh and Inanna registered on the screen as planets far insystem and below, but they were too far out for the little ship to detect any traffic around them.

"We are between the orbits of Tammuz and the asteroid field," Griffin said. "And at seventy-three degrees to the ecliptic. Going for main engine shutdown. Let's just go dark for a while."

"Sounds good to me," Adelita said. Her heart was still racing, but she couldn't stop smiling. That one perfect shot, that was for Eresh and Galion and Cielo and…

Griffin reached across from the control arm. "It's a pleasure, Captain."

"Indeed it is, Captain," Adelita said, clasping his hand wrist to wrist. "You're a fine pilot."

His face darkened. "Glad to hear it," he said gruffly. "Now let's see how our passengers have fared and if they have any idea where we're going."

"You are insane!" Bister said as she unstrapped. "Attacking a frigate with a dispatch boat? You are both completely insane!" Griff came around to help the Navigator unstrap. Adelita stood in the doorway of the rear compartment. It looked like she was trying to suppress a smile. "I thought you were a responsible person!" Bister said. "Steel Captain! Surely that might indicate that you're not crazy!"

"Scared you to death, did I?" Griff trailed a hand along her arm, then stopped as he realized he had. The Navigator was still shaking. Bister was just fighting mad. "I'm sorry."

"It was the only way," Adelita said. "Our jump windows were limited and we could not dodge missiles for very long. Sometimes the best defense is a good offense. Your friend Griffin is an excellent pilot, but that can only make up for being so far outclassed for a short time."

"And you're an excellent shot," Griff said as he folded the Navigator's couch into a comfortable upright seated position. "But as you pointed out, we only had two missiles."

Bister took a deep breath. "Well, then."

"We are alive and that is what matters," the Navigator said, and if their calm seemed somewhat forced, Bister approved of the control. Nobody could afford to fall apart right now.

"We need to figure out our next move," Griff said. He sat down on the end of Bister's couch and she nudged him with her toe to show he was forgiven. After all, she'd told him to show his best stuff, and they were all lucky he was as good as he said.

"Yes," Adelita said. She leaned against the doorway. "Navigator, do you have any ideas?" There was a chime from the control room and she swung around. "What is that?"

"Proximity sensor." Griff barged past her on his way forward. "There's another ship close enough to be on passive sensors."

"Surely not *Sounding Dark*?" Bister said. It couldn't be that easy. She got up to follow him.

"Nah, it's a merchanter," he called back from the control room. "Looks like somebody else is lurking around out here."

"Probably came out of jump for Eresh and then saw the Calpurnian fleet," Adelita said, crowding down the corridor behind Bister. "Got a schematic?"

"On screen," Griff said. He'd folded his couch up into the seated position and pulled the control arm across him.

The merchant ship was five times the size of the dispatch boat, running silent except for passive sensors as well, its energy signature damped. You'd have to be practically on top of it to find it, a very reasonable precaution. Griff switched to the forward camera for a visual.

"That's *Perisad's Pleasure*," Bister said, recognizing the familiar stubby hull. "I know them."

"Smugglers?" Griff asked.

"Absolutely," Bister nodded. "Inbound from Morrigan with contraband for Inanna and goods for Eresh."

"Their manifests are always perfectly legal," Adelita said. "As I recall they often carry high-end home furnishings."

Bister laughed. "They do! High-end furnishings for Eresh packed full of pharma for Inanna! I've shipped with them a bunch of times. In fact, I'm the one who thought of putting vials of pharma in the seat cushions of every lovely couch and chair."

"Of course you are," Griff said.

"But it wouldn't stand a manual inspection," Bister said. "Just..."

"...the kind of cursory look we usually give you." Adelita seemed amused. "We inspect, we find nothing, everyone gets what they want."

"But if they're stopped by the Calpurnian Navy, they'll confiscate the ship," Griff said flatly. "So they're lurking out here waiting for a jump window or to see what happens."

"Hail them," Bister said. "I want to talk to Perisad. He's probably wetting himself thinking we're a Calpurnian dispatch boat."

"Hailing," Griff said. He nodded at the second seat. "Bister, sit down so you're on camera."

"What are we telling them?" the Navigator asked from back in the corridor behind Adelita, who shrugged as if to say this wasn't her party.

The screen image resolved into Perisad's worried face, close-cropped black hair and lined forehead. "Bister?" he said incredulously, having no doubt expected an officious Calpurnian subaltern who wanted to know his business.

"Hey, Perisad!" She gave him a big smile. "So I've got this Calpurnian dispatch boat with a couple of friends. How's it going?"

"How do you think?" Perisad asked. "Do you see the Calpurnian fleet all over the inner system?"

"Actually, I don't," Bister said. "Too far for our sensors. You've got a better view than we do. We lifted from Inanna and microjumped out here. What's going on?"

"We came out of jump and saw this mess," Perisad said. "There are seven or eight large ships, though there might be another couple behind Inanna or docked with the station. It doesn't look like a fight. I'd say Eresh surrendered without a shot, which seems pretty unlikely to me. I don't get it. Especially since there are a couple of Name Ships on long-range."

Adelita looked like she was being held up by leaning on the doorway. "Which ones? Where?"

"Looks like *Steel Nine* and *Salt Seven*," Perisad said. "They're as far out as we are but twelve degrees below the ecliptic. There might be another ship beyond them, but it's too far for us to get a good look at them."

"They got off. Thank the Lady they got off," Adelita breathed.

"Beats me what they're doing," Perisad said. "Except maybe they figure two ships on seven or eight is a suicide run."

It was the moment of decision, and it passed in a blink of an eye. Bister knew it even as she framed the words. "They're waiting for reinforcements," she said. "Which we're on our way to get. And then we're going to take back Eresh."

Perisad's eyebrows rose. "Take back Eresh?"

"You heard me," Bister said. "Look, what's it going to do to all of us if we lose Eresh as a port of call?"

"How? There's half the Calpurnian Navy sitting around Eresh!" A movement behind Perisad showed that his crew was listening, clustering in.

"Exactly. And if we destroy half the Calpurnian Navy, they're done here," Bister said. "Eresh isn't worth it to them. Whoever of the autarchs is leading this expedition will go down in disgrace and the other one will distance themselves from the whole idea. Eresh will be independent in fact whether they admit it or not."

"How are we going to destroy half the Calpurnian Navy?" Perisad demanded. "That's crazy talk."

"It isn't," Bister said. "Look, we've got four Name Ships, and that's the equal of six Calpurnians in terms of armament. And we're going to get reinforcements now." Bister paused. "And then there's you."

"We're a merchanter." Perisad's brow furrowed.

"I know perfectly well you mount two missile tubes and that you were probably considering whether to blow us up before we could get a call out when I hailed you," Bister said. "You've got a pair of 250s at least."

"Well, an honest man…"

"…in these troubled times, yeah," Bister finished. "But you're not the only one. I know *Naga* got off and they've got a forward mounted 250 and a rear mounted 500. And there's *Lainey's Luck* and *Elusia* and *Enniak* and…"

"Yeah, but they're not here," Perisad said.

"They could be." Bister leaned forward. "Perisad, you know every quasi-legal ship that trades through Eresh has a stake in this. And you know they're heavily armed and have no love for the Calpurnian Navy."

"Yeah, but to take on their Navy? What do we do for a home port if we're wanted in Calpurnian space?"

"I can answer that." Adelita cleared her throat and leaned over Bister's shoulder into the camera view. "You may know me. I am the Steel Captain. If you help free Eresh from the Calpurnians, you will always be welcome on Eresh. We would be delighted to extend home port status to you, along with full merchant rights in the Glitter Rim and the entire Inanna system."

"Trading rights to Inanna?" Perisad's eyes widened. "What about the Isolation?"

"If we win, it ends," Bister said.

Adelita's hand closed on her shoulder. "As she said, if we win, it ends. Inanna will be fully open for trade."

Bister heard a faintly choked sound in the corridor, as though the Navigator was refraining from pointing out that Adelita did not speak for the Council. On the other hand, if they saved Eresh, Adelita could probably write whatever ticket she wanted with the Council. She could probably hammer the radical position through at that point.

"That does change things," Perisad said. He paused thoughtfully. "So ideally what would you want us to do?"

"Fight beside us when the time comes," Adelita said.

"And what time is that?"

"When we get back with the reinforcements," Bister said. "So what we're asking you to do right now is exactly what you're already doing: lurk here outsystem and wait until we get back. If you're able, we'd like you to pass on a message to *Steel Nine*. Our comm systems won't reach them."

"We can do that," Perisad said. He shrugged. "We were planning to wait around for a while anyway and warn off anybody else inbound."

"Instead of warning them off, how about getting them to wait with you?" Bister asked. "Jamila Ravit will do it. It doesn't hurt anybody to wait around for a little bit and see how the situation unfolds. There's minimal risk for the independent businessperson and enormous possibility."

"There's the possibility of getting blown to pieces by a Calpurnian missile," Perisad pointed out.

"There is that, Captain," Bister said cheerfully. "Just like always. But no risk, no gain."

"I would point out that *Steel Nine* also has missiles," Adelita said at her shoulder.

Perisad nodded gravely. "That is a point, Steel Captain." He looked up, exchanging glances with someone unseen behind him, then turned back to the camera. "Very well. We will pass on your transmission to *Steel Nine* and we'll wait here at stationkeeping for five Calpurnian Standard Days. Unless," he held up a finger, "the Calpurnian Navy starts patrolling out here."

"In that case I would advise you to convoy with *Steel Nine* and *Salt Seven*," Adelita said. "I will include in my transmission that they are to take innocent merchanters under their protection. I would guess the ship you can't quite see is *Silk Five*, so you may rest safely under their missiles."

"Much appreciated, Steel Captain. We'll await your transmission." Perisad nodded to her. "Bister, we'll wait for your reinforcements."

"We'll be back soon," Bister said, and cut the comm.

"Lord's balls," Griff breathed. "Bister? Do you know what you just started?"

"I know exactly what I just started." Bister felt light as sunshine, the sense of being exactly in the right place at the right moment, tall as mountains. "We're going to free Eresh and Inanna both."

"How do you plan to defeat the Calpurnian Navy? I'm just asking." Griff spread his hands. "Because it's kind of a problem."

"This is not totally crazy," Adelita said. "Four Name Ships and a bunch of these merchanters...."

"Pirates," Bister supplied. "And smugglers who all run heavily armed. I mean, the problem is that none of them can beat a naval vessel alone. But in concert with the Name Ships, they could."

"Oh, I agree with that," Griff said. "I agree you can start one hell of a battle. But four Name Ships and half a dozen privateers can't take out ten capital ships. And you're right—if they did, whichever autarch it is would run for home with their tail between their legs if they survived. But it's not enough. That's not enough firepower. It's not enough for a decisive victory."

"It is with *Sounding Dark*," Bister said. Her voice sounded sure, even to her.

"We don't have *Sounding Dark*," Griff said.

"So we must gain it," the Navigator said from the doorway. "We must, Griffin. For our loves and our lives. We must trust that the Lady of the Void chose well when she put her faith in Bister. As have we." The Navigator looked at her and slowly bowed, hands together before their waist. "Gracious Lady, Queen of the Long Night, hear our prayers and petitions and lead us safely to you."

Part of Bister wanted to protest, and part of her took it in a strange kind of silence. "I'll do my best," she said. "So help me figure out how to find *Sounding Dark*."

They put the charts up on the screens in the rear compartment because there was more room for all four of them in there. Bister sat on the couch she'd had for launch, now folded into a comfortable seat. The Navigator took the other couch, but with it folded out so Adelita could sit behind them while Griff hovered standing, going back and forth between various controls. Adelita was munching on a nutrition bar. Bister wasn't hungry, but she did open a packet of rejuvenation juice for the hydration and electrolytes. The super-sweet fruit flavor wasn't her favorite, but once it was open it was hers. The Tainted never wasted food.

"So," Bister said. "On a long orbit around the system. That's a lot of space to search."

"Which is probably why *Sounding Dark* hasn't been found," Griff said. He got a nutrition bar out of the cabinet and offered it to the Navigator, who shook their head. Unfazed, he opened the wrapper himself and took a bite. Griff was acting like he completely believed in the existence of the ship, which was a considerable comfort.

"Let us begin like good treasure hunters," Adelita said. "And plot the ship's last reported positions." She gave Bister an impish grin. "Is that not what bold adventurers would do?"

"I think you're having far too much fun with this," the Navigator said. "What will Galion say if you decide to run off and be a treasure hunter?" Adelita's face fell, and the Navigator said quickly, "I only meant that Galion will enjoy this story when you tell him. As you will, back on Eresh when it's over."

"He will." Adelita took a determined bite of her nutrition bar. "So. The ship's last reported positions."

"There are some questions about the veracity of various reports," the Navigator said, touching the control panel to bring a set of green dots up on the chart of Inanna's system and the local cluster. There were at least twenty of them all over it in no discernable pattern.

"You mean they were stories told by drunk spacers in the bars of the Glitter Rim," Griff said. "About the ghost ship."

"Some of them were," the Navigator said. "And some were not."

"Can we focus on the ones that were reliable?" Bister said. "Navigator, can you take us through them chronologically? We can remove the dots that seem like tall tales."

"Logical," Adelita said. She stretched out her long legs. "I can tell you what the first one was. Three years after the mutiny brought them to Eresh, the crew of *Steel One* had a sighting. It was fifty-six years ago, but the story is part of the lore of Steel's Company."

"That is one of the first reliable ones, yes," the Navigator said. At their direction one of the green dots began pulsing, far above the plane of the orbits of the major planets and as far from the primary as the comet cloud. "They had a jump malfunction and came in far outsystem from where they were supposed to be. They were stranded for days while they recalibrated the drive. During that time they observed a "sensor ghost" a number of times. The reports of *Sounding Dark* were made by no less than five crew members over several hours."

"Then they saw something," Bister said. "That many trained people wouldn't have imagined a ship."

"Certainly not," Adelita said. "They saw something. They were sure it was *Sounding Dark*. Remember, at that point *Sounding Dark* had only been lost a little more than a hundred years. It wasn't legendary. It was historic."

Bister nodded. "So what's the second really reliable one?"

"In my opinion," the Navigator said, "and this is just my opinion, the next reliable one was only four years later and not far from the same site." A second green dot near the first one began to pulse. "A renegade made a blind jump and came out far from the system primary. They reported their sensor contact on Eresh after they made port."

"So that's only four years and not far outsystem of the first," Bister mused.

A third green dot began to pulse. "Sixteen years later there was another reliable sighting. *Salt Two* suffered a massive hull breach and the crew had to abandon ship. Three crew members survived to be picked up by *Bone One*, and they said that they had seen *Sounding Dark* and the Lady of the Void had saved them."

"Saved them how?" Griff asked.

"They had no power for their beacon. They'd sent a burst from their lifecraft, but they turned the beacon off to divert power to life support for an additional hour. *Bone* found them almost at the end of the time and their beacon was transmitting."

Bister felt a chill run down her spine. She took a sip of the sickeningly sweet drink. "Sounds familiar," she said evenly.

"That was here," the Navigator said, gesturing to the chart.

Adelita frowned. "That's halfway around the system and on a completely different plane."

"That doesn't make sense," Griff said. "You'd have to burn to get there, at least for course correction even if you just burned and then drifted along purely ballistic."

"There's nothing that says that *Sounding Dark* doesn't steer," the Navigator said.

"Yes, but a long burn would be noticed by other ships and by Eresh Control," Adelita said.

"But what would you assume it was?" the Navigator asked. "There are so many freetraders in and out. There's an unidentified burn. That's not the kind of thing you keep records of for fifty years."

"They didn't use a burn," Bister said quietly. Everyone looked at her. She shrugged. "They didn't. I just…"

"Then how did they get halfway around the system?" Adelita asked.

"I don't know." Bister shook her head. "Let's go on with the list."

"The next two are quite similar," the Navigator said. "Twenty-nine years ago there were two sightings only three days apart. They were here." Another dot pulsed. "One was from an inbound merchanter and one from *Silk Four*. *Silk Four* attempted to hail the ship and follow it but became disoriented and returned to Eresh."

"I remember that one," Adelita said. "All the children wanted to investigate it. Of course we weren't allowed to."

Griff frowned. "How did a Name Ship become disoriented? In their home system?"

"Apparently they had a major sensor glitch. All of their long-range sensors and communications failed, even the navigation fix. They had to get back to Eresh on manual."

Bister shook her head. There was a strange sense of unreality suddenly, as though she'd had this conversation before or she had heard it somewhere else. "And that was insystem of the others and close to the orbit of Tammuz. There's no way a ship could get there from the other location without a course correction."

"I agree," the Navigator said. "So there is some kind of steering active."

"But how would we not notice it?" Adelita said.

"Sensor failure?" Bister asked. "How many times in the last twenty-nine years has somebody had a sensor failure?"

"Plenty of times," Adelita conceded. "And that's the most common excuse for the Glitter Rim adventurers who claim they saw it or tried to find it and failed."

"Maybe they're not failing. Maybe it's jamming them," Griff said.

"If it is, it's not using any method we're aware of."

"That's my point," Griff said. "First Ship. We don't know what it's technically capable of. If *Sounding Dark* wants us to not see it, we don't see it."

"Then how are we supposed to find it?" Adelita demanded.

Bister took a sip of the sweet drink, then put it aside. "Maybe we're going about this wrong. What if it wants us to find it?"

"Why would it want us to find it?" Griff sounded intrigued.

"Why did it save me? If it did, which was your theory in the first place," Bister said. "The question isn't what we want from *Sounding Dark*. The question is what it wants from us."

The Navigator put their head to the side. "What *Sounding Dark* wants or what the Lady of the Void wants?"

"Both. Either." Bister searched for the words. "It's just a feeling. But I think she needs something from me. She wants me to do something. I needed her, absolutely. But she also needs me. I don't know why. I don't know what she wants. But I know that if I'm going to do it, I have to be able to find *Sounding Dark*. So if there are countermeasures, jamming, who knows what—it's not going to use them against us because that would be completely counterproductive. If I can't find *Sounding Dark*, I can't do what the Lady of the Void wants me to." She looked at them. Only Adelita didn't look frankly skeptical. "So maybe the way to go about this is to ask where *Sounding Dark* would be if it wanted me to find it?"

"Near where we picked you up," Adelita said. "Or at least in that direction. We have to assume there's a range to *Sounding Dark*'s capabilities. That was outside the system but not a full light-year away. If we jump to that location and then backtrack toward the primary…"

"…we'd be pretty close to the first sighting you showed me," Bister said, pointing at the chart.

Griff nodded. "That makes sense."

"Can we do it?" Bister asked.

"What, jump out to the debris field? Or to the site of the first sighting?" Griff asked. "Sure. We can make three or four jumps easily. It's a lot of sublight maneuvers where we start dealing with fuel issues."

"The first sighting," Bister said. There was a feeling, a sense, like someone watching. Waiting. Hoping.

"Navigator, do you have the coordinates?" Griff asked.

They nodded. "We can jump there."

Bister looked at Griff. "Do we have enough fuel to burn at sublight going toward the debris field and then just drift on the course for a while?"

He shrugged. "Sure. It's slow, but if what you want to do is just troll along, we can do that. Remember, the ship's sensors are short range."

"I know. And if we don't find anything, we can jump to the

debris field," Bister said. "Does that make sense, Adelita?"

"As much as any of this does." Adelita huffed. "We are far beyond what is sensible, but what is sensible is not acceptable."

"Surrendering to Calpurnia," the Navigator said.

"No," said Bister. "We'll never surrender."

CHAPTER EIGHT

Tal had been waiting on the Autarch's pleasure for nearly four hours when the antechamber doors opened. It took him a moment to register the strangeness. He was used to seeing the Ivory Elder in the council chambers anteroom. Only this time she was escorted by four Calpurnian guards. One of them spoke into their comm politely. "Altissima, there is one here who wants to speak with you."

Tal looked at Doro, trying to read her expression. "What's going on?" She shook her head slightly.

The inner doors opened and Altissima Gnea sauntered out. "I believe you are styled the Ivory Elder?"

"That is my title, yes," Doro said. Her voice was even but her hands were clenched. "I have come to ask you what you are doing with the children. Your crewmembers are separating them from their parents, even young babies who are breastfeeding. Why are you doing this and where are you taking them?"

"For the moment they are being lodged together in your own educational facilities," the Autarch said. She walked around Doro, as though deliberately contrasting her whip-lean disciplined form and black uniform with Doro's flyaway hair, ample figure, and brightly colored clothing.

"Babies that young cannot be taken from their mothers," Doro said. "I understand one little girl only seven weeks old has been taken. They must eat every four hours. And a baby who has only ever nursed…"

"They will be provided adequate and standardized nutrition." The Autarch stopped again in front of her.

"The damage to their emotional development…"

The Autarch's tone was pleasant. "…is far greater if they live among criminals and degenerates." She clasped her hands behind her back. "You are pirates. You are criminals, a lawless subculture, inbred and addicted to various substances, unstable, and mentally and cognitively subpar. It is the judgment of this autarch that you constitute a real and present danger to the children under your care. At best, they are exposed to harmful influences and to the pervasive dangers of living in unhealthy levels of radiation. Therefore, every child under the age of fifteen will be relocated from this installation to appropriate facilities within the Calpurnian Mandate."

Doro reeled back as if she'd been struck. "You can't do that!"

The Autarch put her head to the side. "I'm curious as to why you believe I can't."

"You can't just take hundreds of children away from their families!"

"It's interesting that you believe I can't. An example of dangerous delusion. I most certainly can, and I will. They will grow up in the Calpurnian Mandate where they will have healthy and appropriate role models rather than criminals."

Doro seemed to be struggling for breath. "Parents have a right to bring up their children as they see fit."

"Not if their teachings are detrimental to the children's mental health and well-being." The Autarch smiled reasonably. "I understand, for example, that you allow polygynous and polyandrous household groupings, and that these groupings include children with different biological parents. Obviously that's problematic. Many children are in fact raised by grandparents or a grandparent and their sexual partner because their parents are absent."

Tal jumped in. "Because we're all exposed to higher ambient radiation than on a planetary surface, most of us don't produce viable genetic material much past thirty. Children are incredibly valuable and wanted. Lots of people have children young and then pursue their careers while their own parents are the caregivers. That's the pattern. You have your kids young, they're raised by their grandparents, and then in turn you raise your grandchildren. They're all part of a Ship's Company."

"An unhealthy pattern which perpetuates generational delinquency," the Autarch said. "Without intervention, there is no doubt these children will grow up to be criminals as well. I am doing my duty and intervening. The youngest ones will no doubt find good homes with childless Calpurnians."

"And the older ones?" Doro's voice was tight.

"Will receive appropriate institutional care." The Autarch smiled again. "So if I were you, I'd display a constructive attitude."

Doro was shaking. "This is evil. To take children away from their homes, from their families...."

"Hyperbolic speech," the Autarch said. "Have you been evaluated for mental health issues? If not, it might be helpful."

Doro took a step toward her. "The gods will not forgive what you do. You will suffer for this."

"Making threats?" the Autarch asked pleasantly. "Restrain her."

Immediately the two guards each grabbed one of her arms, twisting them behind her, forcing her down to her knees. Doro screamed as they shoved her down hard on her arthritic knee. "The gods condemn you!"

Tal started forward and was seized by the other two guards. "I believe you need to learn that you are no longer in charge here," the Autarch said. "Your criminal enterprise is over."

Reason, Tal thought. *Reason may be the only way out.* "The right of self-determination is enshrined in Calpurnian law," he said.

"The Alliance Accords of the First Pruvian Council establish that every people has the right to ethnic and cultural freedom and to establish representative governments based on those freedoms."

"Which do not apply to criminals and the mentally ill," the Autarch said, at least momentarily distracted from Doro. "Freedom is for the fit."

"Freedom is for everyone."

The Autarch took a step closer, looking up at Tal held in the guards' clutches. "Not for children. Not for the insane. Not for those convicted of crimes. Not for the deviant and diseased. Surely that's the lesson you should have learned on Eresh."

Tal felt a red wave wash over him. "What we learned is that freedom is for the strong."

"Is that a threat of violence, Robber?"

"If you choose it to be." His arms tensed in their grasp.

The Autarch's face was sad. "I regret the necessity," she said. She turned to one of the guards by Doro. "Felicitis, if you will?"

"Altissima." The soldier handed her the energy flail from his belt.

"You have a choice, Robber. You or her." She gestured at Doro, grimacing on her bad knee.

"Me, of course." Tal went to his knees willingly. He'd heard of such things. They were part of the lore. No doubt his great-grandfather had survived many a flogging. If he was nothing but Robber, then that's what he was.

"So be it." The Autarch made a couple of practice swings. "Strip him. And turn the cameras on. It will be instructive to the entire installation."

Tal took a deep breath. He hadn't counted on that. "I'll do it myself."

"You won't."

And of course he didn't. That was part of it, naturally, to be stripped as though he were nothing in front of everyone, the whole installation, his childhood teacher looking away from his naked privates though she'd surely seen them when he was tiny, the guards holding his hands away, prodding at his scrotum with their batons.

Instead of telling him to kneel, they simply kicked him in the back of the knee so that he dropped gracelessly, his left shoulder hitting the floor because his hands were still linked behind him. He heard the sizzle of the energy flail igniting.

"For communicating threats of violence, by the power vested in me by the Senate of Calpurnia, I hereby condemn you to nine lashes," the Autarch said solemnly, "the sentence to be carried out immediately. Justice is served."

The first stroke hurt. The second set every nerve on fire, and Tal clenched his teeth. The energy flail on its medium setting was designed to inflict pain, not to cause permanent injury. It was supposed to hurt. That was what it did.

It was the fifth before he screamed, his eyes watering. It was the seventh before he wet himself. He was sure the camera lingered. It was the ninth before he collapsed on the floor heaving, vomit pooling beneath his face. And then he was hauled up and thrown out into the hallway. Tal just lay there for a moment, feeling coming back to his wrists and shoulders.

There was a touch on his arm. Doro was crying. "Tal, I'm sorry. I'm so sorry. It's my fault." She was beside him, her touch tentative, as though she were afraid even it would scar.

Tal turned his head. The red haze inside was solid now, a mass deep in his belly ready to rise when he called it, dark and bright as banked fire. "I'm okay."

"Tal."

"Help me up," Tal said. "And back to my office." He staggered to his knees stark naked. His clothes had been left in the anteroom. But he would walk through the station this way. He could hear them just down the corridor, people of his Company and others who had come to help, to do something, to make some premature move. They'd seen his humiliation and it hadn't frightened them, not most of them. It had made them angry. He would walk through them and let them see every burn. Doro got her shoulder under his arm and helped him up. "They don't understand Eresh," Tal said quietly. They had awakened the dragon.

The jump had been unremarkable and they had simply been trolling along for hours, taking turns watching the sensors as though the chime wouldn't alert them if they saw anything. Griff was taking a turn watching them now. The Navigator had gone to sleep on one of the rear couches, curled up on their side under one of the emergency blankets.

Adelita was forward at the control station, and frankly Bister had been paying very little attention to what she was doing. The sounds of the engines and the ventilation system were soothing, the acceleration couch comfortable, and she had been drifting on the edge of sleep when she heard the sudden scuffling noise and Griffin cry out. It was more a cry of surprise than fear. "Griff?" she called, sitting up on the edge of the couch. "Is everything all right?"

There was no reply. Bister got to her feet, turning into the long lateral corridor that ran forward. "Griff?"

"Do not make any sudden movements," Adelita said.

"What?" She stopped in the corridor, hardly able to believe what she saw. Adelita had Griff in a tight hold just beyond the entrance to the control station, his hands before him, her long knife at his throat. Griffin wasn't struggling. He simply stood passive in the hold.

"Do not come closer," Adelita said calmly. "Or I will kill him."

"What are you doing?" Bister demanded. "Griff is our ally."

Adelita raised her chin. "Is he? He's not really Griffin, is he? That is not his real name. Calpurnian, yes. But he is not anyone named Griffin. He is Dalys Morgan, Captain of the *Melanike*." Her eyes did not flinch. "I found enough in the logs to know it. And you—you do not deny it, do you?"

Griff didn't move. "Guilty as charged," he said.

There was a whisper behind Bister, the Navigator coming forward, their long skirts brushing against the walls. "Guilty of what?" They glanced around. "What are we talking about? Adelita, why are you holding a knife on our pilot?"

"You don't know what the *Melanike* did?" Adelita's hand tightened. "Tell them."

"It was a Calpurnian frigate," Griff said. His eyes met the Navigator's over her shoulder. "It fired on and destroyed a Menaechman passenger vessel." His voice was as toneless as if he were giving a report. "Thirty-two people were killed. One escape craft survived."

"And why did that happen?" Adelita held the knife to his throat still, though he did not move.

"Because the Captain…because I ordered it." For a moment his eyes flicked to Bister's.

The Navigator drew a sharp breath. "You ordered your crew to fire on a passenger vessel? On an unarmed ship?"

"You do not deny it?" Adelita's voice was harsh.

The Navigator shook their head. "Why would you do such a thing?"

"Why does it matter?" There was a spark in Griff's voice now. "She has the right of it."

"Because it doesn't make any sense. Because it doesn't match what I know of you." The Navigator came to stand close beside Bister in the corridor.

"I was ordered to. We were ordered to attack anything with Menaechman registry." Griff raised his head, grimacing as he felt the blade. "It wasn't long after the war with Morrigan. I'd made Captain then. They were good fighters with good ships and some really superior pilots. It was a tough fight. We took the outer system but we couldn't get through their defenses to the inner system. They had missile platforms, ships as good as ours, and electromancers who'd burn the skin off your bones in a boarding action."

"What does that have to do with it?" Adelita demanded.

"Wars cost money, Steel Captain," Griff said bitterly. "We withdrew after two years with nothing to show for it. Altissimus Cordelius was disgraced and retired. The treasury was practically empty. We knew Menaechmi didn't have a fleet and it wasn't the first time that we'd shaken them down. But this time somebody didn't want to pay. So we were ordered to demonstrate the consequences." He grimaced. "We were told to take out a few ships to encourage them to pay up. I knew it was a passenger vessel."

"But?" the Navigator asked.

"But I did it anyway." His shoulder moved in what might be a tiny shrug. "The Steel Captain is correct. I admit it and submit to her justice."

"This does not make any sense at all," the Navigator murmured.

Griff met the Navigator's eyes. "You think I'd have gotten in trouble? Unthinkable, dishonorable and all that?" He shook his head. "I'd have been decorated. That wasn't the Navy I joined. I thought…I thought we were better than that. I wanted us to be better than that. So I took the ship's dispatch boat and deserted. I don't even remember where I went. I drifted around for a while, I guess. A couple of years later I thought I'd go to Inanna and stay there. They're all criminals, right?"

Adelita's eyes sought Bister. "And you are not surprised," she said flatly. "You knew."

Bister took a deep breath. "I strongly suspected." She looked at Griff, but he dropped his eyes. "I didn't need to know the specifics."

"You mean you did not want to know," Adelita snapped.

"I didn't tell her," Griff said. "And I didn't meet Bister until I was on Inanna, years after. She's guilty of nothing more than not wanting to know the details of my crimes."

"There was no reason to ask," Bister said. She saw the faint whitening of Adelita's knuckles. "Adelita, we need him. We need his help. This is his ship. And we needed a pilot. And it doesn't matter, not now."

"The lives of those thirty-two people don't matter?" Adelita demanded. "There were children! They don't matter?"

"He had already exiled himself to a penal colony!" Bister shouted. At last fear uncoiled in her. "What else was he supposed to do? Kill himself?"

"It would be just!"

The Navigator put their hand on Bister's arm, their voice very calm. "I think the actual question is what we do now."

Griff looked at Bister. "I'm sorry, Bister," he said quietly. "I should have…"

"Hush," Bister said.

The Navigator's face was calm, as though they were considering some conundrum in a data pack centuries old. "If you kill him and take the ship, you can probably bring it into *Sounding Dark*. We don't need him for the docking. You can do that. I suppose the two of us could get his body to the airlock and space it. And then what?"

"What do you mean?" Adelita's hand wavered, though her voice did not.

"What will she do?"

"You mean Bister?"

"I mean the Lady of the Void. What will she do if you kill her avatar's lover at her threshold?" They glanced sideways at Bister. "And yes, it matters what Bister does too. I don't think she's going to just stand there and let you kill Griff. Are you?" They asked casually, as though it meant little. "Four people have a melee in the corridor of a ship. You kill Griff, and then what? Bister attacks you? You kill Bister? Which makes this entire mission pointless. You wound her and drag her aboard *Sounding Dark*? And the Lady of the Void is perfectly content with that? Even if Bister doesn't use *Sounding Dark*'s defenses to kill both of us in retaliation, do you think *Sounding Dark* will help us? Do you think She will help us? Have you forgotten that we address her as Mother of Mercy?"

"And so we just let this man, this criminal, have his way and escape punishment? He committed a war crime!"

"We send him to prison," the Navigator said.

"He already sent himself to prison," Bister said. The fear in her voice was tinted with anger now. "He exiled himself to an Isolated planet for the rest of his life. He'd never have left Inanna if we hadn't asked him to help us. Yes, it was a terrible crime. And he is serving his time. But don't you think it's more to the point for him to make restitution? If he helps us, he can save hundreds of lives. And no, that doesn't undo the crime. It doesn't make those people not matter. But he can do something of worth, something that saves your child in those children's names!" Adelita's eyes widened just a fraction, and Bister knew she'd hit home. She shoved the point as though she fought with blades rather than words. "Adelita, there is no good in this. We answer blood with blood and we will doom everyone. What we need right now is to find *Sounding Dark* and work together."

"Work with a war criminal?"

"If that's what it takes." Bister raised her chin defiantly. "I am Tainted. And I do not say I would have done any differently than my ancestors if I had lived in their times. And I am willing to do whatever it takes to win this and drive the Calpurnians from Eresh."

"You are not from Eresh."

"We need Eresh and Eresh needs us." Bister took a step closer. Soon she'd be in reach of the knife hand, even if Griff wouldn't move. If she had to, she would play it that way. "Inanna and the plains and the secret places and Eresh and the Glitter Rim—we are all one thing. We are parts of one body. If Eresh falls and the Glitter Rim ceases to exist, we will keep right on dying of diseases that kill nobody in civilized places." Her voice choked.

"Your service is to Eresh, Steel Captain," the Navigator said. "How does this guard those you are sworn to protect?"

Abruptly, Adelita stepped back. Released, Griff fell to his knees so swiftly that for a moment Bister thought she had slit his throat, until he raised his head, his eyes disbelieving. "May the Void rot you, monster!" Adelita said. "Child-killer."

"Steel Captain," Griff began.

"Do not address me." She took another step back. "You have your life. We will find *Sounding Dark* and do what we must. I am watching you!" She turned and made her way forward into the control room. With a swift glance at Bister, the Navigator followed her.

Griff stayed kneeling on the floor where he had fallen, Bister with her hand still on the hilt of her energy flail. She had almost drawn it. Almost. She looked down at him, her heart still beating fast. "Are you all right?"

"Yes." He looked up. "Better than I deserve to be."

"You were just going to let her kill you."

"Yes."

Bister shook her head, pacing away across the compartment. "You are impossible."

"She's right."

"I don't care."

"That much is obvious." There was a touch of amusement in his voice, and he slowly got to his feet.

She turned to face him. "Why did you do it? It wasn't fear."

Griff huffed mirthlessly. "Would you believe for the tonnage?"

"The tonnage?"

"If you destroyed a certain tonnage of shipping you would be decorated and promoted. I was almost there. If the *Melanike* had one more kill, I'd be a Tribune. I'd wanted that my whole life. The award, the respectability…. I grew up in a slum, Bister. You couldn't see the night sky because there were always lights, everything brightly lit at every hour to prevent recidivism. I wanted to be somebody." Griff shrugged. "In the Navy I was somebody. I was a damn good fighter, good pilot, good officer. I rose way above my station in the Morriganian War, further than anyone who didn't have a powerful family could ever expect to. On Calpurnia it's all about who you know. It's all about money. Well, I didn't have any, but for once talent mattered. When you're nose to nose with a Morriganian boarding party, hand to hand with Black Guard and an electromancer overloading the flail in your hand, what matters is what you can do, not who you know. But after the war it didn't matter anymore. I was stalled out. I was slipping. And so I got given 'an unsavory but necessary piece of business'. And I did it."

Bister closed her eyes.

"Disappointed? I told you long ago that I was not worth your time." She heard his footsteps on the deck. "When you've killed or stolen or whatever other crimes are actually yours, not some ancestor of yours dead a hundred and fifty years, you've done it to survive. Not to get rich." His steps stopped. "I did an evil thing. And I am willing for the Steel Captain to pronounce judgment."

"But I am not." Bister opened her eyes. He was standing very close, and she had to look up into his face. "I am not willing to lose you and whatever good you may yet do. You have done no wrong to us. You have given selflessly and asked nothing more than sustenance in return. You even agreed to help with this insane mission knowing that it might get you captured by the Calpurnian Navy and that at the very least it broke your self-imposed exile."

"It's not about your feelings, Bister. Justice is about more than your feelings."

"But mercy is not." She shook her head. "I don't know how to be the avatar of the Lady of the Void. I don't know how this works. I was never trained for the priesthood like the Navigator. But I have worshipped her my whole life and I do know this: you don't have to be worthy to be loved."

At that he bent his head, his forehead almost touching hers. "And that would be why she chose you."

"I don't know why she chose me. I just know what I have to do. And that I can't do it alone." Bister put her hand on his chest. "You can't fix the past. But you can help me save Eresh."

"You know I'll do what I can. Whatever I can." His voice was rough. "It's not enough, but...I'll swear to her if you want. I'll make this chance worth something."

"Then we have an accord," Bister said, and stepped into his arms. They held her tight, the only thing between her and the void.

Adelita sat in the first chair, her eyes on the passive scan. The Navigator came in quietly. "I liked him," Adelita said flatly.

The Navigator sat down on the second couch, kicking their feet up to lie in it properly, looking for once annoyed with the full skirts of their office. "And now?"

Adelita switched to full spectrum scan, her eyes on the controls. "I have read a great deal about the Lindorn Massacre over the years. Different historians, different analysis. I cannot say that I know who was right in the war, the Politists or the Federationists. They believed different things about how people should be governed, and frankly I think both of them were mostly wrong. And yes, it was ninety-four years ago and both ideologies were discredited long ago. I don't know why it mattered so passionately to my great-grandparents. But I do know this: ordering those civilians out in the snow and killing them was wrong. There are things that are abhorrent no matter whose name you do them in or what excuse you give yourself. Killing children, old people, babies in front of their mothers, finishing them off with knives—it is wrong. I would not have done it." She turned her head to look at the Navigator. "If I had been there, I would not have done it."

"Probably not," the Navigator said mildly. "There are always a few like you, whose moral compass is stronger than orders or ideology or self-interest. But not many, Adelita. Most people do what others around them do."

"And that is why leaders must do better," Adelita said. Her voice was harsh. "If most people will do what they are led to do, then they must be well led."

"You're not the first person to think of that," the Navigator said. They leaned back on the couch. "Myself, I think our Council is best. One person or several may go astray, but as long as most don't, we can pull ourselves back from the brink."

"And if most do?" Adelita asked. "Then you have the Corporation. Bister said that if she had been her ancestors, she would have committed the same crimes."

"Nobody thought of them as crimes," the Navigator said. "Or at least most people didn't. People in that era didn't think that working for the Corporation was evil or that people being trapped into debt-service their whole lives was wrong. It was just the way the world worked. And remember, the Alliance were no saints either. The moment they took Eresh from the Corporation they turned it into a penal colony where people were sent to hard labor in the mines because they sold naughty pictures or stole something worth a day's work. The Calpurnians got rid of their undesirables by sending them to prison for the rest of their lives, out of sight and mind of everybody else. I'm not sure that's actually more moral than what the Corporation was doing." The Navigator arranged their skirts. "I was born to Ash's Company, a Pornographer on my mother's side. My great-great grandmother generated images of polysex. Do you think that deserved life in prison?"

"Not compared to the Lindorn Massacre, no," Adelita said mirthlessly. "And what's wrong with that anyway?"

"Nothing, by our lights," the Navigator said. "I doubt Bister's ancestors thought there was anything wrong with charging interest on a loan. Or with requiring people to pay for food and then charging interest on what they owed."

"Food is a basic right," Adelita said. "Every member of a Company, no matter how useless or obnoxious they are, has a right to Ship's Mess. It's in the Compact. And it's there because our ancestors believed it. They may have been horrible people or just people who wanted to make images of threesomes, but they believed that everyone should eat."

"And so here we are," the Navigator said.

"But that does not excuse Griffin. Or Morgan. Or whatever his name is." Adelita pushed the control arm away frustratedly. "His crimes were not centuries ago. It was eleven years ago. The families of those he killed still cry out for justice!"

"And there is absolutely nothing we can do about that right now," the Navigator said.

"When we are done—"

"When we are done, we can decide what to do with Griffin."

"I know." Adelita let out a long breath. "It is just…"

"…that you liked him."

"Yes." She shook her head. "I imagined that people who would do such things were monsters."

"I don't think it's ever been that simple," the Navigator said. "And only the gods know our hearts."

"We must judge actions, not hearts." Adelita looked out at the screens showing empty starfield. "And his actions condemn him." A set of lights on the board lit, a soft chime sounding. Adelita swung the control bar back across her, her fingers dancing over the screen.

Bister and Griff appeared in the doorway as if by magic. "What is it?" Bister asked.

Adelita adjusted the scan, sending an active ping. "A ship," she said wonderingly. "Of a design I do not recognize."

Chapter Nine

Bister leaned forward over the second chair. "What is it?"

"I don't know," the Navigator said. "If you'll move, I'll get up and let Griff in." Bister's brows rose, but she stepped back. Apparently the Navigator still trusted Griff to fly his own ship. Adelita said nothing as they traded places, her eyes on the screens. They lit suddenly with the forward camera view.

Something moved in the darkness, a shape that eclipsed the distant stars. Bister was reminded of nothing so much as a vast sea reptile, one of the leviathans that hunted the deep seas of Inanna, left alone by anyone with any sense these last two hundred years. She glanced at the readouts over Griff's shoulder. "That's…four times the size of a Calpurnian capital ship," she said quietly.

"Just about," Griff said.

"I have never seen anything of that design," Adelita said. "Where is its propulsion? I don't see any thrusters or drive pods or maneuvering jets of any kind."

"Is it just drifting?" Bister asked. It was incredibly beautiful. Up close, there was no attempt to hide it at all. Instead of the normal blacks and grays of starships, it was painted a lambent, sparkling green, shading from deep emerald on what she supposed was its dorsal surface to almost gold below. Adelita was right, she thought. There were no thrusters, nothing that suggested that any sort of propulsion fired. It simply held a slow and steady course.

"It's on momentum alone," Griff said. "Out this far even atomic friction is practically negligible."

"So it could have been on this course a long time?" Bister asked.

"Theoretically, centuries," Griff said.

"But we know it is not centuries because *Sounding Dark* has been seen all over the system on courses that are not this one," Adelita said.

The Navigator smiled. "And so you're sure it's *Sounding Dark?*"

"Unless you happen to have another ancient ghost ship?" Adelita snapped.

The Navigator held up their hands. "Peace, my friend!"

"It's *Sounding Dark,*" Bister said. She could feel the murmur of ions along its sides like wind against her face, as though it were indeed some great beast that nuzzled up to her. How could it shine so after so long? How could it be so beautiful? "The question is how we get aboard."

Griff frowned. "I don't see any docking ports either."

"There must be docking ports," the Navigator said. "If pilgrims came and went, they docked with *Sounding Dark* somehow."

"I don't see any," Griff said again. "Look for yourself."

"I am looking," Adelita said. "He is correct. There are no docking ports."

The camera view slowly changed. "I'm taking us alongside," Griff said. "Maybe we're just not seeing it. It's shielded or something."

"How would we not see a docking port?" Adelita demanded.

"I don't know, Steel Captain," Griff said icily. "The same way you haven't seen the entire ship for generations?"

"This is not helpful," Bister began. She broke off as a section of the dorsal skin began to open. It slid softly back, a space wide enough to admit a ship five times their size.

"What in the…" Griff began.

"We are supposed to dock inside?" Adelita said doubtfully. "It opens? I did not see a plume."

"Sensors confirm no atmosphere was vented," Griff said. "It was already vacuum."

"Well, perhaps the docking port is covered," Adelita shook her head. "I have never seen anything like it, but covering docking ports does make sense."

"If you're worried about long-term damage," Bister agreed. "Griff, can you take us in there?"

"Absolutely." Griff's hands flew over his controls. "If there are no objections?" He glanced sideways at the Steel Captain.

She lifted her hands from her board. "None."

Carefully, he maneuvered the little dispatch boat. It appeared to sink into the bay, landing thrusters making the tiniest of puffs to slow them. The boat's external lights came on, the camera showing a huge empty space.

"Again, no docking port," Adelita said, peering at the readouts. "I see what appear to be several airlock doors, but no port."

There was a vibration. Above, the section of dorsal skin began to close. Griff swore. "We're trapped."

"It's supposed to do that," Bister said, glancing upward involuntarily. "Just wait." A glittering strip ran across the floor they settled upon, leading toward the airlock doors. "It's okay. Really."

The vast doors slid shut. "The bay is flooding with air," Griff said. He frowned over the screen. "It looks like perfectly breathable atmosphere."

"On a ship deserted for nearly two hundred years?" Adelita's eyebrows rose.

He shrugged. "Reclamation? Storage tanks? How should I know, Steel Captain?"

Bister cut Adelita off before she could tell him not to address her again. "It doesn't matter how. It just matters what."

"I recommend that we use suits anyway," Adelita said. "Even if this compartment is pressurized, there is no knowing if other compartments will be."

"I only have two suits," Griff said.

"So we leave the Navigator and you on the ship," Adelita began.

"I am not staying on the ship," the Navigator began. "You need me to…"

"None of us are staying on the ship," Bister said decisively. "If you want to wear a suit, you can wear one. I won't." There was no need. It was like a low thrumming just below the range of sound, the ship beckoning. It wanted them aboard. It would make the way safe.

"Bister," Griff said. "I know that a suit bothers you right now, but you should wear one just in case."

"It's not necessary." She straightened up from the boards. "Controls say pressure has equalized. So let's go."

"Just like that?" Adelita said.

"It seems so," the Navigator said with a smile. "I'm ready." Adelita shook her head but made no move to the locker to put a suit on if the others were trusting to *Sounding Dark*.

Bister cycled the hatch and jumped down the two feet to the deck, activating a handlamp and shining it about. Only the glittering strip they'd noticed before glimmered with a faint light. Either *Sounding Dark* was meant to take many ships at a time or was built for much larger visitors—easily four ships the size of theirs could fit in here. Indeed, the smallest of the Name Ships might manage.

"I have never seen anything like this," Adelita breathed. "The technology to either keep atmosphere in when the doors are open or to constantly refill this…."

"We can learn so much from *Sounding Dark*," the Navigator said. They looked utterly pleased, clambering down in a flurry of rose and scarlet skirts.

Griff stood beside her. "Which way, Bister?" he asked quietly.

"That door." There were several doors to the bay, but one stood at the end of the glittering strip, a plain airlock door like any other, but that was where the line led.

Adelita flashed her light over the ceiling fully thirty feet above. "How old is this ship?"

"If it is indeed one of the First Ships, about two millennia," the Navigator said. "That's what the first settlements on Agni date to, at least as far as we know. The Agnen guard their world carefully. I don't think anyone from outside has been able to do any archaeology there."

"I've been to Agni," Bister said. They all turned to look at her with surprise. "Just the port and traveler's pale, not into the underground cities," she said, "but it's amazing. And really, really inhospitable to human life on the surface. Enormous glaciers and huge volcanos so that when it's not freezing it's on fire. It's not quite as difficult as Eresh, but nothing like Inanna."

"I'm not sure why humans chose to live there first," the Navigator said.

"It was the first place they found that was plausible." Bister kept walking toward the door. "And no, I don't know why I think that." She almost felt Griff and the Navigator exchange a look.

They walked along the strip to the airlock door. It was conventional enough, red for cycling, green for pressurized. "This can't be two thousand years old," Adelita said.

"Maybe three hundred," the Navigator said. "I'd guess it's contemporary with the oldest parts of Eresh. Corporation work?"

Bister flashed her light around it. "It's functional."

Griff frowned. "You don't know...."

"Yes, I do." She turned, putting her hands on his upper arms, looking up into his face. "Griff, the Lady of the Void wants me to do this. She's not trying to trick me. She's not trying to lure us into a trap."

"That doesn't mean everything on a ship this old works," he said.

The Navigator ran their hands along the sign inside the airlock. "It says that pilgrims should wait for the airlock to cycle, then turn to the left on the other side." They looked triumphant. "It was a temple."

"More to the point," Adelita said, "the readout says the atmosphere is equal on the other side. For whatever reason, we can simply cycle the door."

"Then let's do that." Bister waited while it opened, then stepped through. The glittering strip led straight ahead, a long line like an arrow pointing directly forward down the ship, while the cross corridor went both left and right.

"Are we following the line?" Adelita said. "That is probably where the ship's control area is."

"The sign said to go left," the Navigator said.

"That's for pilgrims," Griff said.

Bister hesitated. They were all looking at her, waiting for her to make a decision. The ship was waiting too. She moistened her lips. "We take the pilgrim path," she said. "As a mark of respect." They turned to the left through an arched door that slid open at their approach.

"The ship has power," Griff said. "So why aren't the lights on?"

"Nobody's told them to come on?" Adelita suggested. "It's on wait status until we get to a control panel and can give it new input."

"Maybe," Bister said. There was another door across what seemed like an anteroom, the door panel itself elaborately ornamented with red and gold whorls. It slid open at her approach.

"Oh my," Adelita said.

The room was spacious by any standards, the walls covered in faded scarlet cloth. Benches wrapped around the walls while another arched doorway was in the right-hand wall. The ceiling and floor were both black, though they were made of some shiny material, as though they were giant screens. Bister took a step forward. A rippling chord of music sounded, lavender whorls spreading from where her foot touched, fading off across the room as the music faded from hearing.

"Lord's Balls," Griff said, "What is that?" The Navigator took a step into the room. Chimes sounded like tambours, red sunbursts spreading and fading.

Bister laughed. "It's amazing!" She took three running steps out into the center, green tendrils wreathing outward to the corners of the rooms like vines, a run of chords accompanying her.

"But what is it for?" Adelita asked.

"Pleasure? Beauty?" Bister spread her arms. "Try it!"

Griff stepped onto the floor, coming out to stand by her. A glissade of electronic drops followed him, blue and white fractal patterns curling around him. He looked bemused. Adelita followed more skeptically, golden vines like swords or lilies breaking from her steps and then fading off as she stopped and the music did as well. "Why does it do different things for different people?"

"Our weight? Our speed? How warm our feet are?" The Navigator walked out to join them in the center of the room. "It's gorgeous."

"But it does not help us find the control center," Adelita said. There was a regretful note in her voice. Surely, Bister thought, she must have some lightness about her when she was with those she loved. No one could be so serious all the time.

"Then I suppose we should try the other door." Bister walked over to it, ascending electronic notes accompanying her, pink starbursts dancing around her feet. She ran her hand over the panel and frowned. "It's not opening."

Griff looked over her shoulder. "The panel says 'program incomplete'. What program?"

"It won't open until we do a certain thing," the Navigator said. "It's a pilgrim path, remember? This is a temple. Pilgrims are supposed to do something at each station. No doubt when *Sounding Dark* was regularly visited, there were priests or even the Lady's avatar to explain how they were supposed to make devotions."

"How are we supposed to know?" Griff said.

"We could go back and try the other corridor," Adelita said.

Bister took a few steps more. Pink, strobing, bright. Adelita took a step, the drumbeat of her footfalls accompanied by red spears that merged with the pink strobes for a moment before fading. It reminded Bister…. She smiled. "We dance," she said.

The Navigator laughed. "Of course!"

"There is no music," Adelita said.

"There will be when we move." The Navigator smiled. "Like this." They raised their arms above their head, hands curved inward, graceful and true, their posture shifting. "And this." Slowly, they took a step forward, hips moving more than the foot, head turning. Red and gold sunbursts spread from their foot, chimes sounding like finger cymbals. "Oh you know, don't you," the Navigator whispered. "You know the Lord of the Dance."

"He's the Lady's lover," Griff said. Adelita looked at him quizzically and he coughed. "In the stories."

"He is indeed," the Navigator said. They slipped their sandals off. "Let's see if this works." They arched their foot, putting it down carefully, weight shifting as their hips moved. The chimes sounded again, a single drum beat behind, a golden flower or star opening beneath their foot. Their chin lifted. The other foot moved. Slow and then quickening, the Navigator's feet moved in time with the music. Or rather, the music moved in time with the Navigator's movements, swelling as they quickened. Wide skirts spread. Their steps sped, hips swaying, hands moving. The colors erupted, spreading and colliding with one another, greens and golds and purples calling to reds and oranges, suns and leaves and vines and bright stars.

It was a story, Bister realized. The Navigator's movements told a story, the Lord of the Dance calling to his distant lover, begging her to return from the depths of the Void. He spoke to her of sunshine and verdant land, of wind blowing over plains of grass, of storms rising empurpled and wild, blessing the land with rain. A series of running steps, and quick and blazing lightning flared. Slow, sensuous movements, and she was drawn in, the Lady of the Void pulled toward flesh and bone, to trees rising against the sky, the scent of lilies opening after the rain. The Lord of the Dance called, and she answered.

The Navigator's steps were faster now, hips moving, abdominal muscles moving, hands shifting. The beat kept pace, music rising. It was a heartbeat; no, two heartbeats entwining. Patterns of light flared, red and pink, a kaleidoscope of colors, one flower melting into another, one star blazing, pulsing, its rhythms matching the other. The Navigator's feet flew. The lights strobed.

Bister blinked. Pink. Gold. Gold. Orange. Pink.

*P*ink *light enfolded her, flashed around her. The lights of the Glitter Rim ran like water around the walls, the dance floor crowded, the music loud enough to lift like wings. Bister threw her head back, sweat running down her neck. Purple lights shone on the long, pink hair of the girl beside her. Astrea. She moved closer, her body almost against Astrea's, black against the strobing patterns of the lights sewn into Astrea's bodice. Desire rose in her like waves, fierce possessiveness, wild need.*

Astrea leaned in, her voice barely audible over the music. "Come with me!"

"Where?" Bister shouted back. She was young and it was the Glitter Rim and there was dark, intoxicating dark, a million stars beyond the station and a million stars within it.

"Anywhere!" Astrea spun, her bodice flashing enticing patterns like a deep-sea fish, her long legs bare beneath a tiny flared skirt, the glitter on her

eyelashes iridescent. "We can do anything!"

Anywhere. Anything. Young and strong and full of desire, full of need, full of something to fill up on, to be the lift under her wings....

"Come with me!"

The universe was enormous beyond Eresh, beyond Inanna below. Astrea had outbound tickets and a job waiting for her in the Adelpha Rim.

"And what if I get there and there's no work for me?" Bister was eighteen. She was no pilot, no crewmember, no one who was anyone.

Astrea spun again, coming closer. Her voice dropped. "I need you. And you'll find something." Of course she would. Of course. What was jumping with no suit? Surely if she jumped the air would hold her up. "Come with me!" Astrea shouted again. Her eyes were bright. She brushed against Bister. "You can take care of me."

"And you'll be mine?" Astrea laughed, spinning under the pulsing lights. Whatever she said was lost in the music. The lights flashed, falling down the walls in cascades of blue and silver.

"Just jump!" someone yelled. Bister did, the floor opening like the void, as though black tiles were suddenly the darkness of interstellar space....

She landed on hands and knees, purple novas flaring from her hands, dark minor notes rising. Adelita leaned over her. "Are you all right? Did you trip?"

"Look!" The Navigator pointed, their steps slowing, Griff still turning as though entranced. The door on the far side of the room had opened.

"I'm fine," Bister said. She had been in the Glitter Rim, in that club which had closed ages ago. With Astrea. Thirty years and more past.

Griff shook his head like a man shaking off sleep. "What just happened?"

"We danced," the Navigator said. "The door opened."

"It was very strange," Adelita said. She offered Bister her hand, and Bister got to her feet. "For a moment it seemed like I was somewhere else."

"Me too," Griff said. He was frowning. His mouth opened as though he meant to say more and then thought better of it.

Bister went and leaned against him for a moment, feeling his heart beating hard in his chest. He must have been dancing. What had he dreamed? "It takes you. It transports you," she said.

"Where?" Adelita said. "I don't know what you mean."

"You do." Bister looked at the Navigator. "You understand what it does."

"Dance is a window," the Navigator said. "But usually only for initiates. This…" They looked around the room, now quiet and dark, "…this makes trance more accessible? Bio-feedback? I don't know how it works."

"But it was not a surprise to you," Bister said flatly.

"I have trance-danced before," the Navigator said. "But I did not expect it to have this effect, no. Not on you."

Adelita lifted her head briskly. "Well, no one is hurt and the door is open."

"So we go on," Bister said. Griff's arm was around her back as though he planned to catch her. Or perhaps he, too, needed reassurance. "Did you see something bad?" she asked quietly as they went to the door.

He shook his head. "Just...a long time ago."

"Yeah." Maybe she would tell him about it sometime. Maybe she'd tell him about everything that had gone down with Astrea. Maybe she'd tell him where she'd been and what she'd done, but he could probably guess most of it anyway. And it wasn't a conversation to have in front of the Navigator and Adelita. Maybe he would even tell her what he'd experienced. She squeezed Griff's hand. "A long time ago."

Places that were gone, people who were gone, all drifting away on the seas of time, an era, a place…. No, the Glitter Rim still existed. It was still that for some people, even if the intoxication no longer worked for her. She knew too much. She was too much behind the scenes to be lost in the dance anymore, to be transformed.

…you are already transformed, something whispered behind her. *You already are.*

Bister spun around, Griff's hand still on her waist. No one was there, of course. "What is it?" he said, suddenly alert but plainly hearing nothing.

"Nothing," Bister said. "Just music."

The door led into a corridor that turned sharply right, occasional pools of bluish-white light coming from the ceiling. Walls and floor were a dark matte grey.

"We are going forward," Adelita said with satisfaction. "The control center should be this way."

"On a modern ship," Griff said. "We have no idea where it would be on a ship that has no drive section."

"Why don't we wait and see?" Bister said. "This is the pilgrim path. We will go where it leads."

"Well said," the Navigator said, bringing up the rear behind her and Griff. If they sounded a little smug it was well earned for having figured out the last puzzle. And the next? Bister frowned. Of course there would be a next puzzle. Nothing was what it seemed. Dark grey floors. Bluish-pale light. It was like descending into a tomb.

The corridor ended in a door. "There is no choice of direction this time," Adelita said.

"If there is no choice, what is the point?" the Navigator mused aloud.

Bister stepped away from Griff, examining the door. Black on black, it was cold steel. Not the cold of the void, but the cold of the tomb. Embossed on it was the universal symbol for danger, the skull and pair of long knives. "Death," she whispered.

The door slid soundlessly open. "That's…" Adelita stopped. The room was long and narrow. Niches filled each wall, each covered by a glass door that allowed one to see within, each niche seven feet long and two feet high, the bottom of it a metal grid covered in ashes. Cool blue lights illuminated everything.

"What is this place?" the Navigator said, their tone hushed.

"A crematorium." Adelita's voice was calm.

"Why would you?" Griff said. "It's—"

"People die in space," Adelita said harshly. "Or had you not noticed? What do you think should be done with them? Should we space those we love? Or perhaps recycle and eat them?"

"Maybe cremation is not a Calpurnian custom," the Navigator said. "As it is the custom of Eresh and Inanna."

"My uncle operates the crematorium on Eresh," Adelita said. "It is much like this. I was raised by him and he hoped that I would follow after him in his service, as my brother did. I grew up among the dead and the reverence they are due. There is nothing terrifying about this place." She glanced around at the chambers.

It would burn so hot and so quick. Bister put her hand against the cold glass of the nearest chamber. Smelting hot. It would reduce all to nothing so fast. Not like a pyre. Not like a pyre of precious wood. She closed her eyes against a sudden wave of vertigo. Sparks spinning up to the sky like stars flying upward….

She sat alone under the spring stars, a flannel blanket in her hands, her back to the fire. The smoke billowed the other way. She did not smell it. She did not smell roasting flesh. She curled inward over the blanket. She had

taken it from the pyre. He would not need it, not now. His lovey since he was born, he would not need it now. He would never need anything again.

The scream curled round and round inside her, never breaking out. ***My baby my darling my only my love my heart.*** *If she spoke, she would scream. If she screamed, she would never stop screaming.*

There was a soft sound. The lorist, Ista, stood beside her. She sat down quietly. "Bister." There was nothing to say. Except that she wished Ista was dead. She wished Ista was burning instead of Breden. She wished the world was on fire. "I know there are no good words at a time like this," Ista said quietly. "Bister, if there is anything I can do...."

"You could go away and leave me alone," Bister snapped. "You could leave me alone forever."

"If that's what you want...." Ista stood up, her worn shoes leaving impressions in the long grass.

"I want Breden back." It came out between clenched teeth.

"I know," Ista said quietly.

"No mother should lose their child," Bister snarled. "A curse on them who did this, a curse on them who keep this, a curse on any who speak for this."

"Bister, accidents happen," Ista said gently. "You know that Marrin did everything he could. If he'd had antibiotics or anti-spasmodics, he would have used them. You know there wasn't anything else...."

"I'm not talking about Marrin," Bister said. She dug her hands into the earth at her sides. "I'm talking about our accursed ancestors who got us Isolated. I'm talking about everyone who keeps us Isolated. Every last one of them. I want their children to die. I want them to die themselves. I want to watch them swell up and stiffen and shake in tremors and struggle to breathe...." She caught on a sob that was the start of the scream.

"Bister," Ista reached out to put her arms around her.

Bister jerked away. "Don't touch me. Don't help me. Don't say one more word about how tragedies happen."

"I wasn't going to say that," Ista said. "I was going to say that on Inanna..."

"I hate Inanna!" Bister jumped to her feet, the flannel blanket clutched against her chest. "I hate this planet and every person on it. I am leaving and I am never coming back!" She walked out into the night, the pyre behind her. Everything behind her. Every person. There was only the plains and the dark and the skies. It was a long way to Taralis Beacon, but she could walk it before morning. There was nothing to keep her here, not one more moment, not one more breath....

Something caught at her knees and she doubled over, falling...

...against Griff's hair. He was on his knees, bent like a bow, his face clenched in agony, eyes unseeing or seeing far beyond her into something else, a pain too sharp for tears etched in every line of his face. "Griff? Griff?" She drew a deep, shaking breath, leaning over him where he clutched at her knees, easing down to kneel in front of him, her arms around him. "Griffin, it's not now. It's in the past." It was the past. Fourteen years in the past. Breden would be a young man now. He died fourteen years ago. And still Griff shook. The Navigator lay on the floor beyond, their hand outstretched, trembling in some nightmare. Adelita knelt beside them. She looked up, pale but composed. "Why aren't you doing this?" Bister asked.

"I told you," Adelita said. "I don't fear death."

Bister tightened her arms around Griff, feeling him shudder back into himself. "The nova and the accretion disk. Life and death." She wore them on her body, inked into either shoulder, the signs of the Lady of the Void. "Justice and mercy."

"Mercy," Griff whispered.

She bent her head over his, her hands on either side of his face. "There, now," she whispered.

"You are mercy," he said. His eyes were closed.

The ashes were cold. Nothing burned. The world was not on fire. The chambers were long empty. The pain was long ago, transformed into purpose. And this—this was rain on ashes. Bister pressed her face against his hair.

The Navigator moaned. "I am here," Adelita said to them. "Nothing is wrong. It was another test of some kind."

"A test?" Griff lifted his head. "What?"

"This is the pilgrim path," Bister said. She slid her hand down to clasp his. "It's hard. It's hard because life is hard." She took a deep breath. "We need to go on. Catch your breath, and we'll go on."

Adelita helped the Navigator to their feet. "I'm sorry," the Navigator said.

"For what?"

"I didn't anticipate…."

"Of course you didn't," Bister said. "You serve the Lord of the Dance." The Navigator shook their head. "It shows you the worst moments of your life," Bister said, looking up and around at the walls bathed in cool blue light. "Whatever those were." Griff made some sound that might have been a snort. His breath came more normally. He would not appreciate her asking any questions now. Maybe there would be time later. "So if we're all in one piece," Bister said briskly, getting to her feet and guiding him up, "you may notice that the door at the other end is open now. We're done here."

"I cannot say I am grateful," Adelita said.

"I am," the Navigator said. "That it was no worse."

"There's no point in dwelling on it," Bister said. Her eyes were on the Navigator but her words were for Griff. "Come on. We're here to do something so let's do it."

"Right," Griff said. He didn't let go of her hand as they went out through the door, the Navigator and Adelita coming behind. "Do you think there are any more of these things?"

"What, worried the next one will make you sing?" Bister asked. She squeezed his hand and didn't let go. It might look silly, walking together like children, hand in hand, but just now she didn't care.

"I might be good at that one," Griff said, the corner of his mouth twitching.

"Hidden depths."

"Would you believe I was an actual choirboy?"

Bister looked at him sideways. "Seriously?"

"All the children had to take music. But renting an instrument cost money, so the ones whose parents didn't have money to spend or who thought it was a waste were taught to sing." His face was bland and he didn't look at her. "It's very gratifying to hear a choir of the proletariat sing for their betters. A heartwarming educational opportunity."

"I see," Bister said. The corridor was dark purple, faint reddish and blue lights deeply recessed in the walls. It was very theatrical. Of course one would expect that of a temple.

"Actually, I was pretty good."

"Then I'll leave the singing to you," she said.

It wasn't far before the corridor branched. Bister stopped at the junction, considering. "Four corridors?"

"Don't you mean five?" the Navigator asked, coming to stand on her other side.

"Three," Griff said, "unless you mean to count the way we came."

"That is ridiculous," Adelita said. "There are only two ways to go."

"There are five," the Navigator said. "And of course I'm not counting the way we came."

"Then there are three," Griff said.

"Two," Adelita said, a confused sound in her voice. "What are you talking about?"

Bister shook her head. It was as though a gray mist enfolded the junction, the doors wavering and not quite clear. "More illusions," she said. "It's the next test. Discernment."

"So we're supposed to measure it somehow?" Griff asked. "We don't have any portable instruments with us."

"We just walk boldly through the doors and trust our path will be true," Adelita said. "We must trust our hearts instead of our eyes and do what we know to be true regardless of what we see."

The Navigator frowned. "It seems to me that we are supposed to resist somehow. Only I'm not certain how."

Bister looked at the wavering mist. Was she the only one who saw it? "I think this one is for me," she said.

Griff glanced sideways at her. "Bister?"

"It's a pilgrim path." She let go of his hand, stepping out in front of him. "It's a choice to go on." She lifted her hands away from her side, away from the energy flail at her belt. "I surrender," she said, and stepped forward into the mist.

Chapter Ten

Bister dreamed, and in her dream she got up and climbed up through the old installation, out through the farmhouse into the night. It wasn't high summer. It was Harvestide. Fires danced in the pit behind, in the big fire-ring at the crest of the hill. The sound of music filled the air, steel and electric fiddles and the low heartbeat of drums beneath the wild cries of dancers. They spun around the fire, arms and legs and hair flying, the wild music lifting them like wind under feathers.

Bister smiled. The taste of honey-wine was sweet in her mouth, and her sleeveless blue shift was made for dancing, her arms cooled by the night air away from the heat of the fires. Her heart jumped in time with the drums. She was home and it was Harvestide, among faces she'd known all her life, the hunter returned.

There was one who did not dance. He was a big man in a homespun shirt, smiling through a brown beard as he clapped time, but he didn't dance. "Griffin," Bister said. That was his smile, his way, his face as she'd first seen it. There was only a little gray in his hair then, his face less weathered by planetary elements.

"Griffin," the woman said beside her. Her voice was curious. Bister looked at her sideways, and the woman smiled. She was small, her head barely at Bister's shoulder, fine boned and light as a child. She had a round face, eyes that tilted at the corners, and her hair was a river of night down her back held up with titanium combs that flashed and flickered in the firelight.

"Do I know you?" Bister asked.

"Of course." Her smile widened. "Tell me about Griffin. What happened?"

"I asked him to dance." And she was there, standing in front of him, talking to him about nothing with her voice but about everything with her eyes. It was Harvestide and she was home. She'd brought pharma and another battery and some odds and ends like data chips and a reader more precious than water in the desert to tell stories of the universe beyond. Now it was time to dance.

"I don't know these dances," he demurred.

"I'll teach you," she said.

"How can a man refuse an offer like that?" he said and took her hands.

Whirling, swirling, round and round the flames, bodies together and then apart, orbital comets about a glowing sun…. They broke away at last, stumbling out into the cooler dark. The grass was tall. It smelled of summer, as the fires smelled of winter to come. His lips were soft on hers and his hands were hard and rough from labor. She pulled him down beside her, looping her leg over his, getting her hands beneath his shirt.

"You are so beautiful," he whispered.

"You are too." She meant it. Falling into him was like falling to earth, plunging like a meteor toward a gravity well, caught in the scent of grass and warm skin and honey wine on his lips….

"And so that is Griffin." Bister stood a little way away, watching herself making love to him in the shadows beyond the fire. She looked at the woman who spoke. She was tall, older than Bister by a decade, her body ample and her hair shorn as short as Adelita's. Her gown shifted from black to indigo as she moved. "Your lover. Your dancer."

"He does like to dance," Bister said. It didn't seem strange to talk like this, but then this was a dream, a memory of a night nearly seven years ago. "And he loves it here. Sometimes I think he loves Inanna more than I do. I watch him working with the wind on his face and I see a kind of peace." She paused. "And at the same time I feel better leaving the clan here in his care. I know he'd do anything to protect them."

"Anything?" The woman's voice was curious. "Even kill?"

"If he had to." Bister glanced at her. "As I would. Don't mistake me for a tame thing."

"Never," the woman said seriously.

Bister lay on Griffin's shoulder, looking up at the night, their heartbeats slowing from the peak of passion. "I've never seen you here before," he said.

"I don't come back to Inanna very often," Bister said. This was only the fourth time back, the fourth time in seven years. She expected it to hurt more, but perhaps even pain fades in time to a dull ache.

"You travel then?" His shoulder was warm beneath her. "Despite the Isolation?"

"You can get around the Isolation if you know how." Bister shrugged. It felt good to lie like this, with him beneath her as warm and solid as the planet. "I've never belonged to just one world. And you?"

He hesitated a moment. "I've been everywhere I'm going. I reckon I'll stay here. It's a good place with good people. I've got skills they can use."

"You're the one fixing up the bunker we found." Bister opened her hand against his chest. She could feel his heartbeat under her hand.

"Yeah. It's a mess. And I'm trying to make two-hundred-year-old tech work with modern stuff. It doesn't help that the Calpurnian tech and the Morriganian are on two entirely different systems." He turned his head against her hair. "I can make it work."

"Well, I'm off to Morrigan next," Bister said. "Give me a list and I'll see what I can do." She leaned into his caress. "It's for the clan."

"Sure," Griff said.

The heavens arched above them. "Look," she said. "A shooting star."

"It's probably just some space junk burning up in the atmosphere," he said, and his arm was firm beneath her, her head against his shoulder.

"That's what I said." Bister tilted her head back. "It's a shooting star."

His arm tightened like a man who cannot believe his good fortune. "Maybe it is at that."

"I think perhaps you were right," the woman said. She was Bister's height exactly, wearing a black shipsuit that was so dark that it seemed to have depth. "He loves Inanna. And you?"

Bister looked up at the night sky, distant stars beacons for every wanderer. "I have been yours since before I knew your name, and every step of my life has been your pilgrim path."

The woman smiled then, a mysterious and secret smile, amber eyes in a dark-skinned face. "So I see."

"Why do you look different every time I look at you?" Bister asked.

"You see the faces I have worn. These are the women who have been my avatars before, from the days when the First Ships first sailed the seas of night, came into my realms and worshipped me. I remember them all." She shifted, her face changing to the one Bister had seen first, a round face with dark eyes, a delicate chin and broad cheekbones. "Yin Yue, who dreamed true, *Sounding Dark*'s Navigator. I was ancient but I was alone. She heard me. I heard her." For a moment Bister saw a different place, a park in a city, a red ball rolling on green grass, the sky above framed by tall buildings. "She was a child when she came into the Long Night, a young woman when she went into the interface. She reached for me and I reached for her." The woman who was and wasn't Yin Yue tilted her head. "They needed me, such fragile creatures so far from home. How could I not help them? How could I not be shaped by what they desired? Yin Yue called me Mother, and so I was."

"Queen of the Night, Lady to Guide Our Path," Bister said. "Mother of Mercy."

"You gave me purpose and so I have loved you." She smiled, her face changing again, dark hair, weathered skin, a face rather like Bister's.

"Am I your avatar?"

"Do you wish to be?"

Bister licked her lower lip. "I don't know. What do I have to do?"

"Free me."

"And then?" She looked away from those luminous eyes. "I don't want to spend my life alone on *Sounding Dark*. I don't want to be apart. If that's the price of your help, I will do it. But I don't want to."

"My dear daughter," she said, and her crown of stars rose above a pale face and high glittering collar, "Nor do I. I do not want to remain alone, able to reach out only in dreams or to those near death. I want to dance with my children again, plunge to earth and lie in my lover's arms, sing to them in their sleep as they travel my roads. I want freedom. Surely you understand that. You have always wanted it yourself. I want you to set me free."

Bister frowned. "And you will be in me?"

"Sometimes. But not always." She lifted her chin. "Or rather, I suppose a part of me will be in you, but most of me will be out there, out in the darkness beyond heliopause, until something draws me close and takes my hands in love."

"And we will come there," Bister said. "Into the Long Night.

And you will be waiting for us like a mother."

She nodded. "I will watch over you, as I always have."

"Will you help me free Eresh?"

"Yes." Her proud mouth twisted in amusement. "But know that nothing will return to the way it was."

Bister frowned. "Will you kill them?"

"What do you take me for? Some of them will be killed in the battle, and that cannot be helped. Those who fight are the willing sacrifice, blood for the birth of the world that will come. Birth requires blood just as death does." She held out her hands, one with the accretion disk of a black hole swirling slowly within it, the other cupping a newborn star.

"I know," Bister said. And she did. Of course she did. "I will take your bargain," she said. "Lady, I am yours."

And with a thundering thud she rushed back into the present. The corridors of *Sounding Dark* led in all directions, but the film that had obscured the junction like a net of false night was gone.

Adelita had taken her arm. "Bister? Are you all right? You froze for a moment."

Only a moment. "I'm fine," Bister said. "And I know the way to the control room."

It was forward and two decks up, but nothing hindered them. The corridors were simply empty, arched doors leading off in all directions, glittering with gold or green or lavender. "I wish we had time to explore," Adelita said.

"Maybe we can after we get *Sounding Dark* back to Eresh," Griff said. He seemed to have forgotten that he wasn't supposed to address her, and though she didn't reply, the Steel Captain also didn't protest. Or perhaps that was merely a result of the strangeness of the place. The walls seemed to flicker, whatever surface they were coated in shifting with the movement of their handlights, a few dim panels here and there giving off a pale sheen.

"There is room for hundreds of people in here," Adelita said.

"Hundreds of people lived here once," the Navigator said, "if this is indeed one of the First Ships. There was a fleet that set out together and the youngest children had grown old and died before they reached their first port, or so the stories tell us." They looked around the walls with fascination. "Imagine what we can learn from *Sounding Dark*. To touch her secrets...."

"I think it's this way," Bister said. The corridor ended in a high arched door, its frame picked out in gold while the door itself was blackened steel, the designs upon it black on black.

"The accretion disk," the Navigator said. "And the star." Their voice hitched just a little.

"How do we get in?" Griff asked.

Bister reached out, touching first one and then the other. "Life," she said, and the star blazed silver at her touch. "And death." The accretion disk glittered, and the door slid open.

"Oh my," Adelita said.

It was a dome two decks tall, a dark hemisphere rising from the floor in all directions lit only by two panels beside the door which gleamed silver over small cabinets. At the three opposite points around the circle there were padded benches. In the very center of the room was a single acceleration couch. Bister walked out into the center of the room, her steps loud on the steel deck. She knew what she would find.

On the couch lay the desiccated body of a woman, her arms straight along the control arms of the couch, shrunken fingers resting on pads of silvery iridescent gel. There was no heads-up display. Her face was raised, white hair haloing around her head. Bister looked down, and at the same time she felt that she looked up with sightless eyes.

"The ship's last avatar," Adelita breathed. "The one who

took *Sounding Dark* away into the Long Night to keep her from Corporation and Alliance alike."

"She died in the interface," Bister said. "And that trapped the Lady of the Void with her. In the interface. In *Sounding Dark.*"

"What are you talking about?" Griff said.

It felt like she was still dreaming, or perhaps this was the realest moment she'd ever had. Griff, her terribly flawed sweet lover. She felt a rush of love for him, *Mother of Mercy, Lady of Compassion, She Who Walks the Darkness at Our Side....*

"We need to move her," Bister said. "Respectfully. I need to use the chair."

Gently, Griff bent. The Navigator carefully disengaged her fingers from the gel, mindful of fragile bones. And then Griff lifted her like a father with a child, carrying her over to one of the side benches. Adelita knelt, arranging her, and pulled up a silver embroidered throw until it shrouded her to the breast.

The Navigator bent their head. "Queen of the Long Night, Mother of Stars, Lady of the Void," beginning the Litany for the Dead. They were calling her. They needed her. And she needed to answer.

So much love for the three who stood around her body, the Navigator in the impractical, flounced skirts of their office, every word of the litany held in their heart. Griff, his hands clasped like a boy who has been told to behave. Adelita in her black shipsuit, her back straight, Justice's champion who would never flinch from the night. So much love for these fragile lives.

Bister sat down on the couch. They were facing the other way, engrossed in the litany. It carried her. "...the paths of the unknown are long, the darkness overwhelming. Lady of Darkness, be our guide in the trackless paths...." She lay back just where the dead woman had lain. Bister took a deep breath, her head on the support, stretched out her arms along the control arms, and slid her fingers into the iridescent gel pads.

The dark dome overhead lit with a thousand stars. The entire expanse was a screen, showing the full starfield beyond the ship, as though suddenly she lay on a couch open to space, nothing between her and the profound darkness beyond heliopause. There was Inanna and Eresh's primary, their sun shrunk to a single bright star. It sang to her. All the voices sang to her, a chorus ranging from the primary's strong baritone to the soft whispers of stars too distant to see, their voices a million years gone, singing out to her through time.

Sounding Dark was her body, strong and old, empty rooms where her children had once played and loved and given birth and died and made songs to keep the void outside their hearts. Now they called her. Now they needed her.

For a moment she could see Tal Robber bent over his office desk, his eyes squeezed shut. "If you really exist, Lady of the Void...." And there were others, a fearless black-haired boy who waited with other children in a big room, wondering if he could short out the door panels...Cielo, she thought, and she knew him as if she'd clasped him to her breast a thousand times, Adelita's son, the children of Eresh hostage for their parents.

As we all are, Bister thought. *As we all are made to pay for the sins of our ancestors.*

"What is going on?" a distant voice said. Adelita, she thought, though she could not see her. Her eyes were millions of kilometers away. "Every control panel has lit."

"Bister's doing it." That was Griff, his voice torn between fear and relief.

I love them, she thought, though whether it was Bister or the Lady of the Void she could not say.

It is both of us, daughter. Her voice was inside. *I do not have time to teach you all of **Sounding Dark**'s mysteries if we are going to save Eresh. I am sorry the transition is so harsh. You are not trained from childhood as a dreamer should be. I would be gentler, but we have no time.*

It's all right, Mother, Bister thought. *I can take whatever you need to do.*

My brave one. Her voice was tender. *I am afraid I must hurt you a little.*

A prickling spread up from her fingers, *Sounding Dark* testing nerves and synapses as though they were her own connections, her body part of it as though she were a peripheral component that could be plugged in to the complexity that was *Sounding Dark.* It tingled just on the edge of pain. *This was what the Navigator was,* Bister thought, *back when it was more than a priestly title. The Navigator was the living interface with the ship.* She could feel the flow of electrons on *Sounding Dark*'s skin like water moving in a stream, vast currents that defined the trackless ocean between the stars.

No, not trackless. There were solar winds, patterns that showed where stars were, tiny variations of gravity that marked the islands of worlds in their orbits, almost imperceptible differences that indicated cloud albedo, liquid water, atmosphere. She felt them like wind against her face, like the flow of water against her legs. It wasn't hard at all.

It's not pain, Bister said in her mind. *It's wonderful.*

She felt the Lady of the Void's delight. *You were born for this,* she said, and a wash of love encompassed Bister, love for her and for all those who had lain on this couch and given themselves to this mystery. *My dreamer, born to sound the great darkness, an accident of genetics, a miracle. I wish I had time to show you so many things, but we have so little time.*

I understand, Bister thought. *Not a million kilometers away, but here. Here. Now.* Bister stretched out her arms. No, *Sounding Dark* did. Bay doors opened, panels extending. Solar sails unfolded like vast golden wings a kilometer across, as though *Sounding Dark* were the body of some huge, winged creature, every surface aglitter as they spread to the solar wind, to sail on its song straight toward Eresh.

"We are picking up speed," Adelita's voice was behind her.

"And changing course."

We need to rendezvous with the fleet, Bister thought. *With **Steel** and the other Name Ships and **Perisad's Pleasure** if it's still there.*

And the screen shifted, long range sensors stretching out. She did not need to see displays on a screen. She was part of them, the sensors her eyes and ears. There, further in toward the primary and below them, eight ships waited. She knew them, each precious container holding atmosphere in the darkness, *Steel* and *Silk* and *Salt* and *Ash*, each Name Ship faithful to its charge. And *Perisad's Pleasure* tucked in beneath *Steel*, *Naga* riding on the perimeter as a guard, and *Horatius* and *Valhalla* and *Enniak* and *Lainey's Luck* and *Elusia* scattered about as though in convoy—Bister's heart contracted.

There was Lainey. She stood beside her in her control room, a big woman with faded blond hair braided up with blue cord. There was Perisad, worried as usual. There was Mek'am of *Enniak* with his fierce tattoos, a dangerous fighter who loved romantic novels and secretly believed in lost treasures and wild stories. There was Jamila Ravit, calculating profits and jump points at the same time. They were hers. They were all hers.

"Is she in pain?" Griff's voice seemed close and far away at once. "She's crying."

Bister opened her eyes. "I'm crying because it's beautiful."

"Bister." He was kneeling beside the couch, his hand almost against her shoulder as though he'd been told not to touch her in the interface. The handsome lines of his face were drawn beneath his beard.

"It's just overwhelming. But I'm fine. She's going to help us. We're going to have to fight, but she's going to help us." Bister could talk. She could separate. She was still herself, still able to step away from the dazzling brilliance of the interface.

"Is the Lady in the ship?" the Navigator asked.

"Yes. No. She was, but now she's in me." It was hard to

explain. "She was in the avatar when she died in the interface. Or at least mostly." Adelita and Griff both looked completely blank, the Navigator serious. "I don't know how to explain. But she's free and she's going to help us. She wants to help us."

"Why?" Griff asked. He sounded genuinely confused.

"Because she loves us."

"I don't understand," he said.

Of course you don't, Bister thought. She lifted one hand from the gel and touched his face. "You don't have to," she said. "Trust me, Griff."

Adelita was at one of the lit screens. "We are approaching sensor range of the Name Ships. Bister, do you have a way for us to hail them?"

"Of course." That was easy. Hailing was easy. Countermeasures were hard. *Sounding Dark* liked hailing better than countermeasures. Jamming shut out their voices. It did not like to be shut out. It showed Bister how, what thoughts to think to make it happen. "You have an open channel," Bister said. "Just speak. Anything said in the room is on the comm as of now."

Adelita took a deep breath. "*Steel Nine*, this is the Captain. *Steel Nine*, are you receiving?"

"What in the…?" a woman's voice began and then was interrupted.

"This is Oxa Usury. Captain, is that you?" a man's voice said.

"Usury, this is the Captain. I am aboard the ship approaching your position," Adelita said. "You should have us on sensors soon if you don't already."

There was a chorus of chimes, of other voices, each ship hailing each other and *Steel Nine*, voices raised in fear or incredulity. *Sounding Dark* swept toward them, four times the size of the largest ship, her golden wings stretched above the little fleet.

"You are on the common channel," Bister said, glancing up and back at Adelita. "They can all hear you."

"This is the Steel Captain," Adelita said. "We have recovered *Sounding Dark*."

"I need to return to *Steel Nine*." Adelita had done her best to answer the cacophony of questions from the other ships, and now her hands were itching. It was time to plan the counterattack, and her place was on her ship.

Bister did not open her eyes, stretched on the couch, her hands in the gel pads where the dead woman's hands had been. "Griff can take you over in the dispatch boat."

"I'm not leaving," Griffin said. He sounded like he half wanted to pick her up and rip her out of the interface, and half as though he was fascinated.

"I can take it myself if he will show me the protocol for a zero-g start," Adelita said. "It's different to undock than a planetary launch." She didn't add that there was a big difference between a little dispatch boat and a ship the size of *Steel Nine*.

"That works," Griffin said.

"When I am on *Steel Nine*, it will be easier to plan the attack."

Bister nodded, her eyes still closed. Adelita wondered what she was seeing. "And I'll talk to the merchanters in the meantime. Jamila Ravit first."

The hardest sell or the easiest? That was Bister's business. Adelita glanced over at the Navigator. "You'll be here?" In case of the unexpected, she meant. Everything on this ship was unexpected.

"Of course." The Navigator nodded. They at least seemed to harbor no doubts.

Adelita and Griffin retraced their steps through the ship, reluctant to take a different route even if there might be a more direct one. The doors stood open, their programs run. "I wonder if they have to be reset," Griffin said as they passed through the dancing room, the floor dark.

"I would not know," Adelita said, and he was silent the rest of the way back to the ship.

He opened the hatch and they climbed up the short jump to the deck. They made their way forward to the control room. "Can you win?" he said.

She studied his back. "Probably."

He stood aside to let her slide into the first seat, where he had been before. "But?"

"Nothing is certain." Adelita shrugged. "I know the Name Ships and I can guess the smugglers' capabilities. They've traded on Eresh and I've inspected all of them at one time or another. But I have no idea what *Sounding Dark* can do."

Griffin shook his head. "Or what it will cost." He met her eyes. "I'm not going to let her take a suicide mission."

"You will instead."

"It's a fair use of a useless man, don't you think, Steel Captain?"

Adelita nodded slowly. She could respect that. "You will be remembered for your sacrifice, not your crimes."

"Bister will live." He pointed to the readouts above as they came online, the beginning of the docked start procedure. His eyes were on the screens. "She's had a hard life. She deserves better."

"They all deserve better." She thought of the carefully tended installation, the work it must have taken to rebuild it, the absent inhabitants whose comfort and care it was meant for. And that was an assurance she could give him that would mean something. "If we win, Inanna will have better. I swear it."

"That's your oath, Steel Captain?" he looked at her sideways, a half-smile on his face, his hands on the docking controls.

"That is my oath," Adelita said. "Unless death keeps me from it." As it would him. He was a doomed man and went to it willingly. No doubt the Navigator would have some pithy thing to say about the Lady's Lover as the sacrifice or some other mythical reference. What she saw was an old spacer who was going to die. And maybe she would as well, but she certainly didn't intend to.

He gave her a quick nod. "That's that." He pointed to the screen above. "And it looks like the docking bay door is keyed by our main engine burn, so I need to get out of the bay before you start her up or I'll be decompressed. Good luck."

"Thank you," Adelita said, settling back in the couch. She watched the monitors, knowing when he departed, sealing the hatch behind him and watching him hurry across the bay. She waited until he had disappeared and the airlock had fully cycled before she went for main engine start.

As Griffin had predicted, the bay doors above her began to retract. It was easier than she expected to slip out. The little dispatch boat moved like a dream. As she rose above the horizon of *Sounding Dark*'s broad back, she saw *Ash* and *Steel* at stationkeeping, one to each side, and put the little ship over. "Permission to dock with *Steel Nine*," she requested.

"You are cleared for the starboard forward airlock," Adulterer's voice said on the comm. "Welcome back, Captain."

Bister watched Adelita and Griff leave together, relieved that at least for the moment they seemed able to work together. She respected Adelita, liked her even, but if it came to a choice between her and Griff....

The Navigator was walking slowly around the dome, examining each touch screen that had appeared at waist height, an expression of delight on their face. "Getting to know *Sounding Dark*?" Bister asked.

"I've wanted to find *Sounding Dark* all my life." The Navigator didn't turn from the screens. "That story Adelita told about the children being fascinated with sightings? I was much younger

than she was. The older kids gave up on the idea pretty quickly.
I suppose the younger ones did too, but I didn't. My grandfather
told me it was just a story made up by spacers who wanted to
impress people. I didn't believe him. I knew she was out here." The
Navigator ran their hand along the wall screens like a caress. "I
spent years compiling the list of sightings. I went through logs and
accounts and hundreds of reports from Eresh Control decades old.
I tried to get people to help me go look for her, but no one would,
not even Tal."

"And now you're vindicated," Bister said.

The Navigator glanced over, a quick smile. "We're going to
take *Sounding Dark* straight to Eresh!"

Bister put her head to the side, aware that in some way she was
speaking the question that wasn't hers, letting the Lady use her
voice. "And why was it so important to you?"

The Navigator looked thoughtful. Bister supposed questions
like that were part of their trade. "I suppose because nobody
believed it. We don't really believe in the gods, not so much
anymore. Curses and funerals and births, but we're not what you'd
call a devout people. And it's wonderful to worship the Golden
Lady, but there's more to her than profit. The Glitter Rim is a good
thing, don't get me wrong, but there are things that matter more
than ventures that bring in luxury foods and fine furniture. I serve
the Lord of the Dance."

"Hardly an ascetic service," Bister said dryly.

"Exactly. I don't think people should avoid pleasure or not take
delight in good things. But they need to remember to say thank you!"

Bister laughed. "As you'd say to a child when you hand them a
cake, 'What do you say?'"

"Yes!" The Navigator said. "And this ship—this is a living
temple. It's proof that the gods are real and that they care for us.
A lot of people don't believe that anymore. It's hard to remember
to say thank you when nothing is there to remind you to, and even

harder to remember that when you curse in someone's name you're doing a real thing, asking for real intercession to send misfortune on someone. People can look at this, come aboard, and walk the path as we did. It's finding the Mysteries again and giving them back to anyone who comes seeking them."

"That's important."

"This ship is important. The Calpurnian Navy, all the rest of it—these are temporary troubles. *Sounding Dark* has existed for thousands of years. It's bigger than us and our lives. It needs to be preserved. Honored. Learned from."

Bister nodded slowly. Some part of her was sad. "It's still just a ship," she said quietly. "It's not the Lady of the Void herself. The temple is not the god."

"The Mysteries, the Pilgrim Path, it's to bring us to the god."

"It's a tool," Bister said gently, "and people can find their way without it."

"Some can." The Navigator's eyes were bright with tears. "And some can't. Those are the ones I see, and I have no help for them. They need a guide. They need a transformative experience. They need the hallowing. If I had the tools, I could help. But the best shipwright in the galaxy can't build a ship with no tools."

"And you are not the best shipwright."

"No." The Navigator sat down on the end of the couch. "I do my best. But with things like this—what do you say to hundreds of people who have lost their families? Their friends? Their lovers? How do you even begin to comfort everyone in Horn and Bone Company? I don't have words. I can say the same hollow things over cylinders of ashes or cylinders of nothing because no remains were recovered, but I can't fix anything. I can't explain to elders why their only daughter was taken or tell a barely-walking child that mother will not be back! I can't do anything." Their voice broke, and Bister leaned forward, taking her fingers out of the gel and putting her arms around the Navigator.

After a second the Navigator turned in her embrace, their face against Bister's shoulder, their body wracked with sobs. "There now," Bister said, smoothing their long hair. "There now. You have done everything that anyone could do."

The Navigator bent their head. "Mother, it's not enough!"

"It will never be enough, my dear," Bister said. "You can't take their pain away. Not even if you bring them a god." She dropped her face against the Navigator's hair. "And that's what you're trying to do, isn't it? Bring them a god so that they won't hurt so much."

The Navigator nodded. "And so you won't hurt so much." Bister's arms tightened, just as they had around Breden when he was little. "You needed the path for you, devoted to life and love. But wildfires sweep the plains, and from the burned stubble the flowers grow. You were meant for fields of wildflowers, not for pain. But it is all part of the same dance. Even the Lord of the Dance must descend and grow anew."

The Navigator lifted their head, pushing back to arm's length, their hands clasped. The dark lines around their eyes were smeared. "Are you her?"

"Yes," Bister said. "I am the Lady of the Void."

The Navigator closed their eyes and swallowed hard, tears still seeping beneath their eyelids. "Then I am blessed beyond belief."

"You have sought the Mystery with your whole heart and walked the pilgrim path," Bister said. "and so you have found what you sought. Now you stand at the heart of the maze. What is it that you want?"

The Navigator opened their eyes, drawing themselves up as though trying to find the dignity appropriate to a holy place. *So young,* Bister thought. *Not much more than twenty-five, and so much on them, so much responsibility for so little life behind them, so earnest, so dedicated.* She knew what the Navigator would ask.

"Great Lady, Queen of the Long Night, please help me to be good so that I can best help those who need me. And," they hesitated, "let me be happy."

"My dear, if we survive this you will be both good and happy for many long years," she said. The surviving part was the trick. Fortunately, Bister thought, she had a few ideas up her sleeves that the Lady of the Void didn't.

It was with a supreme sense of relief that the Steel Captain regained her bridge. Usury and Adulterer sprang to their feet as she entered, "Captain, the ship is yours."

"Thank you," Adelita said. She looked around, checking each face. They were no longer grief-stricken, no longer uncertain. Some were filled with wonder. She had returned from an impossible mission with a ship out of legend. *Sounding Dark* was real, riding just off their starboard beam. The Steel Captain could do anything. The weight of it was heavy, but she needed every ounce of their trust now. "You have performed admirably," she said. "And I know that you will continue to do so in the battle ahead."

Butcher cleared his throat. "The battle, Captain?"

"We're going to retake Eresh."

Usury frowned. "There are still ten Calpurnian ships. They've sent off the pinnaces, no doubt to take word home, but they've ten ships. We have four. Five, with *Sounding Dark*." He struggled a little over the name, as though he could hardly believe it even though he saw it.

"And there are the merchants," Adelita said.

"Yes, but will they fight?" Butcher shook his head. "Better for them to just get clear." Fortunately, Adelita didn't have to answer that.

"Captain," Adulterer said, "*Sounding Dark* is requesting fleetwide access."

"Granted," Adelita said. She put her hands behind her back, standing before her couch looking up at the wide forward screens.

They shifted, showing one after another of the ships' control rooms. She was acutely aware that they were all watching her. There was Captain Ravit of *Naga*, there Themis of *Elusia*, and there the tattooed visage of Mek'am of *Enniak*, a beaker of something in his hand as he scowled into the camera.

And then *Sounding Dark* joined the link, Bister in tight close-up, the back of the couch behind her, something bright moving to the side that might have been the Navigator's skirts. "Can everyone hear me?"

Of course everyone replied they could, their responses stepping all over each other. Perisad of *Perisad's Pleasure* overrode the others. "Bister, we've waited here like you wanted. And no lie, you've got a ship like we've never seen. But in case you can't tell, there are ten Calpurnian ships out there. Have you got a plan or not?"

"That's a fair question," Bister said.

"It is," Perisad said. Adelita could see Ravit and the Ash Captain both nodding. "A better plan than *Let's just attack them*. Because I can tell you, most of us aren't going to survive a straight-out attack on a Calpurnian capital ship. We're not armed like the Name Ships."

"We're not pirates," Lainey of *Lainey's Luck* put in. "We're armed merchant ships. Attacking a Calpurnian frigate is suicide."

"There are only four Name Ships," the Silk Captain put in. "Isn't the plan that we're going to wait days or weeks until the Calpurnians draw down their forces?"

"I'm not waiting anywhere a week," Jamila Ravit said. "That's ridiculous. The longer we sit here, the greater the chance that the Calpurnians will attack us."

"Much less weeks," Perisad said. "We're bringing in cargo and we don't have stores for weeks of sitting around."

"My crew will mutiny," Mek'am said starkly.

"Bister, I agreed to wait a few days," Perisad said, "and I asked the others when they showed up to wait and hear you out. Nobody is going to sit around for weeks or flat-out attack the Calpurnian Navy. As we see it, that's the Name Ships' problem."

"Especially when we can't win," Lainey said. "Why should we die for Eresh?"

"Eresh is all you have," the Salt Captain said. "What will you do if we fall?"

"Trade out of Freya," Lainey snapped. Adelita could feel it slipping, getting out of hand. In a few minutes they'd lose the alliance. But what would bring them together? They weren't her crew.

"You're right," Bister said. Adelita sucked in a breath. "You're absolutely right." Bister was worn, familiar, a Tainted smuggler, except for something different around the eyes. She looked straight at the camera, as though she was addressing each of them alone. "If we attack ten Calpurnian capital ships, a lot of us are going to die. And I don't have the right to ask that of you. It's not worth it to die for a trade port, even if it's the most profitable one you have. There are other places to go that the Calpurnian Navy isn't yet. You can run and keep running and you can probably stay well ahead of pursuit. The Name Ships—" Bister shrugged. "Well, you've got to make a suicide attack, don't you? Your families are there. Sooner or later you're going to have to take them on, four on ten, and you know how it will end. You all know how the Steel Captain will die."

Adelita felt a chill run down her spine. She could already feel the missiles slamming home, *Steel* shuddering under each blow, controls blowing in showers of sparks until she stood on her bridge alone, waiting for the final shot, a moment when the air burned for a split second before *Steel* exploded.

"You will go to the Lady of the Void," Bister said. "You will go into the Long Night. Your families will toil on a penal colony and your children will go into exile and try to remember your names." Her voice was dreaming, inexorable, savage. "Your blood will fall on Inanna as bitter rain." Adelita closed her eyes. She was not an imaginative person. Yet she could see it. "Or you can fight," Bister said. Adelita opened her eyes quickly.

Bister was her usual, practical self, her voice crisp. "The Calpurnians can't see *Sounding Dark* yet. It's invisible to their scans this far out, and they've never seen anything like it. I'll take *Sounding Dark* straight into Eresh. It doesn't have any weapons they can see and they can't get a life reading. When we get close, they'll try to board. That's their procedure, and we know how Calpurnians love their procedures." There was a smile in her voice, and she glanced up. *At Griff*, Adelita thought. *He knows all about Calpurnian procedures.* "And when they do, we attack."

The Ash Captain nodded. "And then?

Adelita could see the next move as clearly as if it were on a game board. "We microjump insystem," Adelita said. "We jump in behind the Calpurnian fleet while they're engaged. That should also put us close to Eresh so that we can guard the station against strikes."

"We let them have it right up the rear," the Ash Captain said.

The Silk Captain nodded. "That could work. If *Sounding Dark* can do some significant damage, we'd be in a good position." The Silk Captain's voice was firm, her scarlet shipsuit pristine.

"And what about us?" Jamila Ravit said.

"You can leave if you want," Bister said. "But I expect there will be considerable rewards for those who help save Eresh."

Adelita nodded. "Full trade rights to Eresh and Inanna both. That was what I told Perisad. Eresh will be an open port and we will open Inanna to trade."

The Ash Captain's eyebrows rose. "That seems a fair deal," the Silk Captain said. "But only for those who participate, of course. Full trade rights are valuable."

"I'm in," Mek'am said. "Come on, you lily-livered refuse! Big risks, big prize! And that ship you've got—if we've got the Lady of the Void with us, it's not our blood that will be spilled!"

"It's not lily-livered to be cautious, you old drunk," Lainey said. "But if we're to go in with the Name Ships in an ambush, that's a different matter than a straight-out attack."

Bister said, "Most of you have known me for years. Have you ever known me to make a fool's wager?"

Jamila smiled. "I've known you to do some crazy things, but somehow it works for you."

"Because I know what I'm doing," Bister said. "I've played this game thirty years. I know a good bet from a bad one, even when it looks risky. If I thought it was a bad bet, I wouldn't lead the assault myself."

Lainey nodded slowly. "Then I'm in."

Perisad looked around, apparently gauging the acceptance on his bridge. "We are, too."

Adelita did not permit herself a sigh of relief. No matter how much Bister spun it, a lot of people were going to die. She drew herself up. "Then we have an accord," she said.

CHAPTER ELEVEN

Tal waited on the Autarch's pleasure in the Council Chamber, the Ivory Elder, the Ash Elder, the Steel Elder and three guards present. Not that they expected trouble from the elders. Doro was hardly going to attack someone wearing a shipsuit and carrying an energy flail with her bare hands. The antique weapons displayed on the walls were just that: antiques from the ancient prison, and no threat to a person with modern energy weapons. And Tal—well, Tal had been brought to heel, hadn't he?

The Autarch had chosen to work from the Council Chamber to make a point. She worked at ease, the cameras no doubt focusing on her reading statistics on her personal device, composing her triumphant report to the Calpurnian Senate and people. It was no doubt salutary to everyone on Eresh to see her firm control. She seemed oblivious to the cameras, projecting unshakable confidence, while Tal and the Elders stood about uselessly.

The door slid open and an officer entered, a perplexed look on his face. "Autarch, *Fidelitas* is signaling. They have a ship of an unrecognized type approaching."

The Autarch didn't look up. "Tell them to hail and identify."

"They've done that, Altissima. It does not respond. And it is completely different from any ship they have ever encountered."

At that the Autarch did look up. "Different?"

"It has some sort of solar sails for propulsion. It's very large. It has no drive pods or thrusters that we can tell. And it does not answer our hails at all."

The Autarch frowned. "Its course?"

"Straight for Eresh."

Tal felt a frisson run through him. It couldn't be. Could it? He glanced at the Steel Elder, who was clearly thinking the same thing. The man met his eyes, and he shook his head infinitesimally. They both knew Adelita Massacre well. Could she have…? Best to say nothing.

"Order *Fidelitas* to intercept." The Autarch looked away, maintaining an air of unconcern.

Tal was silent. He resisted the urge to pace, to try to get a look at a screen, anything that showed an interest. It was probably nothing. And yet his heart beat faster.

"I see them," Bister said. Or rather *Sounding Dark* saw them. She lay in the interface, her senses one with the ship's. She saw the Calpurnian capital ship's thrusters flaring as it changed course, turning toward them to intercept. They were hailing again, trying different dialects. "Do not respond. Let's keep them guessing."

Griff's voice sounded as though he were at her elbow rather than at a terminal across the room. "Power reservoirs are charging quickly because the sails are picking up more and more visible light as we approach the primary. But we're still only at nine percent capacity."

"I would guess it would take several hours to fully charge," the Navigator said.

"We don't have several hours," Bister said. "Griff, what's Calpurnian procedure here?" She opened her eyes, still lying back in the chair.

He turned from the screen. "They'll hail and maintain a course toward us. If we don't respond or make a hostile move, they'll try to match course and board. But they're not going to see any boarding hatches either."

"Match course," Bister said. "All right, let's let them. No response, no hostile moves. We don't have any weaponry they can see. Just hold our course toward Eresh."

"There are ten Calpurnian ships," Griff said. "If we get between them, we're in real trouble."

"If we get between them, they've got a problem with firing missiles," Bister said. "Unless they'd like to risk taking each other out by accident if they miss us."

"They're not going to miss something this big."

"*Sounding Dark* has a few tricks up her sleeves." Bister leaned back again. "We hold course. Let them come alongside. We're getting as close to Eresh as we can."

"Autarch, the ship is maintaining course and not responding."

Tal couldn't help but glance at Doro. She met his eyes, then glanced from one to another of the Calpurnians. One, two, three, four and the Autarch. Against three Elders and him. Tal shook his head minutely. The station was full of Calpurnians. Even if he could take out a guard or two, there were twenty who could respond.

The Autarch frowned, getting to her feet. "Tell *Fidelitas* to investigate. *Lightning* and *Piper* will back them up." She shook her head. "No hostile moves?"

"No, Altissima." The officer listened to his earpiece. "The ship appears to be unarmed. There are no missile tubes or other weapon emplacements."

"Perhaps it's a drone." The Autarch shrugged. "Or an old

vessel on automatic somehow. Tell *Fidelitas* to board and claim it if possible."

"Yes, Altissima."

Tal took a step backwards. It was in fact possible to get closer to the antique weapons display. Even an antique weapon was better than none.

"Put it onscreen," the Autarch said. "Give us *Lightning*'s feed."

The screen at the end of the room lit with the camera view, and Tal heard the Steel Elder catch his breath. A vast, glittering shape swam toward them through the void, sails like the wings of some fantastic creature. Beside it, beneath the mighty spread, a Calpurnian capital ship maneuvered closer.

"One of the ships is coming alongside," Griff said unnecessarily. Bister could see it clearly. "Two more moving to intercept."

"They won't be able to find a docking port." Bister's voice was cool. "Let them get close."

It was a capital ship, one of the largest in the Calpurnian Navy, and yet it was less than half the size of *Sounding Dark*. It rode at stationkeeping beside them now, no doubt trying to figure out how it could possibly dock.

Griff shook his head. "Range nine hundred and forty-two meters. Bister, they're practically in our underwear."

"No response." She glanced over at the Navigator. "What's the charge?"

"Ten percent." The Navigator bent over another screen, intent on the work.

"It's enough." She looked at the timer she'd set flashing on the dome above. "We need another four and a half minutes."

"We're not going to have it," Griff said. "They're extending drones with cables. We'll be clamped in less than two minutes."

"Ninety seconds." Bister's fingers twitched in the interface, telling *Sounding Dark* where to reroute power, sending it rolling like a vast electrical wave to the rail guns. "Ninety seconds and we open the ports. The rail guns are charging."

"They'll see the energy signature," Griff said.

"They won't know what it is." *Sounding Dark* was confident, happy. No one had used weapons like this in a thousand years, no more than they used sails. They wouldn't recognize what was happening quickly enough. One of the drones caught, pulled closer by its magnets. She felt it like an insect touching her own skin. The clock was still running. Three minutes twenty seconds. "Open the ports!"

Twin rail gun ports began to retract on either side of the ship, four shielded panels opening, smaller than the dorsal docking port, guns fully charged behind them, sliding forward on their mounts into the firing position. There was a sudden flurry of communications from the Calpurnian ship, the drone freed suddenly as its cable was released at the source.

"Fire," Bister said.

Tal watched with incredulity as *Fidelitas* suddenly incandesced in flame, a balloon of superheated gases and oxygen igniting, then snuffed as quickly by the void. Debris flew in all directions, and the unknown ship slipped through it on its inexorable course toward Eresh, massive starboard sail tattered by flying chunks of metal. The stern compartments of *Fidelitas* drifted, burning plumes lighting it, a haze of liquid around it.

"What…" The Calpurnian officer stifled a curse. "What is that ship?"

"*Sounding Dark*," Tal said.

"You know something about this." The Autarch had come to

her feet, her eyes narrowing.

On the screen the massive ship turned, presenting her port side to the camera. There was a flash along her side. The screen flared white, then went dark. "*Lightning!*" the officer shouted. "*Lightning, respond!*" The earpiece was silent, the camera view cut. "*Piper!*"

"All ships, respond," the Autarch said, "Take that ship out, whatever it is. Battle stations. Battle stations all!" She turned to Tal. "What do you know about that ship?"

"It is *Sounding Dark*," Tal said. "The Lady of the Void has come for you." All around him the alarms began, the high, keen sound of danger.

"Come around," Bister said. "We need to get the third ship on the starboard side where the rail guns have had more time to recharge. What's the charge?"

"Seven percent," the Navigator said. "Bister, we're using power at a furious rate."

"And the sail...." Bister had felt the shrapnel rip through the tender fabric of the solar sail as though it had been her own skin as the rail gun at point blank range had simply blown through the Calpurnian capital ship as though it were foil. But the sail could be fixed, given peace and time. Three hundred or more Calpurnians could not be, blood sacrifice to the Lady of Night.

"We can recharge but at about half-speed," the Navigator said. "There are torn cables to the right sail." Bister didn't spare time to answer. The clock was still running. Two minutes and eleven seconds.

"Ship number four is launching missiles," Griff said. The screen showed four pulling away from Eresh on an intercept course. "A pair of 750s."

Bister held her breath. The nose was turning, the forward

starboard rail gun just bearing. *Come on,* darling, she whispered to *Sounding Dark. Fire on the missiles.* The other avatars had known to do this. She knew it.

One rail gun answered, light streaking across the void. It caught the missiles eleven kilometers into their run, just outside the range Griff had said that the Calpurnian Navy considered standard to arm. They blew, their warheads detonating under the nose of the ship that had fired them. Bister noted with satisfaction that there was a plume of atmosphere, though the ship did not explode. Rather, it reeled, sensor suite gone, forward compartments vented.

"Yes!" Griff shouted. And Bister felt an impact in her bones, a smaller missile striking *Sounding Dark* far aft. The third Calpurnian ship had fired as well. *Sounding Dark* screamed. Bister felt it like lightning running up her own nerves. Empty compartments closed against vacuum, life support systems sealing. It hurt, but it was far from fatal.

"Fire the port rail guns as they bear," Bister said. "Griff, reroute the power." He nodded, the ships' systems blinking green and indigo.

"Five percent," the Navigator said. The third Calpurnian ship incandesced briefly, then tumbled away, cut in half by the rail gun's fire.

"Bister, we've got ships five, six, seven and eight on intercept courses," Griff said. "Missile launches detected."

"I can get them," she said, her eyes the ships' eyes, her hands the rail guns. "But it's going to take everything we've got, and then we're unarmed until we can recharge." The rail guns spoke, the missiles exploding on their courses, unfortunately not close enough to the ships which had launched them to do any real damage.

"They don't know that," Griff said.

"When we don't shoot again they can guess," Bister said grimly. Her eyes met his across the domed room. Then she looked up at the time display and smiled.

"What is that thing?" The Autarch was on her feet shouting. "Where did that ship come from?"

"It's always been here," Doro said. "It is *Sounding Dark*."

"Altissima, we have three ships destroyed." The officer sounded incredulous. "And *Regal* is badly damaged."

"Go after that ship!" the Autarch ordered. "All ships, concentrate fire on that ship! They're outnumbered six to one! Get that ship!" On the screen, Tal could see that *Sounding Dark* had taken damage. The glittering skin was streaked black, one solar sail hanging in tatters like feathers from a skeletal wing. "Take command of *Invincible* yourself," the Autarch said. "Cast off from the station and engage!"

"Autarch." The officer bowed sharply and hurried out.

"Good call," Tal said.

The Autarch spun around. "What did you say?"

"I said good call," Tal said pleasantly, glancing up at the screen. "Because if you look, you'll see you're going to need every ship you've got."

On the other side of Eresh, behind the Calpurnian fleet, eleven ships had just come out of microjump, *Steel Nine* first. Arrayed behind her were *Salt* and *Ash* and *Silk*, seven armed merchanters following them in close order.

The Autarch whirled around. "Carmen, hail those ships and tell them we have the children of Eresh." She looked up to the ceiling cameras. "Your families are hostage for your behavior."

"Not for long," Tal said. She'd been distracted a moment; the guards, too. It was long enough to grab the antique boarding pike, heavy steel and old leather grip in his hand. But it was sharp. It was sharp as he drove it into her back, straight between her shoulder blades with all his strength.

The cameras were still rolling.

"This is the Steel Captain. All ships, engage."

Adelita watched as streaks of fire lit the evernight. Missiles converged. The Calpurnians turned, half one way and half another, their formation divided. "Butcher, fire missiles as we bear."

"Captain." Butcher's stubby fingers flew over the board. "Opening launchers one and two. Two 900s clear and in the tubes." There was a moment of hesitation, waiting as *Steel Nine* came about a few more degrees, bow on to the Calpurnian fleet. "Firing one and two."

"Reload," Adelita said. "Two more 900s. Distribute?" she glanced over at the crewmember on the short-range scanners, and the screen shifted, showing Distribute's plot.

"The 900s have acquired, Captain," Distribute said. The lines converged on the screen, the missiles running straight and true, one for each of the Calpurnian ships designated six and seven. There was a sprinkle of electronic static, the Calpurnian ships launching countermeasures.

Adelita shook her head. One of the 900s detonated prematurely as it hit the countermeasures, the explosion no doubt rocking its intended target but not causing any real damage. The second 900 veered left but came through the cloud. It hit the Calpurnian warship just astern of midship, laying open four decks to vacuum and taking out the ventral missile launchers.

Butcher led a cheer abruptly truncated by Usury cutting in. "Eight has launched missiles, Captain. We've got one on us."

"I see it," Adelita said, looking at the screen. "A 750."

"Countermeasures, Captain?" Usury said.

"Save them." The missile was too close. It would reacquire. "Full thruster burn. There's nobody ahead of us."

"Going to full burn in three seconds," Distribute said. "Two, one."

Adelita was pushed back in her seat a little despite the internal compensation as *Steel Nine*'s massive engines fired, the ship leaping forward. The missile attempted to compensate, turning to follow rather than pass aft of *Steel Nine*. As she'd intended, it turned directly into the thruster blast, the superheated plasma detonating it behind the most heavily shielded part of the ship. "Damage report?"

"No damage, Captain."

"Braking thrusters," Adelita ordered. They didn't want to overrun the Calpurnian fleet. Already the burn had brought them well ahead of their own ships, closing on beleaguered *Sounding Dark*.

Blood, so much blood, pumping out on the white carpet, the pike through her body....

Doro was struggling with one of the guards, trying to get the energy flail out of his hand. He'd raised it and now she had his wrist, holding it with all her strength. One of the lambent threads fell forward against her shoulder, her green sleeve sizzling as it scorched.

Tal threw himself forward, tackling the man body to body. They fell to the floor together, Doro to the side, Tal on top. He punched the guard in the face, knocking protective face gear out of the way, exposing brown skin and stubble. He punched him again, the Autarch's blood on his hands, on his shirt, spattering across this man's face, battering and battering.

Doro had the flail out of his hand now. "Tal!" she shouted. "Stop!" Tal stopped, his fist raised, his heart pounding. The man flinched, his eyes frightened, lips moving over broken teeth. "Do you surrender?" Doro panted.

The man nodded. Tal got off him, looking around. The other elders had the remaining guard at knifepoint and were busy shackling him with his own restraints. The Autarch lay unmoving, blood pooling as it had soaked through the rug to the deck underneath.

All over Eresh people would be watching, Calpurnians and Companies alike. Tal raised a bruised fist, red before his eyes. He knew the words. Every child on Eresh knew them. "It is the Taking!" he shouted to the camera. "We rise!"

"We rise!" Doro shouted, the energy flail in her hand, a long burn down her shoulder, her hair wild as the dangerous beldames of literature. "Eresh!" Through the walls of the Council chamber Tal heard the stir in the corridors outside. All across the station people answered.

Sounding Dark was hurting. Bister could feel it as though it were bruises on her own skin, her own bones that were crushed, her own flesh bleeding atmospherics and liquids into space. But she was old and strong and very, very large. She could take more than this. Bister winced in the interface, her eyes closed, seeing the ships around them as though the ship's sensors were her own eyes. *Steel Nine* was coming to their aid, plowing through the floating debris of the destroyed Calpurnian ships, her dark form silhouetted against Inanna.

Beyond, she could see *Salt* and *Perisad's Pleasure* engaged with another ship, while *Naga*, *Enniak* and *Elusia* seemed to be grappling to board the ship *Sounding Dark* had blinded earlier. That was Jamila, Bister thought. She'd split the prize rights with Themis and Mek'am. Mek'am would probably lead the boarding party himself. It would be a bloody melee, and whether the Calpurnians would ask for quarter or the pirates give it was an open question. Themis might, but not until Mek'am had taken the ship.

Bister was vaguely aware that the Navigator had initiated a data transfer, a handshake with the autoreceiver aboard *Ivory*, still in Eresh's dock. It required a code for *Ivory* to receive, and the Navigator put in the clearance. Irrelevant right now, Bister thought. Whatever the Navigator was sending, it was probably all right. At this moment there were other things much more critical.

"Bister!" Griff said. "We've got another pair of 750s incoming!"

One percent power. "I can get one of them," she said. One missile detonated under the rail gun's fire, the other coming straight on.

There were ways to reroute power, to pull it out of unused compartments, to cut it off to unused things like docking control, but it took time. She didn't know the routes, didn't know them like the vessels beneath her skin. She was new to this, new to the interface. She wasn't fast enough.

It slammed into *Sounding Dark*'s nose. For a moment the power blinked completely, screens darkening, gravity flickering. *No, no, no, not again*, Bister thought desperately, adrenaline shooting through her body. *Not again on a dying ship in the dark, not again the rush of air and the cold….*

I am here, the Lady said within her. *See? Here is the way.* Compartments to seal against the night, conduits to close. Bister squeezed her eyes shut. *This. And this.*

"External sensors are down," Griff said faraway in some other place.

"Reinitializing," Bister said. She could restart them. The bow cameras were destroyed and the forward sensor suite, but there were other views. *Sounding Dark* had others.

Steel Nine was firing missiles at one of the Calpurnian ships. Another was close in by Eresh, too close. It meant to fire on the station. Vectors and angles shifted, information pouring through

Bister as quickly as *Sounding Dark* felt it, the Calpurnian ship moving into a firing position.

"Bister!" Griff yelled. "*Lainey's Luck* is in trouble. And we've got one closing on us."

"No," Bister whispered. They were too close. There was no way the Calpurnian would miss the station. The Glitter Rim, Ivory Junction, the Array—all of it would be gone. But surely some blast doors would hold. Surely some would hold in the deep mines. There might be some survivors. Maybe a few.

No rail guns. No power left. *Sounding Dark* bled from a hundred rents. *Lainey's Luck* was venting atmosphere from a hole far aft. *Silk* was tightly grappled with one of the damaged ships, both of them battered. And *Steel* was too far away, a Calpurnian ship between. No one else could intercept.

"We still have steering," Bister said, and turned *Sounding Dark* directly toward the Calpurnian ship. "We can ram."

They could all see the Calpurnian flagship moving into firing position. They could all see it targeting Eresh. They were too far away. There were too many ships between, and they were fully engaged with the one their systems designated Calpurnian ten.

"Their own people are on the station!" Distribute said incredulously.

"That won't matter," Adelita said. She swallowed hard. A hundred of their own was nothing to Calpurnians compared with victory.

"Captain, *Sounding Dark* is changing course," Butcher said. "It's heading straight for seven, the one that's probably the flagship."

"I don't see…" Usury began.

"I do," Adelita said. "Take us beneath ten. Get me a firing solution."

"No!" The Navigator's hand on her arm shook Bister back into the moment, her eyes opening. "You can't!"

"There isn't any other way," Bister said. She sat up. Griff was at the far screen, turning to watch, his hands still on the controls.

"There must be! There has to be!" the Navigator pleaded. "*Sounding Dark* has to be saved. It's irreplaceable! It's our human history. It's a holy place, a priceless artifact."

"It's a ship," Bister said.

"Maybe to you. Maybe that's all she is. We haven't even begun to understand her. Her secrets—how does she work? What stories can she tell us about where humans came from and how we lived and how the Nine Worlds were settled? If you ram this ship, you'll destroy her." The Navigator pulled on Bister's arms, pulling her fingers free of the gel interface. "I can't let you do that."

There was no time. In a battle, moments are forever. "We have to save her," the Navigator said.

Bister let herself be pulled to her feet, away from the couch as the Navigator bent over it and the controls. "I'm sorry," she said, as she activated the Calpurnian energy flail at her belt to full stun and laid it across the Navigator's back. The Navigator jerked, then fell face forward across the couch like a sack of grain.

Griff crossed the room, bending to check an arterial pulse. "They're out cold," Griff said. "And no harm done. Neatly done." He looked at Bister across the Navigator's unconscious body. "So we're going to ram."

"Yes," Bister said.

He nodded. "No need for the Navigator in that mess. There's a lifecraft just aft of here. Why don't you put them in it and launch them? One of the Name ships will pick them up later." Bister looked at him. *Oh my darling,* she thought, *you are so transparent.*

You're planning to do it yourself, but this isn't for you. Not now. Not this.

She bent over the Navigator's body and made a great show of trying to pick them up. "I can't lift them. I'm too small." She didn't look at him. She couldn't carry this off if she could see his face. "You'll have to put them in there for me."

"Well...."

"Hurry!" she said.

Having brought it up he couldn't do otherwise. "I'll just be a moment," Griff said. He lifted the Navigator as easily as he'd lifted the dead woman earlier, their skirts a cascade of color across him.

"Of course." Bister slid back into the couch, into the interface. She watched him hasten out, then closed and sealed the door behind him. It would stand against hard vacuum and certainly against Griff. The internal sensors showed him opening the hatch to the lifecraft. He had to step in, four steps forward to lay the Navigator on one of the couches. He bent to put them down.

She couldn't hear him yell as the hatch irised, but she could see the motion of his mouth clearly. "Bister! Lord's Balls, Bister! Don't do this! Bister, open the door! Bister!"

"I'm sorry," she whispered again, and initiated the launch procedure. The visual cut out as the lifecraft blasted free.

All over Eresh the battle raged. Tal led a group against the guards on Greengate, storming through the carved doors that they wrenched off by main force, boarding pikes splintering the metalwork as the Calpurnians retreated before the mob. Their flails burned, but they were only human, only twenty or so against a hundred. They literally rolled over them, throwing them to the floor, trampling them, beating them with pieces of twisted metal from the doors. Like a wave they crashed into the Glitter Rim, the remaining Calpurnian guards running before them.

Tal was borne up by a fury he didn't know he had within him, the boarded-up shopfronts streaked with blood and burn strikes. And then suddenly there was no one ahead of him. The Glitter Rim curved away, a perimeter still incongruously lit with flashing purple and red and green lights promising pleasure and rest. He stopped as suddenly as if ice-cold water had suddenly been poured over him. He looked around for Doro.

Of course she wasn't there. Of course she hadn't kept up. This was mostly younger people of every Company, though he recognized a young woman of the Tainted, someone with resident status he'd seen around occasionally. And there was Gillys from Ivory, normally a quiet woman who ran the evening buffet line. But she'd had a lover on *Bone Seven*, a woman who'd applied to change to Ivory's Company. Now her clothes were rank with blood, her face set and pale. For a moment he could see Grandma Ema in her. Was this how she'd looked at the Taking?

Tal turned to face those who followed him. "We've got the Glitter Rim!" he shouted. "We've taken it! Now we need to stop and think! What's next?"

"We kill them all!" someone shouted.

Tal held up his bloody hands. "We need to control the power stations and the docking ports. We've got the Council Chambers and Eresh Control. Now we need the ships. If we can cut the power to the docking ports they can't get off." There was a general murmur of agreement. Tal looked at Gillys. "What do you say?"

"That makes sense, Ivory Captain," she said as though she too were coming back to herself.

"*Invincible* is at the Maingate Port," Tal said. "We cut the power to the gate, they can't get on or off the ship. It's too big to take off without a tow. We lock them in the ship. And then we come to terms."

"We kill them," someone said.

"We get them to surrender," Tal said. He could only imagine

trying to take the ship, rushing against a prepared enemy through a single hatch. But the Calpurnians had the same problem. They'd have to fight their way out through a single hatch. No, it would be a stalemate, but one he'd win. "Let's get to the power station!" They followed him.

Bister settled back into the interface. The room was utterly quiet. With the Navigator and Griff both gone, she was alone on the ship. It returned to the silence it had known for nearly two hundred years, as though the stillness had been waiting in corners, ready for the interlopers to leave. Outside and on Eresh, people were screaming and dying. Bister could not hear the pleas of survivors floating in suits. She could not hear the mayhem on damaged ships, the orders and the sounds of struggle as boarding parties and defenders grappled in corridors of dying ships, the lights flickering like strobes on a dance floor. On *Sounding Dark* it was silent.

I hear them all, the Lady said. *I hear every prayer and every curse and every cry for their mothers.*

For a moment, just a moment, Bister was everywhere. She tumbled in the void, head over feet, hoping for rescue. She struggled, heart to heart and chest to chest, aboard a Calpurnian ship, Mek'am's fallen form beneath her feet as the boarding party surged forward. She stood beside Adelita on *Steel Nine*'s bridge, the Captain's voice icy. She locked the boarding hatch of *Invincible* in the Maingate Port, seven inches of metal between her and the hands beating against the door.

They are all mine, the Lady said. *All of you are my children.*

Sounding Dark was silent. The distance ticked off to the Calpurnian ship, moments passing like hours. Somewhere alarms were sounding. The Calpurnian was trying to turn too late. Too late. Too late to arm missiles, too late to change course. *Sounding*

Dark bore down on it, prow to prow. It turned a few degrees, just a few. That only presented a bigger target.

I don't want to end this way, Bister thought. Sky and rain and the sound of her mother's voice…she squeezed her eyes shut and waited for the impact.

"Fire," Adelita said. A pair of 900s streaked into the night, passing under *Sounding Dark*'s belly as it closed. They plowed into the Calpurnian's hull a third of the way forward as it turned, almost cutting it in half. The momentum pushed each section in opposite directions.

And then *Sounding Dark* overrode the Calpurnian. The fireball momentarily blinded *Steel*'s cameras, the view going entirely white until the filters could compensate. Adelita caught her breath. "Get me a sensor reading," she said. "Butcher, get it now."

"There's a lot of debris, Captain." Butcher frowned at his board. "Trying to compensate for radiation and noise. Filters… there you go."

The screen cleared somewhat. There was an enormous debris field dominated by one long, articulated drifting metal arm longer than *Steel Nine*, golden solar sail hanging from it in tatters. Usury compensated at the helm. "Going to one quarter speed, Captain." She nodded sharply. Hitting that would do serious damage. There were lifecraft and smaller bits of debris everywhere, chunks as large as pinnaces drifting, obscuring everything.

"There's a larger section there," Butcher said. Green-gold on one surface, it might be the belly and heart of *Sounding Dark*, some blackened compartments open to space, still as large as a merchanter. "I've got atmospherics within." Adelita nodded. She didn't entirely trust her voice.

"Captain," Distribute said. "We have one of the other

Calpurnian ships asking for terms. *Falcon* is willing to surrender."

"Tell them that their surrender is unconditional," Adelita said. "We will grant quarter, but we will not negotiate further. They can take it or leave it."

"Yes, Captain."

"Usury, get me a channel to *Sounding Dark*. See if you can raise Bister or the Navigator." How was she going to tell Tal? Presuming Tal was alive? She could hear Distribute dictating terms, her voice hard and controlled now. Yes, they were taking them. They frankly didn't have much choice. Quarter was the best they could hope for. They were the only intact Calpurnian ship present, if one didn't count the one which didn't seem to have managed to get off the Maingate Port, hopeless odds for them. She turned on the comm herself, toggling it over from Usury.

"Bister? Bister, can you hear me?"

The voice seemed to come from far away. She floated in a sea of stars, tumbling slowly in the pinprick-lit blackness. And then she bumped against it. Bister shook her head, every muscle in her body aching. She stretched out her hand to touch the sky. It was cool and smooth, slightly curved.

Bister looked down. A dozen feet below her was the elaborate couch, the interface pads glowing softly. She wasn't floating in interstellar space. The gravity was out and she was floating inside the dome of the Array. The screens had rebooted to a simple exterior view, the starfield around whatever camera survived. Chunks of debris floated apparently close enough to touch. And through the debris field swam *Steel Nine*, dark against the stars behind.

Bister took a deep breath. Carefully, she pushed off from the wall, trying to get back to the couch. "I'm here," she said.

"Thank the Lady!" Adelita said. "Are you all right?"

"Close enough," Bister said. "Listen, Griff and the Navigator are in a lifecraft back along my course. Can you pick them up?"

For a wonder, Adelita asked no questions. "Of course," she said. "Usury, scan for *Sounding Dark*'s lifecraft. It should be a unique signature."

"I have it, Captain," Usury said. "It's going to take a while to get there, though. There are a lot of others closer."

"Establish communication," Adelita said. "If there is no medical emergency, pick up our drifters and other craft first."

"What about the Calpurnian drifters?" Usury asked.

Dark ships moving through the night, survivors grasping at drone lines that retracted through their grips, until silence and cold took them all…. It would serve them right. These were the very people who had left *Horn* and *Bone*'s crews to die. It would be justice.

"Pick them up," Bister said. "That's a death I wouldn't wish on my worst enemy."

There was a pause on the comm. "As she says," Adelita said. "Pick up all the survivors. We will grant quarter."

"Thank you," Bister said.

"Are you hurt?" Adelita asked.

"No." Bister pulled herself down into the couch, her fingers sliding into the gel. Nothing happened. There was no tingling, no sudden sense of being part of something much larger, as though *Sounding Dark* were her own body. She couldn't feel it at all. She swallowed. "How bad is the damage out there?"

"Bad," Adelita said. "You're in a section about the size of a merchanter. You must be behind blast doors that held, but there are decks open to vacuum on two sides, forward and dorsal. I have no idea how long your life support will last or how solid the structural integrity of that section is. We still have the dispatch boat docked. I'll send over a crew to pick you up."

Bister closed her eyes. "And *Sounding Dark*?"

"I don't know how much can be salvaged."

She knew that. The silence of the interface told her as much. Her eyes misted. The core, the storage banks, whatever constituted *Sounding Dark*'s mind, was gone. It was physically destroyed. The links in the interface led nowhere. What remained was a lifeless body.

The temple is not the god, the Lady whispered. Tears overflowed her eyes and ran down her cheeks.

"Bister?" the Steel Captain queried.

"I hear you. Come and get me." She lay down on the couch to wait. This time she knew rescue was coming. She left the channel open to *Steel Nine* so that she could hear them. It wouldn't be so very long.

Adelita watched the dispatch boat cast off from *Sounding Dark*. It was one of about ten things she was watching. Drones were out picking up survivors—all of them, as Bister had said. They were retrieving a Calpurnian lifecraft, an armed crew waiting to meet it at the aft hatch. The Navigator and Griffin were already aboard, the Navigator in the life center for neural stimulants since Bister had apparently knocked them out with an energy flail. Adelita was certain that was a long story she'd hear later.

"Captain?" Distribute said. "Eresh Control is hailing us. It's the Ivory Captain."

"Put him on," Adelita said. At least she wouldn't have to explain that she'd lost the Navigator.

"Steel Captain," Tal said, "We have a situation here."

That seemed to be putting it mildly. "So do we, Tal. What can I do for you?"

"We've taken Eresh," he said.

There was a cheer around her bridge that just went on and on. In fact, if it wouldn't be injurious to discipline, she would have joined it. Instead, Adelita said, "Well done, Tal. Well done, Ivory Captain!" and hoped that her voice conveyed how much she meant it.

There was triumph in Tal's voice. "Thanks to the many people who fought, and the many who protected vital parts of the station, including the young and the old. We didn't lose a single child." Another cheer, this one marked with someone's sob. It was absolutely not her. She'd been sure Cielo would be safe.

"Our problem is this," Tal said. "Part of the crew of *Invincible* has gotten aboard their ship. We hold the port and the tows. They can't take off but we can't get in. So we're at a standoff. What's the situation up there?"

"*Silk* has taken one damaged Calpurnian ship and the smugglers have taken another. One has surrendered to us. The other six are completely destroyed."

And that raised a cheer from Tal's end. Adelita waited it out before she asked, "What about the Autarch?"

"Dead," Tal said grimly. "So that's done."

The Steel Captain took a deep breath. "We're granting quarter," she said. "We've got quite a few prisoners. Is there still a long-haul barge with Calpurnian registry at Marblegate?"

"Yes," Tal said, "Though the owner isn't military and swears he had nothing to do with any of this."

"Perhaps the owner would agree to provide passage back to Calpurnia for the prisoners. If we tell the crew of *Invincible* that the others have surrendered and that we'll grant quarter and passage home if they stand down, they'll do it." Adelita smirked. "We want that ship."

"An undamaged Calpurnian frigate, Lady yes!" Tal said. "That's the next *Horn* or *Bone*."

"The two ships that surrendered here are both going to need extensive repair," Adelita said. "I presume the Council will authorize buying the one from the smugglers."

"Adelita, right now the Council will dance a fling-dance if you ask them to," Tal said bluntly.

"Then they'll announce that we dissolve the Isolation," Adelita said. "Which is what I promised Bister. And the smugglers."

Tal burst out laughing. "I'll vote for that," he said at last. "I'm off to negotiate with *Invincible*. Do you need *Ivory* out of dock to do search and rescue?"

"I think we have enough hands," Adelita said. She lifted her chin. "We'll bring them home, Tal."

"I know you will," he replied.

CHAPTER TWELVE

The crowd assembled at the Maingate dock was unexpectedly large, Adelita thought. Or perhaps not so, considering all the people had been through. Perhaps they needed a cause for celebration, bittersweet as it was. The Calpurnian warship formerly known as *Invincible* was once again docked there, a new blazon of paint down its side: *Horn Five. Steel Nine* would no longer be the newest Name Ship.

Cielo jumped up and down at her side in excitement. "Ma, I can't see!"

"Bounce then." She smiled at Galion, who put his hands under Cielo's armpits. "Giant jump." Cielo jumped, Galion lifting at the same time so that he bounced up above the level of peoples' shoulders. "Something is wrong with the gravity," Adelita said gravely. "Cielo seems to be able to leap incredibly high."

"Do it again!" Galion shook his head and did it again.

There were currents in the crowd, new crew coming forward to the airlock. Oxa Usury stopped in front of Adelita, people stepping back to hear. Cielo stopped bouncing. "Steel Captain," Usury said formally.

"Horn Captain," Adelita replied. Then she clasped both his hands. "And well deserved, my friend."

"I never thought I'd leave *Steel*," Usury said, shaking his head. "But with all of *Horn*'s experienced crew lost...."

"They had to make generous Company invitations to a core of crew from other ships. It's your time to be Captain. Now if you'll just take Butcher with you…."

"Not a chance," Butcher said, elbowing his way through the crowd, his bald head shining under the lights. "I'm with *Steel* until they carry me off. Take Distribute instead. She's due for a promotion."

And she might be, Adelita thought, though she'd considered that Distribute might move into Butcher's position on *Steel Nine* when Butcher moved into Usury's. "We'll see," she said. She gave Usury a rare smile. "Don't poach my whole crew, Horn Captain. Steal some from other companies!"

Tal Robber made his way through the crowd and joined them. "Not from my ship, you don't."

Usury laughed. "Can't I have a couple at least? It's a big ship." His face stilled. "And Horn hardly has anyone with ship experience who isn't too old or busy with other ventures."

"How about Cerli?" Galion put in. "She's been doing two years off the ship in botanical while she did an embryonic implant, but the twins are eight months old now. She might be ready to come back."

"I doubt it so soon," Adelita said. "But it is worth asking her." She'd been off the ship nearly four years to conceive and carry Cielo, and she had almost waited too long at the very end of her fertility. The continual exposure to background radiation on ship and station was a hard limit. When she and Galion had started, ninety percent of her eggs were already compromised. But Cerli had parents were who were ready and waiting to care for a baby. Adelita's uncle had been far too old to start again raising another child as he'd raised her and her brother. Still, unlike Cerli, she had a partner whose work was on Eresh rather than on a ship.

"I could ask her now and see if I can get her lined up for when she's ready," Oxa Usury said. "She's too good to let *Ivory* have her."

"Poacher," Tal said without heat.

Galion looked up at the airlock, the Elders assembling for speeches, the new and abbreviated *Horn* crew in their cream-colored shipsuits. "We go on," he said.

"We do." Adelita squeezed his hand briefly and released it.

The Horn Elder asked for silence, and gradually the crowd quieted. "Brethren," the Elder began, "Since the first Horn ship was taken as a prize, there have been four Horn ships. We still mourn the crew of *Horn Four*." They were silent a moment. "However, their memory will be honored by all of us as this captured Calpurnian warship becomes *Horn Five*. I introduce her new Captain, Oxa Usury."

Usury stepped forward, up onto the ramp to the airlock. It wasn't easy to be both Captain and new to a Ship's Company at once, but it had happened before. "I am humbled by your choice," Usury said in his blunt way. "And I'll be true to your charge." He looked at the few crew members assembled. "And if the Calpurnians come back, we'll kick them where it counts!"

There was a cheer, and Adelita smiled. *Yes*, she thought. *We go on.*

B ister stood beside the Navigator in Eresh's Array, looking out the patterned windows at the station spread beneath them. The tow's thrusters were tiny flares, maneuvering carefully to bring the section of *Sounding Dark* to rest on the surface of the airless moon. It slid into place with deceptive ease beyond the longest section of the Glitter Rim, against the jutting section of the original ship named *Ash*, its prow all but obscured with later shielding designed to patch meteorite strikes. Beside it, *Sounding Dark* looked like some vast creature snugged up against the metal, a broken leviathan come to rest.

"*Sounding Dark* has come home at last," Bister said, or rather the Lady said with Bister's voice. There was a catch in it. For a moment, Bister remembered shining sections pieced together in orbit over a blue-hazed world. Shiny new compartments glittered with metal and light, created as carefully as cradles to carry thousands safe into the unknown. She had never known a planet. She had never touched soil, much less atmosphere. She was for the dark.

And now she came to rest, her journey of two thousand years ended, a glittering hulk among the others that made up the station.

"She will remain here in honor," the Navigator said softly. "We will love her and cherish her, all that remains of her. She will be a temple and a monument to all our ancestors who tried the Seas of Night and found new homes."

Bister nodded solemnly. "I know. It is right and perfect. But I will miss her so."

"We will be waiting whenever You would grant us Your presence," the Navigator said. "This airless world—we are between Your realm and the others. We are Your doorstep."

"And you know all about liminal places." Bister smiled. Or rather the Lady smiled. She lifted her head, Bister's sleeveless black tunic showing the tattoos on each shoulder, accretion disk and newborn star. "I will come when I wish. I am curious to see what you will build here." She looked sideways at the Navigator. "I'm sure it will be interesting."

"It will be beautiful," the Navigator said. The Lady smiled again, and then like a flicker of lightning across a summer sky she was gone, Bister alone in her body, swaying a little on her feet as she watched the tows at their work. The Navigator steadied her. "Is it strange?"

"A little," Bister said. She shrugged. "But not hard. I can always feel her just a little, but most of the time it's like hearing music in the next room. I'm aware it's there, but it's not overwhelming."

"And sometimes?" There was a note of envy in the Navigator's voice.

"Sometimes I can't even explain what it's like." Bister took a deep breath and let it out. "Believe me, I didn't choose this. If I could pass it on to you...."

The Navigator shook their head. "She chose you. And for whatever reason, you are what she needs."

"Maybe it's that you already have a service," Bister said. "You serve Eresh. You're what Eresh needs. You have to be here, not out there."

"And are you going out there?"

"Inevitably," Bister said. She looked back down at the section of *Sounding Dark*, the tugs now shifting it just a little into its prepared berth. "Since you saved her charts. We may not have her sails and we may not have the technology that made her, not now, not yet, but we have her charts. Dozens of systems nobody knows! Centuries of data, scans and probes and signals—we don't even know what all of it is yet! But I'll bet anything that there are habitable worlds we don't know anything about. The Nine Worlds aren't all the galaxy, not by a long shot. *Sounding Dark* may not take us there, but she can show us the way. And there are going to be those who are willing to try."

"I'm sure there are," the Navigator said. They smiled ruefully. "Tal, for one."

"Probably." She could see Tal at *Ivory*'s helm, jumping into the dark on a course out of logs and legend. And the Lady would be there beside him, and beside all his successors, venturing ever onward.

"But in the meantime...."

"In the meantime, Eresh is safe from Calpurnia. With Altissima Gnea dead and half the fleet destroyed, the other Autarch was swift to disavow taking Eresh as a fool's expedition. Right about now he's purging everyone who supported the Altissima Gnea and capitalizing on the fury of the families of everyone killed at Eresh to bolster his support." Bister put her hands in her pockets. "The Isolation is old and the Alliance is broken. Nobody's willing to die to keep it."

"So Inanna is free. I wonder what you'll do with it."

"Buy some pharma," Bister said. "Or do you mean are we angry and will we seek revenge? There are certainly plenty of people who are. But revenge is impossible right now, and maybe by the time it is possible another generation or two will have grown up that aren't as angry and deprived. Certainly we see Eresh as our friends and allies. If we can be sisters, maybe that will give us the time we need."

"I hope so," the Navigator said quietly. "We need you and you need us. If your first steps out can be in love, perhaps that will count for something."

"Our first steps already were," Bister said. "That's what the Glitter Rim is. That's what Eresh has been for so many of us and will continue to be. It's like you said: a liminal place. A place where everything is possible."

"A beautiful hell," the Navigator said. "That's what Jorume Murder said, the first Ash Captain. That's what he called Eresh."

"A beautiful hell." Bister looked out over the Glitter Rim. Gold lights picked out *Naga*'s berth, *Silk* next to her with scaffolding all over her, waiting for temporary pressure bubbles for hull repairs, all lit with lambent purple and red lights. "It is that."

The Navigator looked at her curiously. "Where will you go now?"

"First? Back to Inanna. Then..." Bister shrugged again. "I expect I'll be back through soon. I need to go get more pharma."

"Don't tell me you're going back to smuggling."

"I was thinking of being Inanna's first official trade representative to Menaechmi. Jamila Ravit says she knows some people in the Cities of the Coast who would be more than happy to open a new market on Inanna. Maybe make a run to Menaechmi on *Naga* and see."

"Menaechmi was part of the Alliance."

Bister shrugged. "Times change. I seriously doubt the victors care after nearly two hundred years. To them it's history."

"True enough." The Navigator nodded. "But now I think you and I are probably wanted in the Council Chambers."

Bister felt the tension knot back into her shoulders for all that she suspected what the outcome would be. "Yes. Absolutely." She cast one more look over her shoulder as the Navigator led the way to the door, *Sounding Dark* resting under worklights. It wouldn't be the last time. She'd see *Sounding Dark* each time she came in, waiting for her on Eresh.

The Council Chamber was full, every seat along the walls taken. Bister noticed that the carpet was new, a deep green rather than the white it had been. Heads turned when she walked in behind the Navigator. Her black leggings and black sleeveless tunic were no uniform, no formal priestly vestment like the Navigator's tiered skirts, but she wore the Lady of the Void's color, the tattoos bared on her shoulders, one more iteration of the avatar's face. Of course they knew who she was. Conversation stilled. And yet her eyes were for one person only. Griff stood, head down, in the center of the circle of tables, his hands in restraints before him.

The Ash Elder rose, speaking clearly to those assembled and to the invisible cameras. "Brethren, we are called in Council to pass judgment on Captain Dalys Morgan, formerly of the Calpurnian Navy, also known as Griffin. The Elders have reviewed the facts of the case and have heard from the accused and from those who speak both for and against him. We have considered and debated the matter and have each cast our vote in private, as the Compact provides." The Ash Elder paused. "By his own admission of the truth of the facts, we judge him guilty of the crime of murder."

Bister's hands tensed. Griffin did not look up. "The Elders have rendered judgment. Now we defer to the Steel Captain, the Hand of Justice, to pass sentence on Dalys Morgan." The Ash Elder sat down as Adelita came to her feet, her black shipsuit dark under the bright lights.

"It is my duty to stand here," she began, "as the instrument of this Council, the Elders' judgment duly observed." She looked at Griff, who raised his face to hers. "Dalys Morgan, you have confessed and been convicted. Do you deny this?"

"No, Steel Captain," Griff said.

"And do you have any mitigating evidence you wish the Council to consider?"

"I do not, Steel Captain," he said firmly.

Adelita did not look away. "Then it is my duty to impose upon you the sentence of life imprisonment." She lifted her chin. "You are to be transported to the world of Inanna, there to spend your life working for the good of the people of Inanna in whatever way seems most fitting."

His head jerked up. "What?"

The Steel Captain almost smiled. "You don't think life at hard labor is punishment? Our ancestors were sentenced here for lesser crimes. And for greater."

"I don't understand." Griff frowned.

"Your death serves nothing. Your life will." Adelita looked past him at Bister. "I commend him to the custody of the Avatar of the Lady of the Void for transport to Inanna. She has taught me that sometimes justice is best rendered by mercy."

"Without your skill and courage, Eresh would have fallen," Tal said. "We pay our debts. What say you, Brethren?" Tal began to clap, the applause running around the room, thunderous in the confined space.

Griffin bent his head, blinking. Bister stepped forward into the circle of tables. She had thought she'd known what Adelita would do, but he hadn't expected it. He looked so stunned, so unprepared. "I was going to die for you."

"Live for me instead," Bister said, and she cupped his face in her hands and kissed him with the shackles on his wrists while the people of Eresh cheered around them.

Bister and Griff sat on the steps of the old farmhouse. It was full night, the stars bright against the indigo sky, a few wisps of cloud blowing up from the south. Insects sang in the grass. The windmill turned soundlessly in the light breeze. Bister tilted her head back, leaning against his shoulder. She took a deep breath.

"It's going to take some getting used to," Griff said.

"What, me being a goddess?" Bister smiled.

"I don't see much change," he said.

"Well, that's flattering." She laced her fingers around his. "Don't let go. Don't be afraid."

"I wasn't. And that wasn't what I was talking about."

She craned her neck back to see his face. "What do you mean then?"

"Being a free man."

She nodded slowly. "You mean having everyone know?"

"Not hiding. Not worried that people will find out. Being on Inanna—that's fair. That's what I thought when I came here, except that I thought it would be more of a punishment." Griff frowned. "I was raised on Calpurnia, Bister. I never had any idea that there was anything here except things to pity."

"Ignorant, inbred and violent people, descendants of cruel and exploitative people?" Bister shrugged. "That sums us up. I'm certainly inbred and fairly violent."

"I figured it was what I deserved."

"It is what you deserve. Just not how you meant it," Bister said.

He turned his head, looking down at her. "Is that you or her talking?"

"Mostly me. Maybe I'm getting the hang of being an avatar." Bister closed her eyes. Leaning back on him was like being held up by the entire planet. And yet somewhere out there so much was waiting. "But I don't think I'll ever get used to calling you Dalys."

"You could stick with Griffin."

"I could at that." That man was gone. Whoever Dalys Morgan had been, she doubted Griffin bore much resemblance to him. Or maybe he did. Maybe this man had always been there, had always been possible.

Above, a stray cloud crossed the sky like a veil across a dancer's face. For a moment it obscured the stars, the brightest shining through as the invisible currents of the air moved it. Peace. Rest. The scent of green and growing things, the warmth of Griffin behind her. "I can't stay," Bister said quietly. "You know I have to go."

He nodded. "Out there."

"Out there. There's so much to do. There's so much I have to do." Menaechmi first. She saw it as from orbit, brilliant tropical seas separated from desert by a bright band of greenery, lit at night with the thousand lights of the Cities of the Coast, a perilous and beautiful world of stark desert and utter luxury. "Jamila says that she knows someone who might set up a trading arrangement with Inanna, an official one this time. And if Menaechmi will repudiate the Isolation, we've got a lot of new options. So that's my first stop."

Griff's hand tightened in hers. "I'll miss you."

She turned, pressing tight against his shoulder. "I will be back," she promised. "I will always be back. Sure as the Lady to her lover, I will be back."

"It's no more than a season trip," he conceded.

"As though I followed the herds in the summer," Bister said, and knew it was true. The Lady would always bring her home. And she would bring the Lady home, remind Her of the green and growing places Her children made and built and inhabited. She would sound the great dark and then come home.

"I'll be waiting," Griff said.

Appendix: The Nine Worlds

A little more than two thousand years ago, humanity set off into deep space. Nine great generation ships, nine cradles filled with life dared the dark, propelled by solar sails. They carried people and, in their cryogenic banks, a wide selection of animal embryos representing the biodiversity of Earth. They carried plants too, of course. Enormous hydroponic farms fed them, and stored seeds preserved whatever their founders believed would be useful. Each ship was unique, sponsored by consortia of different nations and peoples, and each chose to carry things that were representative of the cultures of its crew and passengers.

The ships were controlled by an advanced biometric interface which allowed their Navigators to plug directly into the ships' systems, experiencing feedback as though it were their own body. Yin Yue, *Sounding Dark*'s Navigator, was the first to encounter the Lady of the Void, the vast consciousness that whispered against the ship's skin far beyond heliopause, in the darkness between the stars. She was not the only one. On each ship there were those who, through some trick of genetics or yearning desire, could feel her, could touch her. One was Sofia Castillo Ruiz, a primary school teacher aboard *Starwolf*. It was she who made the first paintings in light, The Lady of the Void as bright as an icon from a cathedral, the accretion disk of a black hole in one hand and a newborn star in the other. It was not long before they worshipped her—Lady to

Guide Our Course, Queen of the Long Night.

For three generations they sailed the Void, those who left Earth dead of natural causes, until there were none who remembered standing beneath a sky. They were changed, of course. Their cultures, their beliefs, their experiences were shaped by the voyage. The Lady of the Void guided them, showing the Navigators a course that would bring them first to one habitable world, and then to more, nine worlds for the children of Earth.

AGNI

Agni was the first world the generation ships reached. A cold world with mostly frozen liquid water and high levels of volcanic activity, Agni was marginal for human habitation. However, after nearly a century aboard the great ships, many people wondered if they would find better. Agni was not ideal, but its vast subterranean caverns could be terraformed. In the end, every person was given a choice to stay or to continue on into the dark. One in ten chose to stay, preferring Agni's known drawbacks to the great unknown, or perhaps falling in love with Agni's fire and ice. One ship remained to be cannibalized for the colony while the others set forth again, pouring out libations into the void in honor of the Lady as they sailed.

Relatively underpopulated compared to worlds settled later, Agni completely lost contact with the other worlds for more than a thousand years. It developed a matriarchal lineage system and a complex monarchy. Two thousand years later, Agni is still somewhat isolated, the most geographically distant of the Nine Worlds and the most culturally unique. The Agnen do not worship the Lady of the Void or the other gods known through the Nine Worlds, but are monotheists and worship a single creator god, known as the First Lord.

Menaechmi

Nine years after they left Agni, the eight remaining ships entered a binary star system with a single habitable world rich with liquid water. Menaechmi's sole vast continent and world-spanning ocean hold enormous contrasts. The continent has high mountains and deep deserts, but along the western continental rim is an ideal environment where the storms blowing in from the sea drop rain almost daily on a strip between the ocean and the mountains. The twin suns create a complex day/night schedule, and Menaechmi is slightly warmer than Earth, but to the voyagers it was a gem of a world. Twenty percent of them decided to stay, and again one ship remained to serve as a base, its computer core transported down to the planet to be the center of the colony.

While the seas were rich with life, the land held nothing native more sophisticated than large, slow lizards. Hydroponics were converted to grow thawed seeds, hybrids eagerly sought that would thrive in the complex diurnal cycle. In a generation, orange groves grew along the coast, herds of sheep grazed the slopes of the mountains, and grape vines terraced volcanic slopes while fishing boats harvested the sea's bounty. Solar-powered towers of glass rose, balconies spread to catch every ocean breeze. For nearly three hundred years, Menaechmi prospered.

A massive volcanic eruption changed that. The colony was destroyed by a cataclysmic wave of superheated gas and steam, pumice raining from the sky to bury the city ten meters deep. Gone were the solar panels and farms, the technology and the computer core, and nearly half the population of the world. But of course not everyone was close by, and not all of those who were died. Animals grazing far slopes survived. Fishers out to sea watched in horror, then put in through the rain of ash to try to recover survivors. Some fled into the deep desert. Livestock escaped from abandoned farms, and rats and wild dogs and feral cats claimed their territories. Life endured.

Menaechmi survived, though without the technology that could no longer be duplicated or repaired. When the ash settled it was still a beautiful world, still rich and giving. Some people made their homes in the desert interior, while most rebuilt along the coast, coalescing into seven city-states, the Cities of the Coast. By the time Menaechmi was rediscovered by the spacefaring Inannans, it was once again a beautiful and welcoming place, though with a dark current beneath the surface, the ever-looming specter of destruction.

Today, Menaechmi is a wealthy starfaring culture, though it does not have a planetary government. Seven competing republics hold the majority of the population, with an eighth theocratic government in the interior of the continent.

INANNA

The voyagers who wanted to go on from Menaechmi had a choice: long range spectrometry and the wisdom of the Lady of the Void concurred that there were two more worlds as suited to human life as Menaechmi within easy range. The seven remaining ships decided to split up, three going in one direction and four in the other. Inanna was the first one reached by the group of three ships.

It is in every way a world as much like Earth as possible, with a twenty-three hour day/night cycle, a single moon they named Eresh, and a temperate climate with diverse biospheres. It has native life, with the highest life forms enormous reptiles called leviathans that live in the deep oceans that made up sixty-five percent of the planet's surface. Rich Inanna was immediately settled, with *Sounding Dark* the ship that remained in orbit.

Because there was no cataclysm, technology was not lost on Inanna, though communications with other worlds was. With no faster than light communications or travel, it was simply not possible to reach any of the other worlds in a reasonable amount of time to keep meaningful connection.

This changed about a thousand years later. Whether the Inannans invented the jump drive or the Morriganians did (it emerged in both places at nearly the same time and both claimed it) the jump drive changed everything. It allowed ships to use the gravitational fields of celestial bodies along the way to jump through subspace along an ever-shifting series of routes, journeying light years in minutes instead of decades. Inanna, with a population now numbering several billion, quickly became the dominant power in the Nine Worlds. Inanna was a corporate oligarchy, with everyone an employee and shareholder in the Corporation, which amassed complete power on Inanna and its dependencies.

Of course this eventually led to war. An alliance led by Calpurnia, with Morrigan, Menaechmi and Freya as partners, waged the Righteous War against Inanna. Ultimately the planet was laid waste. Its indentured workers were liberated to Calpurnia, while its oligarchs were sentenced to life imprisonment on Inanna. To ensure that Inanna would never again dominate the Nine Worlds, the Isolation was established. All cities and technology on Inanna were destroyed. No future settlements of more than five thousand individuals would be permitted and no technology greater than pre-industrial. No individual of this Tainted blood would be allowed to leave Inanna.

The population crashed as people used to living and working in a high-tech society were suddenly isolated in a pre-industrial society with no medicine, no electricity, and no shelters or food production except what they could build with their hands. Perhaps eighty percent of the population of Inanna died in the first ten years of the Isolation—without a single person being executed by the Alliance. The world was simply bottled up and left, navies patrolling the system around it from the mining colony on Eresh, which Calpurnia converted into a penal colony.

Not quite two hundred years later, Inanna is a wild world populated by clans of migrant hunters and herders and small farming communities that fight among themselves over resources with bows and knives. Life is short and hard. And yet there are those among the Tainted who do escape the Isolation.

ERESH

Originally, Inanna's moon was a mining colony owned by the Corporation. However, in the wake of the Isolation, the mining colony was taken over by Calpurnia as a penal colony. For more than a century it housed prisoners transported from Calpurnia who were sentenced to life at hard labor. As the most remote prison Calpurnia maintained, it also was the last stop for prisoners who needed to disappear, including political prisoners and prisoners of war taken in the cold war with Morrigan whose presence could never be admitted.

Sixty-three years ago a bloody uprising known as the Taking resulted in the prisoners slaughtering their guards and taking over Eresh. They were joined shortly thereafter by the crew of the Calpurnian Naval vessel *Steel*, which had mutinied. Because Calpurnian power was on the wane in the aftermath of the First Internal War, retaking a distant prison was a low priority.

Eresh has thrived, a pirate republic on the edge of human space, its Name Ships defending it and slipping out to prey on merchant traffic, a hub of illegal trade between worlds, including the Isolated world of Inanna. Now it stands at a crossroad as Calpurnian attention turns again to its wayward possession.

CALPURNIA

The fourth-settled of the Nine Worlds, Calpurnia was reached only a year after Inanna and was very similar in many ways. With a twenty-hour day, sixty-two percent water, and a mild and temperate climate, Calpurnia is an ideal world for humanity to colonize. Its dominant life forms are avian, but none of them approach sentience. Consequently, the population grew and spread rapidly, never entirely losing technology, though some back-stepping was the result of focusing on making their new world home rather than looking outward.

By the time the jump drive was invented and contact was reestablished with others of the Nine Worlds, Calpurnia had a population of more than a billion people who participated in a planet-wide representative democracy. A brief war followed as the Morriganian Warlord subjugated Calpurnia, but the Morriganian empire was short-lived. In the not quite eight hundred years since its collapse, Calpurnia has been ascendant. Despite the disruptions of the First and Second Internal Wars, Calpurnia led the Alliance that destroyed Inanna, and has since expanded to rule four of the Nine Worlds as subject worlds in the Calpurnian Mandate, Adelpha, Freya, and most recently Lono as well as Isolated and spoiled Inanna. Representative democracy has evolved into oligarchy ruled by the Altissimi, high ranking members who vie to be Autarch, a supposedly elected position which in essence is a dictatorship. The Calpurnian Navy is the greatest power in the Nine Worlds, backed by a population of eight billion people on Calpurnia itself, as well as another five billion spread among the conquered worlds.

Eleven years ago the Altissimus Cordelius attempted the conquest of Morrigan. However, despite a bloody two-year war, this ended in stalemate and armistice with a Calpurnian withdrawal. It was the ruin of Cordelius' ambitions. Now the other Altissimi look outward, to Eresh and Menaechmi as targets for expansion.

LONO

"Sea-kissed Lono" was the fifth settled of the Nine Worlds. Those who had chosen not to stay on Menaechmi, Inanna or Calpurnia despite their obvious advantages wanted to go on for a variety of reasons. One sizeable group of people who had been raised on the generation ships wanted to live less dependent on advanced technology and to deliberately create a more traditional way of life that was in harmony with a planet's natural ecosystems, rather than terraforming and adapting the world to the colonists. Now numbering almost one-third of the remaining voyagers, they chose the cool and oceanic world of Lono as their new home. With ninety-four percent of its surface covered by water, Lono has long archipelagos of islands but no major continents.

Deliberately choosing to live in harmony with the world, Lono's settlers prospered. Unfortunately, they were left at a disadvantage vis-à-vis Calpurnia, Morrigan, and Inanna when the jump drive was invented. First a part of the Morriganian Empire, then independent again, Lono was subjugated by Calpurnia nearly a century ago.

ADELPHA AND FREYA

The sixth and seventh worlds settled are also now part of the Calpurnian Mandate, though restlessly. Adelpha is a collection of moons and artificial stations around a gas giant. Adelpha has never had a large population and has been dependent on trade with other worlds since the invention of the jump drive.

Freya is a system with two inhabitable worlds, Freya Prime

and Freya Seconde. A temperate world with a population of a billion, Freya Prime in particular has nurtured resentments against Calpurnia and does not rest easy as part of the Mandate. In recent years, Calpurnia has deliberately moved industrial functions off Freya to Lono ostensibly for reasons of environmental preservation, but actually because the Freyar are not to be trusted with the means of production of cutting-edge technology. Calpurnia's great starship yards are now on Lono, though Freya's merchanters are perhaps the most numerous in the Nine Worlds.

MORRIGAN

Like Lono, Morrigan was settled by a group of people who wanted a particular way of life. Unlike Lono, Morrigan's settlers wanted to embrace technology, especially biological sciences, and terraform an inhospitable world into a paradise. As a tidally-locked world, the Light Side of Morrigan always faces its sun while the Dark Side always faces away. The Light Side is too hot for comfortable habitation. The Dark Side is more temperate, but it is perpetually night. Additionally, there are harsh and strange environmental issues. For example, the Dark Side has seas on the eastern edge which flow into the Eastern Transitional Zone. As they reach the hot and sunny side, they evaporate into vast clouds which jet streams carry around the world, cooling as they reach the Western Transitional Zone and falling as enormous storms of rain and snow on the Dark Side, which then flow back to the seas. Brilliant genetic manipulation of Earth fauna and flora for low-light environments created a rich ecosystem unlike any other. For example, in the absence of pollinators that require sun, Morrigan has enormous bioluminescent moths which fulfill the same function.

With the smallest of the ships, *Starwolf*, and only about five thousand people, the settlers were already flirting with genetic inviability. To avoid this, they created an elaborate program of deliberate breeding to preserve genetic diversity, completely divorcing procreation from sex by having every embryo created in the lab to optimize and preserve traits. In particular, they researched and bred for the mental traits that allowed Navigators to interface directly with technology which have now been lost within the broad populations of the Nine Worlds. Today, those people are known as Dreamers, able to manipulate virtuality. There are always stories of even wilder genetic gifts, including the ability to manipulate pure electricity. *Starwolf*'s computer core was never lost and has remained fully functional at the heart of Morriganian systems to this day.

Perhaps the jump drive was invented on Morrigan. Certainly the era in which connections were reestablished between the Nine Worlds was dominated by Morrigan under the first Warlord Khreesos who built a vast stellar empire some eight hundred years ago. His empire did not last, and though he was venerated as a god, Morriganian hegemony was brief.

However, despite enormous pressure over the last two centuries since the Righteous War, Morrigan has maintained its independence from Calpurnia. As one by one other worlds have fallen, Morrigan has held out. Some whisper that it is because of these useful and dangerous genetic gifts which have been honed to high levels of skill, electromancy in particular. Morrigan is a representative democracy with an elaborate and convoluted government in which professional associations, trades and religious organizations elect members of a council which then elects a Warlord or Warlady who is believed to receive mystical guidance from the deified Khreesos. Morrigan defeated Calpurnia in the last war eleven years ago, forcing a withdrawal from Morriganian space and an armistice. However, it is only a matter of time before Calpurnia attacks Morrigan again.

Amurru

Amurru, the ninth world, is the only one with whom contact has never been reestablished. It's unclear where it is located, that information having been lost in the long dark age before the jump drive. Nothing is known of the six thousand people who went there. Their fate is known only to the Lady of the Void.

Acknowledgments

The author would like to extend her thanks to those who helped *Sounding Dark* come to fruition, especially Melissa Scott, who loved the original idea and encouraged me to turn it into a book. I would also like to thank my editor, Athena Andreadis, who took a chance on *The Calpurnian Wars* series and honed *Sounding Dark*. Many thanks are also due to my prereaders, Victoria Francis and Lena Strid, whose suggestions were incredibly helpful. As always, nothing I write would be possible without the support and brilliance of my partner, Amy Griswold

About the Author

Jo Graham is the author of twenty-five books and two online games. Best known for her historical fantasy novels *Black Ships* and *Stealing Fire*, and her tie-in novels for MGM's popular *Stargate: Atlantis* and *Stargate: SG1* series, she has been a Locus Award finalist, an Amazon Top Choice, a Spectrum Award finalist, a Romantic Times Top Pick in historical fiction and a Lambda Literary Award and Rainbow Award nominee for bisexual fiction. With Melissa Scott, she is the author of five books in the *Order of the Air* series, a historical fantasy series set in the 1920s and 30s. She is also the author of two pagan spirituality books. She lives in North Carolina with her partner and is the mother of two daughters.